A CERTAIN MAN'

The last person Virgir
expects to see again is _____strom. Their law
school relationship didn't end well, and Lisa is
now married. She is also the daughter of retiring
Senator Lindstrom and used to getting her way.
So when she is mailed a videotape showing her in
bed with another woman and told that she has
five days to announce her decision not to run for
her father's office, she contacts Robert. He tries to
refuse, but it's a losing battle. That's how he finds
himself in the apartment of Lisa's lover, Cate
Gaulois, who is lying dead on the floor with a
bullet in her chest. All the evidence for the
blackmail—and the murder as well—point to
three men who seem to have known Cate through
the local strip club where she danced: Tommy
Osborn, a ruthless, mob-connected tobacco lobbyist
who introduced Lisa to Cate; Bill Murphy, an old-
school congressional staffer in the opposition party
whose card turns up in the club; and Frank
Nelson, Senator Lindstrom's chief of staff, an
aristocratic Virginian with a strange taste for the
strip-club scene. Three tough, arrogant
Washington, D.C., politicians—which one wants
Lisa out of the race? And which one now wants
Robert Shipley dead?

Timothy J. Lockhart Bibliography

Smith (2017)
Pirates (2019)
A Certain Man's Daughter (2021)

"...a modern master of pulp espionage ..."
 —Kristofer Upjohn, *Noir Journal*

"...this is quality pulp fiction. A thoroughly enjoyable read."
 —Paul Burke, *NB Magazine*

"A riveting, page-turning thrill ride ... Ten thumbs up."
 —Victor Gischler, author of *Gun Monkeys*

"...a great storyteller."
 —*Ship & Shore*

A Certain Man's Daughter

Timothy J. Lockhart

3/8/21

Kathy,
I hope you enjoy the read.
Thanks for your support!
All the best,
Timothy J. Lockhart

STARK
HOUSE

Stark House Press • Eureka California

A CERTAIN MAN'S DAUGHTER

Published by Stark House Press
1315 H Street
Eureka, CA 95501, USA
griffinskye3@sbcglobal.net
www.starkhousepress.com

ISBN-13: 978-1-951473-22-8

Book design by Mark Shepard, shepgraphics.com

First Stark House Press Edition: February 2021

DEDICATION
To Jerry William Boykin

"Sine amicitia, vita esse nullam." —Cicero

ACKNOWLEDGMENTS

The author wishes to thank the people who read and commented on the manuscript of this novel at various stages of its composition and revision:

Elaine Raco Chase

Carmel Corcoran

Annette Freeman

Guy Holland

Lisa A. Iverson

Charles H. Jackson

Dena Lockhart Jackson

Bill Kelly

Erica J. Smith

Warren L. Tisdale

and, as always, Gregory Shepard and the rest of the fine folks at Stark House Press, whose encouragement and support made the publication of this novel possible.

CHAPTER ONE

A simple phone call got me involved with blackmail and murder. Afterward—too late to matter—I wondered whether not bringing my phone on the boat that day would have made any difference. But then I realized the past catches up with you one way or another.

□ □ □

The phone rang as I was beginning to turn and continued ringing until I had swung the boat past the eye of the wind and pointed her on the new tack. *Damn,* I thought, cleating the jib sheet. I grabbed the phone and tapped the keypad to answer. "What?"

"Gosh, I hate calling you when you're sailing. You're bad enough the rest of the time, but out on that boat . . ."

"Sorry, didn't mean to be so abrupt. There's a tricky little breeze out here this afternoon, and single-handing is a bit—"

"I don't want to hear it. I know you were in the office all weekend working on the Melman brief—Jack's reading it now—but we're in the office on a Monday afternoon while you're sailing on the Potomac."

When Georgia paused, I imagined her annoyed expression. She had a quick temper—one of her few flaws—but never stayed mad for long.

"Well, the truth is," she said, "I wish I were out there with you."

"Next weekend, I promise."

"Sure. Where have I heard that before?"

I chuckled and pushed the tiller away a few degrees to keep the shifting wind at my back. "You got me there, but I'll take you out soon, word of honor. Now, what's up? Jack having trouble finding *Black's Law Dictionary* again?"

"No, nothing that serious. A woman—a potential client—is coming to see you."

I frowned at the thought of cutting short a rare weekday sail. "I can't be at the office for an hour or so."

"I know. She said it was important, so I sent her to the marina.

She said she knows the Mount Vernon area and can find it all right."

"What does she want to see me about?"

"She didn't say and didn't seem to be in a mood for questions, so I didn't ask her."

"When did she leave?"

"Right before I called you."

"Then she should be at the marina in about twenty minutes. I doubt I can get back to the slip by then."

"That's okay. She said she'd wait for you at the dock. Robert?"

"Yes?"

"You'll be glad we sent her. She's very . . . decorative."

"Georgie, you know you're the only girl for me."

She swore and hung up. I chuckled again and looked out over the broad river to the marina of the Northern Virginia Yacht Club. The cluster of boats lay about a mile off my port beam, almost in the direction of the fickle wind. Too far to sail, especially having to tack all the way, if I wanted to be docked in under half an hour.

I tugged down the baseball cap shielding my eyes from the mid-October sun and brought the boat into the wind. Then I lowered and started the outboard motor and went forward to drop the sails. I lashed the jib to the forestay and the mainsail to the boom. To help make up for the curtailed cruise, I slid a cassette of *It's Too Late To Stop Now* into the stereo, drowning engine noise with Van Morrison reaching R&B nirvana on "Ain't Nothing You Can Do."

As I motored slowly up the channel, I saw a woman standing at the head of my slip. She had her back to the sun, so all I could tell was that she was tall, possessed a trim, athletic figure, and had shoulder-length blonde hair. But there was something familiar about her.

Aware of her watching me, I backed the boat into the slip. I put the motor in neutral and caught and cleated the spring and bow lines. As I reached for a stern line, I glanced up, saw her face no longer backlit, and realized why the silhouette had seemed familiar.

To cover my confusion, I took longer than necessary to finish with the lines. Then I stood and faced her.

"Lisa! What a surprise! How are you?" I raised my voice a bit to be heard above the throttled-down motor.

"Hello, Robert. It's good to see you again. You jerk."

"Hey, what's that for?"

"You haven't seen me in, what, three years, and the best you can do is 'how are you'?"

"It's been at least three. The bar at the Armed Forces Club—you were there with some of your friends from the Hill."

"Yes, and you wouldn't join us for a drink. As I recall, you *said* you had a date. Funny you weren't meeting her there."

"Well, it is good to see you. Thanks for your Christmas cards and, of course, the engraved invitation."

"To the ceremony you didn't attend. And me marrying a dot-com zillionaire. It was a damn nice wedding."

I had thought about going but somehow had managed to mislay the invitation. "I'm sure. Sorry I missed it. I did send a gift though."

"Yes, you had the address for that—just not the one for the church."

I looked her up and down. "You're as beautiful as ever but now a little bitchy too."

"Hmm, I remember when you might've described me as something other than 'bitchy'."

In our last year at Georgetown Law, Lisa Lindstrom and I had embarked on a torrid affair that lasted several months. It was seven years in the past but didn't seem that long ago. The memory of Lisa in my bed in that stuffy little apartment was fresh in my mind—and probably always would be. The memory of her breaking up with me was also fresh, but I'd been telling myself it didn't hurt anymore.

Seeing her again made me realize I'd been lying.

"Maybe so. Well, give me a minute and we'll talk." I disconnected the fuel line from the outboard and let the motor run until it coughed and quit.

I pulled off my cap and wiped my brow with a forearm. "What can I do for you? Must be important if you drove down here to meet me."

"Well . . ." Lisa hesitated, biting her lip. She seemed nervous, which was unlike her.

"By the way, you look just the same—not a day older. Marriage must agree with you."

She smiled although not as broadly as I remembered. "You've held up well yourself, considering the evil life you lead. Looks like you're still working out."

"When I can. A little running and some weights—mostly twelve-ounce curls." I cupped one hand as if holding a beer.

"No, I can tell. And you must still be in the Naval Reserve, because you haven't stopped getting those cheap military haircuts."

"Please. My barber at Fort Belvoir calls this a 'hairstyle'."

She nodded but didn't laugh.

"Why don't you come on board and tell me what's on your mind?"

Lisa glanced down at her short skirt, then looked doubtfully at the distance from the pier to the boat. I held out my hand. "Here, I'll help you. Better take off those heels though—I don't want you to fall."

"Or mark up your deck, more likely. I know a little about boats. My father always had one although he didn't take me out on the water very often."

That didn't surprise me. He'd been the junior senator from Virginia then and was now the senior. "A man in his position doesn't have a lot of free time."

"That's what he's always told me."

Lisa bent one long leg and then the other to pull off her shoes, displaying a lot of thigh in the process. She extended her free hand to me and swung aboard, giving me a glimpse of her skimpy panties. Standing on the cockpit seat, she leaned over and kissed me lightly on the cheek. She still wore the same perfume—something floral and expensive.

She stepped onto the bottom of the cockpit and sat with her back to the pier. "What a cute boat! You must have a lot of fun on it."

I didn't like hearing *Sea Witch* referred to as "cute" or as "it" but didn't say so. Instead I squinted at the reddening sun and said, "Looks like it's almost five. Want a beer?"

"Okay."

I got two beers from the galley cooler and sat across from her. I opened both, handed her one, and took a long drink. Lisa drank a little of hers, then flicked some condensation from the can with a manicured nail.

After a few seconds she crossed her legs, which hiked the skirt well above her knees. To avoid staring, I glanced at her eyes, blue as a Norwegian fjord, then looked away.

"I suppose you're wondering why I wanted to see you."

"I figure you wanted a beer. Or maybe just to reminisce."

"Actually, I need a lawyer who's capable and discreet to take care of a very sensitive matter."

"And having given up on finding one, you've come to me."

"Stop kidding around, Robert, this is important."

"Sorry. How did you know where to find me?"

"I called Barry Evans."

Our classmate was now a senior associate at the large firm I had joined after law school. "He probably told you I got fired last year. For incompetence—at least that's what the firm called it."

"What did you call it?"

"Refusing to break ethical rules. For a quote, really big client, unquote."

"He thinks you got a raw deal."

I looked out over the river, where the royal blue was beginning to deepen to navy. Then I turned back to her and made an effort to smile.

"Good ol' Barry. He must've also told you I'm partners with Jack Benton now, because here you are."

"Yes, here I am."

"So what's this 'very sensitive matter' you want to discuss?"

"I'm consulting you as a lawyer, so attorney-client privilege applies, right?"

"Yep, unless you're planning to murder someone."

I meant it as a joke, but anger flashed across her face. "Don't be silly!"

There was something more than impatience in her tone. Fear perhaps. Not sure what to make of her outburst, I said, "I'm kidding, Lisa. Now, are you ready to say what this is all about?"

She studied the bottom of the cockpit for a moment, looking at the non-skid as though its pattern might reveal something to her.

Then she lifted her head, looked at me, and said one word: "Blackmail."

CHAPTER TWO

I blinked. "Blackmail? You? For what?"

"Well, you know who my husband is."

I did. Daniel Strawbridge was CEO of Techster.com, one of the fastest growing Internet-based companies in the "new economy." The company's founders had struggled at first, so they'd brought in Strawbridge, an older, more experienced tech executive, to run things. And he'd done it very well, making himself and the handful of initial employees tremendously rich in the process.

"Sure. Sometimes I read more than the sports page."

The Washington Post's "Style" section had reported on the couple several times—some stories cattier than others. Lisa and her husband made good copy—the glamorous, 30-something lawyer, a senator's daughter and now a Senate committee staffer, married to a rich older man who was a legend in the tech companies that dotted Northern Virginia's suburban sprawl and made Fairfax County one of the wealthiest places in the nation. And it didn't hurt that they looked good together—like her, Strawbridge was tall and trim with a bright-white smile, and his short, dark hair with a hint of gray balanced Lisa's relaxed blonde cut.

"Is this about him—about his money, I mean?"

"It's *our* money, and, no, that's not what the blackmailer wants. Or it could be blackmailers plural—I don't know."

"Well, what is he—or more probably they—after?"

"For me not to run for the Senate next year, not try to succeed my father."

"Wait—is your father stepping down?"

"He has to. It's his heart—the doctors have told him that the job will kill him if he doesn't retire soon. So I've decided to run, and Daniel has agreed that we'll spend as much of our money as we need to for me to win."

"What does your father think?"

"He hates the thought of retirement. He's as stubborn as you are, so you can imagine how he took the news."

"Sure—not well."

"That's putting it mildly. But his wife told him he had to do it, and so did I. My mother even weighed in from Miami. If she joined forces with the trophy wife, you know things must be serious."

Lisa was Strawbridge's third wife, so the term might also apply to her, but I didn't point that out. It's taken a while, but I've finally learned to keep my mouth shut—sometimes.

"I understand. But how does he feel about your running for office?"

"He's generally supportive. He thinks I should aim for a state office first or maybe the House. He said that going for the Senate in my first race, especially at my age, is, quote, 'swinging for the fences'."

"He could be right. He certainly knows politics."

Lisa made an impatient gesture. "Sure, but he might be wrong too. Look at Bill Clinton. People told him to wait. They said it wasn't his time yet, but he was elected in ninety-two and reelected last year."

"True—even with the baggage he was carrying."

"We all have skeletons, Robert."

"Yes, we do. That's why I never open that closet door."

When she didn't say anything, I added, "Nobody is interested in my past, Lisa. Not even the part where it intersected yours."

"Good."

"So who knows about this—I mean, that you're planning a Senate run?"

"Well, I talked to some of the senators on my committee about the possibility. Just testing the waters, and none of them advised me *not* to do it."

"All in your own party?"

"No, a couple on the other side. The Senate is a lot more collegial than people think despite what some members say to get press attention."

"And any of the senators you talked to might have mentioned your plans to other people—members of their staffs, for example?"

"Yes, I suppose so. It's not like it's classified information. I have to know in advance whether a run makes sense."

I understood her need to "test the waters," but the more people who knew about her plans, the more there were who might want to stop her early, before she announced a run.

She knew me well enough to guess what I was thinking. She gave me a look as though daring me to say something judgmental, but

I just shifted my gaze to the river, which was darkening further as the day died.

"But I never dreamed someone would want to stop me badly enough to use blackmail."

"Use it how?"

"I got a videotape in the mail on Saturday. It shows me having sex with another woman."

I didn't say anything right away, and in the quiet I heard the sounds a marina makes late on a fall afternoon: halyards ringing on masts, water slapping against hulls, flags flapping in the breeze.

"You and another woman?"

"Yes. You find that shocking?"

"No, not shocking. Surprising maybe, but I know firsthand how you like to . . . experiment. When was the tape made?"

"Sometime in the last month. I haven't known her very long."

"Was there a threat or demand for money along with the tape?"

"There was a note saying I've got until this Friday—only four more days—to announce I'm not going to run. Otherwise, copies of the tape will be released to the media."

"They won't show it. The press does have some standards although sometimes you have to look pretty hard to find them."

Lisa squeezed the aluminum can so hard it crackled. "Maybe no television station will show it, but some tabloid will run a fuzzy picture from the video, and then the *Post* and everyone else will report the tape's existence. Some sleazy porn outfit will probably get hold of it and start selling copies. My political career will be ruined before it's even started—and my marriage along with it."

The air was cooling, and I noticed Lisa's nipples straining against the thin fabric of her blouse. My mouth felt dry, and I swallowed some beer. "You think your husband would divorce you over the tape?"

"Probably. We've always agreed to give each other a lot of freedom—it's not exactly an open marriage, but neither of us keeps tabs on the other. Still, the understanding is that private things stay private—we don't shame each other in front of our friends and certainly not in the press."

"So that's another reason you can't afford for this to become public. Okay, who would blackmail you to keep you from running for the Senate?"

"I have no idea. The other party, I suppose, but I really have no clue."

"Is the other woman, your lover, involved in the blackmail attempt?"

"I've been asking myself that. I can't believe she is. We're friends, obviously, and she's completely uninterested in politics. Or so I thought."

I silently noted the ironies in Lisa's statement. "I take it that you—maybe both of you—didn't know you were being taped?"

"I sure as hell didn't! The only time I ever . . . performed in front of a camera, it was my own. You remember."

Yes, I remembered. We'd videotaped ourselves having sex once and watched it on television a few times. The sight was certainly erotic, always resulting in our making love—a bit distractedly—in front of our images making love. After a while, though, we'd mutually decided we'd rather do it without watching it on TV. We'd also decided to destroy the tape, and I'd done that in front of her.

"Yes, but I didn't know that was the only time for you."

"What?" She gave me an irritated look.

"No offense—I'm just trying to understand the situation."

"Well, if she knew we were being taped, she never let on."

"In either case it's a job for the police. Blackmail's a crime."

"Oh, no." She quickly uncrossed her legs—that skirt again—and leaned forward. "No, I can't go to the police. I can't let anyone else know about this."

"Look, Lisa, I'm flattered you came to me for help, but there's nothing I can do. I'm a lawyer, not a cop, and a business lawyer at that. Jack and I don't take many criminal cases, and most of those are white-collar crime. You should go to the police."

She covered the cockpit in one long step, sat next to me, and grabbed my hand. "You've got to help me—I'm desperate!"

"I don't think I *can* help you."

"I'm sure you can. I remember what little you told me about your work in Naval Intelligence, and you must do investigations as part of your law practice. You can get to the bottom of this awful . . . *thing*. And you'll handle it discreetly, which is just what I need."

I didn't reply. I just looked at the river again, trying without success to regain the calm, on-the-water feeling I'd had before Georgia called.

"Come on, Robert! If I ever meant anything to you, you'll help me now!"

"Bringing up our late, lamented relationship isn't your best argument, considering how it ended."

She sagged onto my shoulder and started to cry. "Please don't hold that against me. You know we couldn't have made each other happy, not forever."

"Maybe, but the breakup didn't seem to bother you much."

"I'm sorry if I hurt you, but all that happened a long time ago. If you really loved me then, you'd still care for me now, at least a little bit. Honestly, I need your help!"

I didn't know what to say. I knew I'd be a fool to take a case in such unfamiliar territory and a bigger fool to get involved with Lisa again, even as her attorney. Plus, I couldn't help thinking it would be poetic justice to refuse to help this woman who'd dumped me, no matter how delicately she'd done it.

But I had to admit I was flattered she'd come to me for help, and somehow I didn't want to let her down. Also, the case sounded challenging, and I've never been able to resist a challenge. Maybe the clincher was that I still felt some connection to her.

I had loved her. I'd seen the tender side of her, the side that people usually didn't notice either because they were so impressed by her beauty and brains or because they were jealous of her and perhaps put off by her drive to succeed.

But I'd been with her when our class had done a service project at an orphanage, and I'd seen how genuinely affectionate she'd been with those children, especially the younger ones. That view of her was just as true—even if, I had to admit, much less common—as the other views most people had gotten.

Yes, I'd loved her, and that counted for something even though I wasn't quite sure what.

When she hadn't stopped crying after a minute or so, I patted her back and said, "All right, I'll see what I can do. Where's the tape? And the note?"

She sat up slowly, sniffed once or twice, and smiled a little. "In my car."

"Who else knows about this?"

"No one."

"Nobody but the blackmailer? Or blackmailers?"

"That's right."

"Then I think we should go to my office and look at the tape."

"Thanks, Robert." She wiped a hand across her eyes and smiled again, brighter this time. "I knew I could come to you with this."

"Give me a couple of minutes to zip up the boat." As I put away the gear, my brain started arguing with my hormones. *You better hope it'll be worth whatever it's going to cost you . . . .*

I snapped the padlock on the main hatch and turned to her. "Let's go."

CHAPTER THREE

I led Lisa's Mercedes in my old MGB convertible, top down. I headed north toward Alexandria, and she stayed close behind me on the George Washington Memorial Parkway as we wound through the curves along the Potomac.

A long line of cars crawled south in Washington's "rush hour," a time when no one could rush anywhere for three or four hours. But inbound traffic was lighter, and eventually we crossed over the Beltway and entered Old Town on Washington Street.

I turned right onto Prince Street and drove the remaining blocks to the office, a Colonial-era townhouse, and took the alley to the tiny parking lot in the rear. I parked and watched Lisa struggle to wedge her Mercedes into one of the two visitors' spots.

Inside we crossed a storage room crammed with office supplies and went down a short hallway, passing a small kitchen on one side. The passageway opened into a reception room that had once been the parlor.

Although the place wasn't nearly as imposing as the reception area of the huge firm where I'd formerly worked, I liked the look of it. The front door, oak with a brass knob, stood between tall windows with wooden shutters. A brick fireplace to the right was flanked by twin upholstered chairs. A large mahogany table used as a desk faced the fireplace from across the room.

Georgia sat on the far side of the table, glancing from a printed document to the computer screen and tapping the keyboard. When she heard us, she stopped typing and looked up. A polite smile came over her subtly Asian features, and she stood to greet us, brushing her shoulder-length black hair back with one hand.

She was wearing a sleeveless maroon dress that set off her ivory complexion and gold jewelry. For a moment I thought she might bow to us, but she must have remembered what Jack had said to her about that and merely nodded gracefully.

"Good evening, ma'am. I see you found Mr. Shipley. Robert, Jack had to leave for a business dinner. He said he'll see you in the morning."

Her slight accent always made me imagine a sound I had never heard: the bells of an Asian temple chiming in a warm wind.

"Okay, thanks. Lisa, this is Georgia Nguyen. I guess you two met this afternoon."

"Yes, and thank you, Georgia, for your excellent directions to the marina. I had no trouble at all finding it."

Georgia's dark eyes widened at Lisa's easy use of her first name. "You're very welcome. May I offer you something to drink? Coffee or tea? Or, in view of the hour, perhaps something stronger?"

"I see she knows your habits," Lisa said, looking at me.

"Yes, she does. In addition to running the office during the day and going to law school most nights, Georgia keeps me out of trouble— or at least tries to."

"She has two full-time jobs then."

"Unfortunately, I'm paid for only one." Georgia gave me a deadpan look.

"And overpaid at that." I kept my expression as neutral as hers. "Georgie, we'll be in my office. Could you please bring us some coffee?"

"Certainly, Robert." The way she said it told me that if we'd been alone, she'd probably have substituted a sarcastic "master" for my name.

I led the way to the second floor, past Jack's office and into my own, which was smaller than his but overlooked the street. Lisa glanced around and sank into one of the two upholstered chairs in front of the desk.

"I like your office. The Navy photos, sailing pictures, history books—it looks like you."

I pulled the other chair back and sat facing her. "Thanks . . . I think."

"Your receptionist is very pretty."

"She's actually our legal assistant, but I'll pass along the compliment."

"She's what? Half Chinese? Thai?"

"Vietnamese American, born in seventy-one as the war was winding down—the American part of it anyway. Her mother died when Georgia was very young. Her father—well, Georgia thinks he was a GI but doesn't know for sure. She's been in the U.S. about ten years."

"No father. What would that be like?" She was silent a few

seconds. "Her English is very good."

"Yes, it is. Georgia worked her way through college and is doing the same thing in law school. She took this job to get some legal experience."

"Very impressive. So—not to change the subject—how do you like practicing in a small firm?"

"As opposed to the big law factory? Oh, I guess I like it fine. The money's not as good, of course, but I have a lot more independence. I know I sleep better—most of the time."

"Good for you." She paused. "Do you ever dream about sleep? I mean, about getting a good night's sleep?" She twisted one of her rings—her wedding ring. "Sometimes I do."

Lisa seemed to be speaking to herself as much as to me. In the bright overhead lights of the office I could see faint lines of strain on her face. *Well, that's to be expected, given what she's facing.*

Neither of us said anything more for the brief time it took Georgia to bring in two cups of coffee, acknowledge our thanks, and leave.

Finally, after I'd taken a sip, grateful that Georgia had made a fresh pot, I said, "Well, let's get to it."

Lisa pulled a fat manila envelope out of her Coach bag. As I took the envelope by the edges, our hands brushed, and I felt an electric tingle in my fingertips.

I stood to lay the envelope on the desk and pull from my khaki shorts the handkerchief that my father had taught me gentlemen always carry. I wasn't sure I was a gentleman, but that one lesson, at least, had stuck. Draping the cloth over my hand, I unfastened the clasp, opened the envelope, and extracted a single sheet of paper and the plastic case of the videotape.

The note, undated, appeared to have been produced on a standard laser printer. I skimmed the text, which said essentially what Lisa had already told me: the videotape would be given to the press at 6:00 p.m. on Friday unless she publicly announced by then that she had decided not to run for the Senate next year. I knew that presidential administrations sometimes release bad news on Friday, hoping it will draw less attention that way, but I also knew that a sex scandal like this would be all the news media talked about all weekend.

"You said the tape came in Saturday's mail. Why did you wait until today to do something about it?"

"I panicked all weekend. I wanted to tell Daniel but didn't have the nerve. This morning I was going to hire a private detective, but then I thought of you."

"I still think you should go to the police."

"I told you, Robert, I won't do that. I've got to take care of this quietly."

I shrugged. "Okay, let's see what's on the tape."

The video player on the credenza hummed quietly while snow swirled on the screen of the television I kept to watch depositions. The screen went black and then showed a dimly lit bedroom viewed from a height of well over six feet. A bed almost filled the frame. A short lamp on a nightstand provided the only illumination.

Muffled voices filtered through the background hiss too faintly to be understood. In a minute or two the voices grew loud enough for me to make out a few words as a woman walked into the room, leading another woman by the hand. Both had their backs to the camera. One was a tall blonde wearing an expensive, tailored suit; the other was a short, athletic-looking brunette in jeans and a T-shirt.

Still holding hands, they walked to the side of the bed and embraced. The brunette reached with both hands to pull the blonde's face down to hers. She kissed the woman on the mouth, long and deep. Then she put her head on the blonde's shoulder and stroked her back.

When the blonde turned her head toward the camera, I recognized Lisa. Soon after I saw the other woman's face—pretty but not striking.

The next several minutes reminded me of the porn videos the enlisted guys had sometimes watched late at night in the intel center—the CVIC—when our aircraft carrier was out at sea. The two women slowly undressed each other, caressing and kissing each other's face, neck, and shoulders. Once they were naked, they slid into bed and were soon tangled in the covers before kicking them away. When the brunette buried her head between Lisa's thighs, the scene had the effect on me that one would expect, and I shifted uncomfortably in my chair.

Lisa glanced over at me. "Sorry, didn't mean to get you all worked up."

"I'll live. Now let me concentrate."

"Looks like part of you is already concentrating."

I shushed her with a finger and turned back to the TV. When

Lisa's moans began coming from the speaker, I said, "I think I've got the general idea. Is the rest of the tape pretty much the same?"

"Yes. Of course, we trade places later."

"Well, I've always admired your frankness, if not your judgment." I punched the stop button.

"Come on, Robert. It was just a fling. I'd always wanted to try it with a woman, and now I have. It's not like you and I never did anything kinky. Remember the time we—"

"Yes, I remember, but this isn't the time to stroll down memory lane. Who is she?"

"Her name's Cate. With a 'C'—Catherine Jean Gaulois."

"When did you meet? And how?"

"About a month ago in Majority Whip. That's a gay dance club near the Navy Yard—most people just call it 'the Whip'. A good friend of mine took me there one night after we left a boring cocktail party in Georgetown."

"Who is this good friend?"

"Tommy Osborn, a lobbyist. That's a whore who works in the daytime as well as at night."

That joke wouldn't be funny outside the Beltway but inside it was. "Good one. But a lobbyist for whom? What special interest?"

"The tobacco industry—this month."

"Going to that bar seems like a pretty bold move, especially considering your political ambitions."

"Well, we'd been drinking . . . quite a lot, actually. Tommy asked me if I wanted to see some of D.C.'s wilder nightlife, things I never get to see with Daniel. I said yes, and he took me to this place. He said lesbians as well as gay men go there."

"Is Osborn gay?"

"No, he's as straight as they come, no pun intended. I've met his wife a few times. I think he just likes that scene."

"Weren't you afraid of being recognized?"

"Not really. I took off my jewelry, pulled my hair back, and wore my reading glasses. I think I looked like a Hill staffer or maybe Tommy's protégé of the month, certainly not like Ms. Strawbridge."

"Okay, you met Cate Gaulois in a gay bar. Did Osborn know her?"

"I don't think so. She just came over to our table and asked me to dance. I figured why not? We danced to a couple of songs, and I could tell she was a good dancer. Really good, you know, like she'd studied it and practiced."

"Keep going."

"Well, the next thing I knew the three of us were sitting there, getting shitfaced, and she had her hand up my skirt. All the way up my skirt. Tommy just sat there with this stupid grin on his face, watching her come on to me."

"What happened then?"

"Nothing. She asked me for my cell phone number. It's private, and I didn't want to give it out, so she gave me hers and made me promise to call. I was intrigued—I mean, she's the first woman who ever flirted with me—so after a couple of days I phoned. That's how I found out she's a stripper."

"A stripper?"

"Stripper, go-go dancer, whatever. She'd given me her work number at the 1776 Club downtown."

"What name does she use when she's working?"

"Cate. She told me once she didn't see anything shameful in what she did and wasn't going to hide behind a fake name."

"So you phoned her at the strip club."

"Yes, and we got together. Cate's actually very intelligent. She's well-read, likes to travel, and paints, mostly portraits. I think she enjoyed meeting someone who could talk to her about art and literature, things like that."

She carelessly crossed her long, smooth legs, and images from the videotape crowded into my mind. I forced myself to stay focused on her story.

"That's how things started," she said, "and they just sort of progressed from there."

"So I saw." I thought for a moment. "Where was the tape made?"

"It's the bedroom in Cate's apartment. You can't see much of it on the tape, but that's the only place we did it."

"Just once?"

"No, a few times." She looked at me as if to gauge my reaction. "I certainly haven't sworn off men, but I did like it, in case you're wondering."

I had been but was too embarrassed to admit it. "Uh, okay. You said you didn't know you were being taped, so the camera must've been hidden. Somewhere fairly high, probably in the wall or the ceiling."

"I guess that's why I never saw it."

"Do you think she knows about the camera?"

"I don't know, but I can't remember her ever saying or doing anything that makes me think she does."

"Well, it seems unlikely she doesn't, but I suppose it's possible. What's Cate's political affiliation?"

"None that I know of. I tried to get her to talk about politics once or twice, but she wasn't interested. She said she'd seen what politics does to people in this town and wanted no part of it."

"Does she know who your husband is? Or your father?"

"No, on both counts—or at least if she does, she hasn't said so. I've never told her about either of them, and she's never asked. She may think I'm some rich man's bored wife, which isn't completely wrong."

"It has been since you decided to run for office."

She paused, then nodded. "Yes, I guess so. That raised the stakes."

CHAPTER FOUR

I went over to the window and looked at the cars moving on the street below, headlights probing the darkness that grew as rush hour ended. I wondered why whoever was behind this crazy scheme hadn't simply released the tape. Why give Lisa almost a week to decide what to do?

Maybe the blackmailers weren't sure the tape would kill her political career—although it was hard to see how she could win an election afterward. Maybe they didn't want to increase the chance that they'd be caught, especially if Strawbridge put his fortune and high-tech contacts into finding them. Or maybe it had something to do with not embarrassing Senator Lindstrom, a well-respected elder statesman who'd built up a lot good will in Washington on both sides of the aisle.

But none of that mattered now. The fact was they'd given Lisa—given me, it now appeared—a few days to try to stop them.

"What are you thinking?"

I turned back to Lisa. "We can't assume Cate Gaulois isn't a player in the blackmail plot."

"Well, at this point I don't care—I just want to get the son of a bitch who's after me!"

"And that's what I'm supposed to do—in just four days."

"Yes! You're clever enough, and once you make up your mind to do something, you don't quit till you get it done."

"You left out how I leap tall buildings in a single bound."

"I wish you could—politics is a rough game."

"You realize that even if I do find out who's behind this, the tape may still become public somehow."

"I have no choice, so I've got to take that chance."

"Then the question is where to start: the opposition or your own party?"

"It's probably someone in the other party. Not necessarily from Virginia but most likely from here, my state." She paused. "Hmm, I noticed I just said 'my' like it was already mine."

"Who in the other party?"

"I don't know. And even though the other side really wants this seat, it could be someone in my own party. Someone who doesn't think being a senator's daughter and having plenty of money for a campaign entitles me to my father's seat. Especially when I'm only thirty-three."

"Just like Jesus."

"What? Oh, yes. But He had God on His side, and I'm not sure I do."

"It's not like you're unqualified. You're a lawyer with experience on the Hill, and you grew up in a political family."

"Maybe I'll ask you for an endorsement."

"Not if you want to win. What do you think your chances are?"

"If I get the nomination and the opposition runs the guy I think they will—he's a sitting congressman—the election will probably be a toss-up. That's why a few people in my party might want someone else in the race, someone they think is a stronger candidate."

"Or maybe someone who'll do what they say once in office. That's not you." I returned to my chair. "You might be right about your side, but I think the opposition is the place to start. After Cate Gaulois, of course. Who knew you were seeing her?"

"I don't know if she told anyone about us—I certainly didn't."

"No one?"

"No. I *can* be discreet, you know. Tommy asked me about her a few days after we met—'that woman you danced with,' he said—and I told him we'd met for coffee but that was all."

"Okay, where does she live?"

"I highly doubt that Cate can tell you anything useful. If she'd been talked—or pressured—into making that tape, I think I'd have found out somehow."

"Look, if you want my help, you have to let me do it my way. Right now this Gaulois woman is the only lead—so I've got to talk to her."

Lisa bit her lip and was silent for several seconds. Then she said, "All right. I guess I can't tell you how to do your job." She took a notepad from my desk, scribbled on it, and tore off the sheet. "Here's the address."

She fished in her purse. "And—in case she's out—here's the set of keys she gave me." She folded the paper around two keys on a ring and held it out to me.

I took the paper from her. "I may not find anything. Even if I do, I may not find it in time."

"Don't say that—you've got to!"

The heat in her tone surprised me. "Look, I'll do my best."

"I know. I didn't mean to sound upset. I realize there's no guarantee, but I think you can do this. Now what about your fee?"

"I'll charge you my hourly rate, same as for any other kind of legal work."

"Let me give you a check for the retainer. How much—five thousand, ten?"

"No, that's okay, I know you're good for it. Let's see if I turn up anything first. I'll just send you our standard engagement letter."

"Whatever you say." Lisa reached into her purse again and pulled out a business card. She wrote something on the blank side and handed me the card. "Here. Send the letter to my home address. And that's my cell phone number. Call me anytime. If I don't answer, just leave a message—no one hears them but me."

I glanced at the card, noting that the address was in McLean, one of Northern Virginia's most exclusive suburbs. Well, that figured. I turned the card over and noted that Lisa had kept her maiden name. That wasn't surprising either, given how prominent Talbot Lindstrom was.

I walked Lisa downstairs and out to her Mercedes. She took my hand. "Thanks again, Robert. I knew that after we'd meant so much to each other . . . well, I knew I could count on you."

She looked into my eyes a moment, then stood on tiptoe to kiss me on the lips. Her mouth opened and her tongue darted out, but I kept the kiss friendly, not passionate.

She pulled back and looked at me again, her mouth still slightly open. "Don't tell me I'm losing my touch."

"You haven't lost a thing, trust me. But there are rules about lawyers having intimate relationships with clients."

She smiled. "Okay, counselor. I'll wait to hear from you. Goodnight."

"'Night, Lisa." I held the car door for her, then stood in the little parking lot until she'd driven down the alley and turned onto the street, taillights vanishing in the dark.

□　□　□

The scent of Lisa's perfume lingered in my office as I locked the note and videotape in my desk. I'd meant it when I said she looked just the same. Maybe the years had aged her slightly but not much—so little that the signs were hard to see.

But after talking with her, I thought the passage of time had changed her in other ways. She seemed . . . harder. Not brusque exactly but certainly more direct. As though she knew what she wanted and was determined to get it, regardless of what others might think.

Well, judging from what she'd hired me to do, she was all that.

I flicked off the lights and headed downstairs, where Georgia was still at work.

"I thought you had class tonight, Georgie."

"The professor had to go out of town. He left us a lot of extra cases to read though, so it's not like we get a free evening. But I wanted to finish these letters for Jack before I go home to study."

"Well, be sure to let me know if I can help with anything. I remember law school as being a lot like learning a foreign language."

"It is. Fortunately, I have some experience with that."

"Yes, I guess you do."

Georgia paused. "Who is she, Robert?"

I didn't need to ask who "she" was, and I noticed that despite her directness, Georgia kept her tone carefully neutral. "Just an old friend—a law school classmate, in fact."

"Hmm, I'd say a very good friend who's quite pretty and far from old. Better think with your head on this one and not with something else."

"Georgie, I plan to be completely professional about this case even though it involves an attractive female client."

She didn't return my smile. "Yes, I'm sure you do. The question is whether you can stick to the plan."

When I didn't answer, she began gathering up a few loose papers. Abruptly she stopped and looked at me. "Seriously, be careful. I've got a feeling in the pit of my stomach . . . I think this woman is bad news."

"Any woman can be bad news to some man sometime, Georgie. Don't you know that?"

She frowned. "When have I ever been bad news to you? Tell me."

"Well, all I know," I said, drawing out the words until I reached the door, "is that in this life we just have to take the bad with the terrible. Goodnight."

I ducked the pen she threw at me and couldn't help laughing.

Closing the door, I heard her say, "I pity the poor girl who ends up with you, Robert!"

□ □ □

I got into the MGB and made the short drive to my townhouse, which also dated from the Colonial period but was on one of Old Town's less fashionable streets several blocks from the business district. Although solidly built, the house needed repairs and paint, which is the only reason I was able to buy it on my small-firm salary.

I cleaned up, put on chinos, a dress shirt, and a tie and grabbed a sport coat out of the closet. Down in the kitchen I made a turkey-on-wheat and poured a glass of iced tea. While I ate I jotted on a legal pad what Lisa had told me about her case.

After finishing the sandwich and my notes, I went into the townhouse's small office, put the pad in my briefcase, and started to leave. Then, on impulse I stopped and pulled a manila folder from a bottom drawer of the desk. I slid out a grainy black-and-white photograph and stood looking it.

The picture was a nude self-portrait Georgia had made in a college photography course. She was sitting in a plain wooden chair set at an angle to the camera, a leg drawn to her chest and a foot on the chair. With her arms wrapped around her knee, she faced the camera and gazed directly into the viewer's eyes.

The photo was simple, natural, and suggestive without being overtly sexual. Georgia looked simultaneously innocent and inviting, her youth apparent in her firm figure and unlined skin but her luminous eyes giving her the look of maturity. I couldn't help contrasting the picture with the images in Lisa's video.

I remembered how Georgia had been half proud and half embarrassed when she'd given me the photograph as a birthday present a few months ago. Not knowing what else to say, I'd simply thanked her and brought it home.

I had never framed or hung the portrait. I'd noticed Georgia looking around for it on the infrequent occasions when she'd come by to drop off or pick up legal documents, but she'd never asked me what I'd done with it. And now we seemed to have an unspoken agreement not to discuss the matter.

I put the photo away and headed out the door.

CHAPTER FIVE

I took the G.W. Parkway north past National Airport, crossed the 14th Street Bridge into Washington and headed up the bone-jarring Southeast Freeway, exiting near Capitol Hill. I cruised through the residential streets, scanning house numbers, until I came to the address Lisa had given me. Located in one of the Hill's several rough neighborhoods, the apartment building was a large, decaying 19th-century house.

Two blocks away I found a typical D.C. parking space: not actually in the intersection but less than a car length from it and not right in front of the fire hydrant but close enough that a small dog could hit it and the MGB in a single stop. I closed the convertible top and took a penlight from the glove compartment.

Back at the building I opened the front door with the larger of Lisa's two keys. The light in the dirty foyer was just bright enough for me to read the names on the row of rusty mailboxes. "C. Gaulois" was on box 202.

I went up the dark, narrow stairs to the second floor. The landing was dimmer and dirtier than the foyer. Loud rock music came from the apartment to the right, and a crack of light shone underneath the door. The apartment to the left was quiet and dark.

I pulled out the penlight, covered most of the lens with a finger, and clicked the switch. In the soft reddish glow I read "202" on the card stuck in a tarnished brass frame screwed to the left door.

I turned off the light and knocked softly. No one answered. I knocked again, a bit louder. Still no answer.

Cate Gaulois might be home, perhaps asleep, but that seemed unlikely so early in the evening. She was probably at work or simply out somewhere. I decided to take that chance.

As quietly as possible, I pushed the other key into the lock and turned it until the bolt snicked back. I opened the door and eased through, gently closing it behind me.

For a full minute I stood just inside the door, letting my eyes adjust to the city light coming through the uncovered windows. A faint acrid odor told me that someone had recently smoked pot in the apartment. I listened for anything audible over the rock music now muffled by the closed door. The only other thing I could hear was a low hum that sounded like an air conditioner running in another room.

Nothing suggested anyone was in the apartment, so I moved to the middle of the living room. Piles of paperbacks and magazines covered the coffee table and spilled onto the scarred hardwood floor. An artist's sketchbook lay on one end of the sagging sofa. Across the room a block-and-board bookcase held a few hardbacks, a boom box, some CDs, and a small, rabbit-eared TV.

The one beautiful thing in the room was the painting that hung above the bricked-up fireplace. I used the penlight to get a better look, careful to shield the glow from the windows.

The painting was a portrait of a young woman in her mid-twenties with short, dark-brown hair, high cheekbones, and a pert nose. She was the brunette in the videotape—Cate. Her plain white blouse gave her a schoolgirl look. Her faint smile reminded me of the *Mona Lisa*, but I saw pain in her eyes.

Something about the picture, perhaps the subject's self-conscious pose, made me think it was a self-portrait. I shone the light on the lower right-hand corner and could just make out "C. Gaulois" in small, elegant script. I looked at her face again, then switched off the light.

As I walked into the kitchen, I sensed a cockroach or two scurrying for cover. Glancing around, I saw nothing out of the ordinary.

When I moved toward the bedroom, I felt a prickling on the back of my neck. As I entered the room I saw why.

The woman in the portrait lay on the bedroom floor. She was on her side, wearing thong panties and a snug white T-shirt cropped at the waist. The front of her shirt and a large patch of the ivory rug beneath her were stained with something dark, almost black.

She lay absolutely still.

My stomach churned, and I wondered if I could make it to the bathroom before I had to vomit. I tried to move, but my feet felt nailed to the floor. I swallowed hard and forced myself to take several deep breaths. That helped—some.

I stood there for what seemed like a long time. When my heart finally stopped pounding, I touched the woman's cheek with the back of my hand. Her skin was as icy as I'd imagined. I pulled my hand away and unconsciously wiped it on my coat.

Then I knelt next to the body, being careful not to touch the dark part of the rug, and shone the light on her chest. In the light the stain on her T-shirt was reddish-brown. There was a small hole, hard to see, in the middle of the stain.

A line from some half-forgotten poem echoed in my head: *"Deadly seed of a crimson flower."*

Cate Gaulois's eyes were open and looked surprised. Her mouth was also open, her tongue black and swollen. She appeared to have been dead for at least a day, maybe two. The window AC unit was keeping the room chilly, so there wasn't much smell—yet.

But there soon would be, and I tried not to think about what the body would look like then.

I played the penlight on her hands and on the rug. I didn't see a gun, which appeared to rule out suicide. Unless, of course, someone had already found the body and taken the gun away to make her death seem like murder.

I stood and looked around the bedroom, confirming Lisa's statement that it was the scene shown in the videotape. I leaned over the unmade bed and from the rumpled sheets caught a whiff of sleep, sweat, and sex.

I turned to look at the opposite wall, most of which was taken up by a pair of folding closet doors. I panned the light across the border of pink roses interspersed with dark green leaves painted—by Cate?—just above the doors.

I went to the closet and peered up at the border. Just above the intersection of the doors I saw a quarter-sized hole in one of the leaves.

Using my handkerchief, I unfolded the doors. Cate's clothes, exuding the scent of her perfume, were arranged more neatly than I would've imagined. Several filmy dresses at one end were cut so low and so high they could only be stripper costumes. Dozens of shoes, some with painfully high heels, were lined up on the floor.

I pointed my light at the closet ceiling. Four small holes marked the corners of a rectangle about the size of a paperback. Faint parallel lines suggested that something, perhaps support brackets, had been screwed into the holes.

Standing on tiptoe, I pushed the penlight into the hole in the decorative border. I leaned awkwardly inside the closet and looked up again. The beam of light bisected the two sets of holes in the ceiling.

I turned and looked at the bedroom. I had the same perspective as the video camera, only about two feet lower. It seemed unlikely the dead woman hadn't known about the camera, but without more facts, I couldn't be sure.

I closed the folding doors and rapidly surveyed the rest of the room. Besides the bed, the room held the nightstand and small chest of drawers I remembered from the videotape. A purse was on top of the chest. Still using my handkerchief, I opened the purse and took out a wallet. Two credit cards, both in Cate's name, and a fistful of cash, almost all singles, were inside.

The top drawer of the chest contained a small jewelry box along with a checkbook and some bills. The box held several pieces of costume jewelry and two pairs of expensive-looking earrings, one pearl, the other diamond. The checkbook showed a balance of just under a thousand dollars and no deposits of more than a few hundred dollars each for the last several months. I put the things back as I had found them.

The lower drawers contained only clothing. The lingerie drawer gave off the same smell of perfume I'd noticed in the closet. For a moment I imagined that the satin and lace still held the heat of Cate's body, but I resisted the temptation to brush my hand across her delicate things.

I remembered how she'd looked in the video. Then my skin felt hot.

Carefully stepping around the rug, I went to the other side of the bed. A small silver-framed photograph stood beside the lamp on the nightstand.

In the glow from the penlight I saw that the photo, a snapshot taken at the beach, was of a girl about six or seven years old and a man in his late thirties. The man was helping the girl build a sand castle. Their faces were shown in profile, and neither appeared aware of the camera.

I opened the nightstand drawer. A package of rolling papers and a small plastic bag of what appeared to be pot lay next to a box of tissues. A slim hardback book was beneath the box. The cover identified it as a poetry collection. I read the inscription on the flyleaf: "To my dearest Catherine. Love always, Dad."

One page was folded down. I read the only poem on it, "A Certain Man's Daughter":

I looked out on the bay this morning
And saw the fog sleeping with the water.
My thoughts turned again to a certain man's daughter
As the tide came slowly in.
I stood there again as evening fell
And the fog crept back to seduce the water.
My thoughts turned again to a certain man's daughter
As the tide came slowly in.
Yesterday I watched a white seagull
As it banked and flashed in the sun;
It turned with the tide to fly over green fields
As though going to search for someone.
But today there is only the fog and the water
As I stand here thinking of a certain man's daughter.

The photo and the book were the most personal things in Cate's bedroom, so they must have been important to her. And her murder and the blackmail attempt against Lisa had to be linked. I didn't think the book would help me find her killer, but the photo might.

I slipped the framed photograph into a pocket of my sport coat, noting the irony that I'd gotten into trouble before for not breaking rules and now I was risking trouble—big trouble—for breaking them. But something told me it needed to be done.

I stepped back around the rug, keeping the light out of the dead woman's eyes.

They can't see, but I don't want to see them.

Back at the front door I snapped off the light. I mentally reviewed what I'd touched with my bare fingers since entering the apartment: other than the photo in my pocket, nothing but my penlight and the doorknob. I left and closed the door behind me, careful not to leave any prints on the knob inside and wiping off the one outside.

I made sure the door was locked, then crossed the hall and started down the stairs.

At the same time a man left the foyer and began coming up. I walked as if I had somewhere to go and kept my head down. Passing the other man at the halfway point, I got a quick impression of someone tall and slim in a business suit.

When I reached the bottom, I glanced up. The man was standing in front of the door that wasn't Cate's. He was half-turned toward me and had his right hand down in his coat pocket. He seemed to be watching me, but in the dim light I couldn't tell for certain. Maybe the man was just reaching for his keys.

I didn't linger to find out. I kept a steady pace out of the building and back to my car. I got in quickly, pulled away from the curb, and accelerated down the street, leaving the lights—including the tag light—off until I was a block away.

Then I debated various next steps, some of which the law would frown on. I remembered having the same sort of debate with myself when I was with the big firm downtown. *But this time you know what you're doing, don't you?* I waited, but no answer came.

I spotted a pay phone outside a shop that was closed for the night. I pulled over, parking in the dark entrance to an alley. At the phone, keeping my back to the street, I dialed 411 and got the main number for D.C. police headquarters. Then I put two layers of handkerchief over the mouthpiece and dialed that number.

"Police. Desk sergeant speaking."

I pitched my voice low to help the handkerchief along. "There's been a murder."

"What? Who's this? Where're you calling from?"

I recited Cate's address and hung up. I wiped off the handset and keypad, shoved the handkerchief into my pocket, and drove away.

CHAPTER SIX

As I left Capitol Hill and headed downtown, I pulled Lisa's card out of my wallet, called her, and got voice mail. *Shit. I don't want her to hear about Cate Gaulois in a recorded message.* I'd have to tell her the next day, and I wasn't looking forward to it.

After finding Cate's body what I wanted to do was go home, lock the door, and have a stiff drink—maybe several. But "four days to go" kept ringing in my head.

I passed the building that housed my former firm, remembering the great view of the city from the senior partners' offices on the top floor. *Too high to see the dirt and corruption . . . or people like Cate.*

I drove to 17th and H and parked about a block from the strip club where Cate worked. No—where she had worked.

I was carrying my coat, and as I walked toward the club, I longed for the first touch of fall to begin pushing aside Washington's sticky summer. I stopped in front of a nondescript three-story building with a polished brass plate reading "1776 Club." I heard dance music pulsing inside.

A large, tuxedo-clad man carrying a walkie-talkie stood at the door. He looked as though he'd probably sacked a lot of quarterbacks in high school.

The doorman eyed me. His "evenin'" was as flat as the expression on his dark face.

"Good evening," I said. "Fine night, isn't it?"

"You comin' in or ain't you?"

"Yes, coming in, thanks."

He opened the door and murmured into his radio, "Coat and tie comin' in. Upstairs."

The music hit me with physical force. On a small stage a brassy blonde wearing only high heels, a considerable amount of jewelry—much of it pierced and not just through her ears—and three or four unattractive tattoos gyrated to the beat. Her tan contrasted sharply with the white outline of a missing thong bottom.

The audience was all male, their clothing identifying them as mostly blue-collar workers, sitting at the bar or at small tables covered with beer bottles and ashtrays. I watched one man walk to the stage and stand, holding a dollar bill.

The dancer sidled over and gave the man a plastic smile. She leaned forward, pushed her Ð-cup silicone breasts almost in his face, and shook them in time to the music. After a few seconds she reached down, deftly plucked the bill from his fingers, and slid it beside the others tucked under her garter. Then she quickly straightened and danced to another side of the stage, another customer, and another dollar.

Across the room a staircase led to the second floor. Another bouncer, this one coatless, stood on the bottom step, apparently waiting for me. I took a ten from my wallet, folded it small, and walked over to the man.

The bouncer looked me up and down and nodded. "Evening, sir. Got a nice table for you upstairs, right in front."

"How about a quiet spot in the back?" I discreetly showed him the folded bill. "I'm looking for a little privacy."

The bill vanished into the bouncer's hand. "Come with me."

At the top of the stairs I saw a smaller, better-dressed crowd watching a dancer who was almost a twin of the first. The music wasn't as loud up here, and a few cocktail glasses were mixed in with the beer bottles.

The bouncer spoke to a short, plump woman in hot pants and a halter top. "Lexie, take this guy over to seven."

"Sure." She began wriggling her way around the tables that crowded the floor, adroitly dodging the occasional reaching hand. I followed, much less adroitly but with no hands to dodge, and sat at the table she indicated, next to a brick wall.

"This is fine. Maybe you could send over a Maker's with a splash of water? Also, I'd like some company." I took out a twenty and looked into her eyes.

"Hmm." She placed her hand over mine. "Anyone in particular?"

"How about Cate?"

"She didn't come in tonight. Guess she's not feeling well. But there's another girl who looks kinda like Cate even though she's a redhead. Short and cute with firm little tits. I'll send her over."

"Okay, thanks."

Lexie squeezed my hand and withdrew hers, taking the twenty with it. She flashed a smile as sincere as a car salesman's promise and strolled away, giving me and the rest of the crowd a chance to admire the roll of her hips in the snug shorts.

A bored-looking waitress wearing a black leather miniskirt and a white tank top brought my drink, and I sipped it while dividing my time between watching the dancers and watching the audience watch the dancers.

When I was halfway through the drink, a young woman came over to my table. As I stood for her, I saw that her short, tight dress, green as a beer bottle and almost as transparent, revealed more of her than it attempted to conceal.

She was the only stripper I'd ever seen who wore glasses. The small, black frames looked good on her, contrasting with her pale skin and the autumn-leaf color of her short, curly hair.

"Hi, hon, I'm Sandi."

I knew without asking that she spelled it with an "i" and probably dotted that letter with a heart. Her real name was probably something mundane like Mary or Susan.

"I heard you're lookin' for company."

She sounded as though she'd grown up on a farm in Southern Maryland. I could see her in a few years waitressing on the Eastern Shore, wisecracking with the tourists and pushing the blue-crab special.

"Yes, I am." I took another twenty out of my wallet, letting her see that the bill had brothers, and slipped it under my glass.

Sandi glanced at the money, gave me a longer look, and we sat. She slid a cigarette from the pack in her purse and pulled out a lighter. I took the lighter from her and flicked it into flame.

She took my hand as she sucked fire into the cigarette, then blew a plume of smoke away from me. "I like it when a man does that. And opens the car door. Little things." She held my hand another moment. "What's your name?"

"Robert."

"That's a nice name." She stroked my wrist with her fingertips before releasing my hand. The scratching of her long nails was not unpleasant.

"Thanks." Even in the low light I could see she had a dusting of freckles and deep-set green eyes. Except for her toned dancer's body she looked nothing like Cate.

"So, Robert, you want someone to talk to tonight?"

"Yes, about Cate Gaulois."

"Cate, the girl who works here?"

"Yes."

"What about her?"

"Her friends, her interests, what she does when she's not working."

Sandi's eyes narrowed. "You some kind of cop? A narc? Or a jealous boyfriend?"

"Nope, just a guy who wants some information."

"Well, I'm not sure I want to talk to you. Even if I did, you'd have to pay for my time."

"I plan to." I took out a twenty, slid the other from beneath my glass, and passed the bills across to her.

Her fingers curled around them with practiced ease and her face brightened. "Okay, but I'm on in a couple minutes. I guess I could talk to you after."

"That's fine. I'll wait right here."

Sandi nodded as she stubbed out her cigarette. She walked away without looking back, disappearing through a curtained doorway.

When the next song was almost over, she reappeared, dressed in a tiny two-piece outfit that glittered as she walked. She stood at the stage while the other dancer gathered the last few bills and acknowledged the tepid applause.

Then Sandi was on. She moved like a cat, all sinuous curves with muscles straining beneath the gleaming skin that shone in the spotlights as though coated with oil. She shed her top and accepted three dollars before the first song was over and then stepped out of both skirt and G-string before the end of the second song, receiving five more dollars.

Now naked except for shoes and glasses, Sandi made the next two songs her own, clearly feeling the insistent beat yet dancing gracefully, her motions smooth, fluid. She had a fine figure, lithe and inviting, with no sign she'd ever been touched by a surgeon's knife.

She frequently swung around two vertical brass poles that flanked the stage and from a horizontal pole mounted like a chin-up bar at the front of it. Her muscles bunched like coiled springs and beads of sweat popped out on her arms and thighs.

Several men lined up to tip her. Sandi bent to whisper something to each of them while she smoothly extracted bills from their hands. Each man left the stage looking like he'd just accomplished something important but wasn't sure exactly what.

Toward the end of the fourth song she dressed quickly and scooped up several remaining bills, smiling as the audience clapped and whistled, and yielded her place to another dancer.

Sandi walked through the crowd, touching and being touched by the men seated closest to the stage, all of them smiling up at her and some putting money in her hands. She worked her way back to my table. As soon as she sat down the waitress appeared.

I touched the rim of my glass and turned to Sandi. "Would you like a drink? You could probably use one after all that."

She exhaled. "Yeah, I could. Michelle, make it a real drink, please. A double bourbon on the rocks—something from the shelf, not that awful house stuff."

I laughed. "Real booze, huh, not just iced tea in a shot glass?"

"Hmm, someone who's not a chump. Nice for a change." She fumbled in her purse and brought out her cigarettes and lighter. I lit her cigarette again, but this time she didn't touch me. She just said, "Thanks," and offered me the pack.

I shook my head.

"Good for you. I'm trying to quit myself." She took a deep drag. "Well, what did you think?"

"Of what?"

"Of my set, silly. My dancing."

"Oh." I mentally kicked myself for not saying something sooner. "You were terrific—really. Graceful but also athletic. You must work out a lot."

Sandi looked pleased. "Yeah, I do although dancing is a workout by itself." She drew on the cigarette again, tapped off the ash, and seemed to hesitate before saying, "Do you think I'm sexy?"

I tried not to but couldn't help thinking of the awful song by that name. "Yes, very. And I'll tell you something else."

She leaned forward. "What's that?"

"I like your glasses."

Her hand went up to the frames. "Really? I don't think most guys do. Thanks."

The waitress arrived with our drinks. Sandi quickly took a long swallow. "Mmm, that's good—just what I needed." She drank more whiskey, then switched back to her cigarette. Glancing around the bar she said, "Pretty good crowd for a Monday. Mostly regulars but a few new faces—like you."

I didn't want to rush her, so I sipped my drink, looked into her eyes, and smiled.

She smiled back and moved her chair closer to mine. "You're nice.

A girl can tell."

"I know one or two who might say something different."

"Well, I'd say they're wrong."

"I appreciate the vote of confidence. Maybe I should use you as a reference."

"Sure, if you think you need to be talking to other girls."

"Just for work, not for pleasure."

She grinned and picked up her cigarette. "I like to mix the two."

"Sometime you'll have to give me the secret for that." I paused. "I hate to change the subject, but I do need to ask you about Cate."

Sandi didn't move for a moment. Then she ground the cigarette out in the ashtray and took another long swallow of her double bourbon.

"Okay, back to business. I should've known. But like I said, time is money around here."

I put another twenty on the table, making a mental note to keep track of my rapidly rising expenses on this case.

"What can you tell me about Cate?"

"Why? What's so damn interesting about *her*?"

I couldn't keep a slight edge out of my voice. "Maybe I'll know when you've told me something."

"Uh-huh." She tilted her glass again, then put it down hard. "Cate Gaulois? She dances naked, just like the rest of us. Makes her living shaking tits and ass at guys who come in here. Especially high-rollers like you." She laughed, and now I could hear alcohol in it.

"That's not much for sixty dollars. Tell me something I don't know."

"Why? What's Cate done? Wouldn't fuck you? Ripped you off maybe, trying to pull herself out of this shit? Well, good for her."

I paused but couldn't think of any other way to put it. "She's dead. Murdered."

Sandi started to say something, then stopped. She stared at me as if trying to discern the truth from my face. After a moment she grabbed her glass with both hands and drained it. She shuddered slightly as she lowered the glass.

I patted her on the back and pushed my glass toward her. She drank some whiskey from it and looked at me again. A tear rolled down her cheek, streaking her heavy makeup. "Cate dead? I don't believe you."

But I could tell she did.

CHAPTER SEVEN

I waited. After a while Sandi said in a small voice, "It can't be true. You're making some sick joke. Cate's not dead—I worked a shift with her just a couple days ago."

"I'm sorry, it *is* true. Someone shot her."

"Shot Cate? How—how do you know?"

"I just know."

"God, who could do such a thing? Who'd *want* to?"

"You have no idea?"

"No, no. Everybody liked her. Cate was so sweet, she was so . . . ." Sandi shook her head, blinked hard, and put a hand over her eyes. Then she let her hand fall into her lap and sat blankly, staring at her empty glass, tears glistening on her face.

I put my handkerchief in her hand, and she dabbed her face and eyes. "Look, I know this is hard for you, but I'm trying to find out who killed Cate and why. Anything you can tell me about her might help. Okay?"

She wiped her eyes again and stared at me. "Didn't you say you're not a cop?"

"I'm not, I'm a—an investigator. I'm looking into whether someone might have been using Cate to hurt someone else."

"Why should I talk to you?"

"Because it might help her."

Sandi laughed bitterly. "How? If she's dead she's past all help."

"Wouldn't she want someone to find her killer? Wouldn't she want you to help if you could?"

She looked into my eyes for several seconds. Then she shifted, straightened, and said, "Okay. What do you want to know?"

"Was Cate especially close to anyone here? Any of the other dancers? Waitresses? Bartenders?"

"No, not really. She was friendly with everybody but nobody in particular. Actually, I guess I knew her as well as anyone. We worked the same shifts a lot and used to talk about stuff between sets."

"What kind of stuff?"

"Oh, what we thought about the other girls, what we were going to do when we got off work, things like that."

"Did she have any romantic interests?"

"You kidding? Cate? Hell, yes, lots—not that I want to be catty or anything."

"No, of course not. Were they all men?"

She gave me a suspicious look. "No, she was bi. Some dancers are. Why? You want to know if we did it? Little fantasy of yours maybe?"

"We can talk about my fantasies another time. Right now I need to know if Cate was really bisexual or just willing to act that way, perhaps for money."

"Well, most dancers will do a lot for enough money, but she definitely liked girls."

"Was she was open about liking women as well as men?"

"Oh, sure. Cate used to say that the rest of us shouldn't knock it 'til we'd tried it—that it took a woman to really please a woman." Sandi absently rattled her ice. "Shit, maybe she was right. God knows no man ever did me much good, in or out of bed."

"Sounds like you know what you're talking about." I finished my drink and signaled the waitress for another round. "Was Cate dating anyone in particular? Male or female?"

"Hmm, there was this one woman. Tall blonde, always well dressed. Cate brought her here a couple times in the last few weeks, which was kind of strange. I mean, we don't get that many women. The ones who're here more than once you remember."

"Did she introduce you to her?"

"No. Cate would get her a table by herself, one here in the back, and tell the bouncers and waitresses to make sure nobody bothered her. This chick loved to watch Cate dance, and Cate loved having her watch. When Blondie was here, it was like Cate was dancing just for her."

"Anyone else like that?"

"Well, I wouldn't say she was *with* anyone else a lot, but I saw her sit with a couple different guys. One was fairly young, about your age or maybe a little older. Tall, thin dude, always wore a suit. I don't know his name or anything. He talked to other dancers, but Cate was his favorite."

"How do you know?"

"Well, he was always touching her when she'd sit with him. I think they were doing it, at least he acted like they were."

"She never said?"

"No, we never talked about him that I remember."

"And the other guy?"

"A good bit older, mid-fifties I guess. Another suit, been coming here quite a while. Actually, he didn't come in that often, but when he did it was just to talk to Cate—and I do mean 'talk'. He didn't even watch her dance. Of course, he really didn't watch any of the other dancers either, which is really strange. He'd just sit at the bar, have a couple drinks, and talk to Cate between her sets."

"Did he touch her like the other guy did?"

"No, maybe he was shy. Some guys are, you know. They come in here and act like they're afraid to talk to a girl they've just seen naked."

"Tell me more about the older guy. Did he and Cate seem close?"

"Well, he'd kiss her on the cheek when he left, but I think he was more of a friend. I only noticed him because Cate didn't seem to have that many guy friends, and the ones she did have were, you know, just normal guys. Not suits and more her age."

"Know his name?"

"Nope. She might have told me, but I can't remember. I think she said once that he worked for the government. She made it sound like he had some really important job—like he worked for a congressman or senator, something like that."

Fresh drinks arrived and Sandi quickly downed a third of hers. "Jesus! I can't believe Cate's gone." She shook her head.

"Did Cate keep any personal things here? Did she have a locker in the dressing room? Photos stuck on the mirror? Anything?"

"Sure, she probably has—had—a few things here. Most of us do." Her words were beginning to run together, and the Southern Maryland accent sounded stronger.

"Listen, this is important to me. How about another twenty if you go look in her things and let me know what you find?"

She frowned. "That's what you want, huh? Just some dirt on Cate? God, I hate this rotten town! Everybody's always trying to screw somebody else—but in the papers, not in bed. I swear, as soon as I get me some money, I'm going back home to Easton. At least there you know when you're being fucked and why."

She chewed her lip, stared at her glass. Then she picked up the drink and gunned the rest of it. "All right, but first give me the money."

"Okay, here's ten. I'll give you another ten when you come back."
She swayed to her feet. "I don't know which is worse, you giving me this or me taking it, but I'm not going to try to figure it out."

After she left, I sipped my drink and watched first one woman and then a second strip to soulless music I didn't recognize. Finally Sandi came back, wearing another minimal outfit and weaving her way across the beer-sticky floor among tables of leering men. She slumped into her chair, took a photograph and a few business cards out of her purse, and dropped them on the table.

"That's all I could find of hers except clothes. Now where's my money?"

I handed her the other ten. "Thanks. Want another drink?"

"Yeah, but I better not. I'm a little high already, and it's hard to dance when you're fucked up. I'm on next, so I'll just sit here a minute."

I nodded. I bent over the table and looked closely at the photo.

The picture showed Cate at a table in what looked like that same bar. She sat between two smiling men, each with an arm around her. Both men were young and had longish hair, one wore a beard. The clean-shaven man wore a shirt with script lettered over the pocket. I squinted but in the dim light I couldn't read the tiny writing.

I tapped the photo. "Who are these guys?"

"I don't know. Just two dudes who were friends of Cate's."

I didn't think I'd get any more than that from Sandi even if she knew more, which seemed unlikely.

I turned to the business cards. Most bore out-of-town addresses, probably of "company reps"—traveling salesmen—who'd given the cards to Cate while trying to get her to do more than dance. I wondered briefly if any of the men had gotten lucky with her. I didn't know why, but I hoped they hadn't.

One card was more interesting: *William A. Murphy* and a D.C. telephone number. Nothing else.

I slid the card toward Sandi. "Know who this is?"

"No. Might be one of those guys I told you about, but I'm not sure."

"Okay. Mind if I keep these?" I used the photo to scoop up the cards, putting everything away in my coat pocket.

"I guess not. I mean, they don't belong to me, but I don't know who'll claim Cate's things. I don't think she has any family—at least she never mentioned any. Her clothes, the other girls will probably just take."

"Thanks again." I smiled at Sandi until she gave up and smiled back, not the bold, sexy smile she used with customers but a small, timid smile that made me imagine a schoolgirl seldom praised by her teachers. "I really appreciate your help."

"You are welcome," she said formally as though she seldom had occasion to use the words.

I rose. "Well, I've got to go. Sorry I can't stay for your next set."

"I'm sorry too—Robert. There's more to being a dancer than you'd think."

"After seeing you up there, I believe it."

Sandi took my hand. "Maybe you can come back and see me again sometime. I always give it a little extra for a regular customer."

I gave her hand a squeeze. "I'll keep that in mind. So long."

□ □ □

The hike to the car cleared my head of some of the cigarette and whiskey fumes. I put the top down on the MGB and drove along Constitution Avenue toward Memorial Bridge to let the cool night air do the rest.

I passed the brooding sculpture of Lincoln near the Potomac and turned onto the concrete span of the bridge. I smelled the musky water and saw the city lights reflecting in it like diamonds set in silver.

Despite the late hour I tried Lisa's number again, and after the third ring she answered, sounding wide awake. "Hello?"

"It's me, checking in."

"Oh." Her voice became as soft as the night. "Working late?"

"Yes, and I have news. Can you talk now?"

"Not long. Daniel had a late business dinner, but he should be home soon."

"I saw Cate."

There was silence, and I wondered if the call had dropped. Then she said, her voice not so soft, "You did? What did she have to say?"

"Nothing."

She paused again. "You mean she wouldn't talk to you?"

"I mean she couldn't talk."

"I don't understand."

"Can't explain now, not on this phone. I have to see you. Tonight."

"Not tonight."

"Lisa, I've *got* to see you. It's important."

"No, Daniel will be back any minute."

"Well, I'll call you from a pay phone then."

"No, call me tomorrow. Robert, I need . . . just call me tomorrow, okay?

I swore under my breath. "All right, you're the client. 'Bye."

I hung up without waiting for her to answer and found my way through the maze of lanes that led back to the southbound parkway.

I thought hard, the road so familiar that the car barely needed my help. *Can't see me? She could have made some excuse. Doesn't she want to know about Cate?*

I passed National, not busy this late but its control tower, lit in red and white, still keeping watch. Then the Daingerfield Island marina came up on my left, its sleek boats lined up neatly in their slips, hulls almost motionless.

My afternoon sail was something that had happened a long time ago. I glanced at my watch and saw that both hands on the old-fashioned rectangular face were approaching XII.

What the hell am I doing? Trying to win some kind of merit badge? I've found a dead body, left a trail of evidence in a strip joint, and risked my law license to do it. All for a woman who dumped me.

A bitter taste came into my mouth and I felt cold and tired. A mist before my eyes made the road hard to see, but I didn't slow down. The lines on either side of the car blurred as I felt myself speeding toward something unknown—riding down the moonlit river toward an ocean uncharted, endless, and black.

CHAPTER EIGHT

I didn't sleep well. My dreams were jittery movies about women—some naked, some dead, some both—flitting in and out of shadows. Shortly after sunrise I quit trying to sleep and rolled out of bed, my mouth dry from the night's drinking. I pulled on sweatpants and a T-shirt and padded downstairs to the kitchen, where I gulped two glasses of water and most of a third. I fumbled with filter and measuring spoon, got the coffee maker going.

I went out the front door to pick up *The Washington Post*. The steps felt cold and damp under my bare feet, and a breeze chilled my face and arms. Although the morning sun shone orange-yellow beyond the red brick townhouses, a few clouds had gathered overnight.

I skimmed the paper's "Metro" section and found what I was looking for. A brief story, probably one of the last to make that edition, reported the death of Catherine Jean Gaulois. The story said an anonymous telephone call had tipped the police to investigate the apparent murder, robbery didn't appear to be a factor, and the dead woman didn't seem to have any close relatives.

I read the story twice, but it didn't tell me any more the second time. I poured a cup of coffee and took it upstairs.

While dressing I switched the clock radio on and got lucky: right after the weather report—rain expected that evening—the announcer read the local stories. The only fresh detail about Cate was that she'd worked in "one of Washington's upscale adult establishments." I imagined Sandi's laughter at that polite description of the 1776 Club.

I ate a quick breakfast of cereal and orange juice and then made the short drive to the office. More a morning person than I am, Georgia was already there.

"Morning, Georgie." I tried to sound happier than I felt.

"Good morning, Robert. Rough night?"

"Do I look that bad? Just short on sleep—worked late. Jack in yet?"

I knew I should tell Jack something about what I was doing for

Lisa, but I wasn't sure how much to say. If I told Jack about finding the body of Cate Gaulois, I might put him into the same bad position I was already in. I decided to say only that I'd taken the blackmail case and hadn't made much progress so far.

"No, not yet."

"All right, I'll see him later." I took out my wallet and extracted Lisa's card. "How about doing an engagement letter for Lisa Lindstrom? Use the handwritten address and our standard form. Call the matter: advice with respect to potential political campaign."

"Sure. How much of a retainer?"

"Uh, none. I don't like to ask friends for retainers. Besides, I'm sure we'll get paid on this one."

Georgia cleared her throat and gave me a look I'd seen before, usually when I was about to do something stupid. "Okay, you're the boss."

I went to my office, pulled the legal pad out of my briefcase, and looked at the scribbles from the previous evening. I added a few more: *professional hit?, framed photo, did Cate have a daughter?, if so, did the father have custody—maybe because of Cate's job?, inscribed poetry book, where was Cate's father?, hidden video camera, Sandi, tall man in a suit, two guys in snapshot, William A. Murphy—works on Hill?*

Lots of questions but still no answers.

I labeled a manila folder "Lisa Lindstrom—File No. 1" and put in the page of notes and the things I'd gotten from Sandi. It didn't look like much to go on, but that was all I had. That and the videotape and blackmail note.

Plus a corpse.

I dialed Lisa's number from memory. I got voice mail again and cursed as her greeting played. After the beep I said, "Hey, it's me. We need to talk." I hung up harder than I'd intended.

I sat there for a minute or two, hoping for some brilliant insight that would crack the case. But the only idea that came to me was that I needed more coffee.

I went downstairs to get some. After I returned from the office kitchen, I heard familiar footsteps coming down the hallway and into the reception room.

"Mornin', folks." Jack Benton's rich, deep-South voice, although loud only when he wanted to intimidate opposing counsel or wake up a jury, always seemed to fill the room.

He took off his tailored suit coat, displaying coordinated shirt, tie, and braces. Apparently still warm from his workout at the Old Town gym favored by businesspeople and politicians, he pulled a handkerchief from a pocket of his trousers and mopped his face. Despite the gray in his thinning hair, Jack's fashionable clothes and muscular build made him look younger than his early fifties.

"Good morning, counselor," I said, "or should I say, 'good afternoon'?"

"By God, I knew it! The swabby beats me in for the first time in his life and thinks he's entitled to rub it in my face."

Jack smiled broadly and cocked a big thumb under one of his braces, making him look like a man who enjoyed good cigars, better bourbon, and the best women—which he did. "Well, son, just for that you're buying me lunch."

"Jack, you know nothing gives me greater pleasure than buying you lunch—especially the way you eat—but it looks like a pretty busy day. I'd better take a rain check."

"'Pretty busy'? I hope you mean with work. Okay, we'll have to go to lunch tomorrow so you can tell me what you've been up to—besides sailing, chasing pretty girls, and generally leaving me to keep this place afloat."

Georgia frowned. "Both of you go to your offices right now and stay there so I can get some work done."

Jack gave me a wink and headed for the stairs. Following him, I said, "Jack, got a few minutes? I want to talk to you about a matter I picked up yesterday."

"Sure, but will it hold for a couple of hours? I need to prepare for an eleven o'clock conference call that may go a while."

I didn't want to wait, but I also didn't want Jack to be distracted while hearing about the blackmail investigation. "All right, I'll stop by when you're free."

Back in my office I pulled Murphy's card out of my wallet and called Lisa again. This time she answered.

"Yes?" Her tone was sharper this morning than it had been the night before.

"It's me. Can you talk now?"

"Yes, what is it?"

"If you've read the *Post* this morning, you know what it is."

"I—I saw a story on the TV about Cate. The police seem to think she was murdered."

"So do I."

"Last night you said you saw her."

"I did, and the bullet hole in her chest. I'm no Kay Scarpetta, but I think Cate was probably killed sometime over the weekend. When did you speak to her last?"

"I tried to call her after I received the tape on Saturday but couldn't get her. I tried again on Sunday, but she still wasn't in."

"Or couldn't answer the phone."

"Is . . . is there any evidence that Cate's death is related to the blackmail?"

"Only circumstantial, like the timing of it. But the police may have found something in her apartment. Meanwhile, do you know someone named William A. Murphy?"

"William Murphy? I don't think so—no, wait, a Bill Murphy is Al Wheaton's chief of staff. Is that who you mean?"

"I don't know. Who's Al Wheaton?"

"I keep forgetting you're not in politics. Wheaton is a congressman from the Richmond area. Nice man although on the other side of the aisle."

"In the other party, you mean?"

"Yes, that's what I said. He's the guy who may run against me."

"So Murphy works for him?"

"Yes, Bill works for Al the way Frank works for my father."

"Who the hell is Frank?" I wondered if I sounded as frustrated as I felt.

"Franklin McWhorton Nelson. Lord, what a name! He's Dad's chief of staff. From an old Virginia family with lots of money."

"A chief of staff does what? Briefs the boss, shepherds key legislation, basically runs the office? That sort of thing?"

"Exactly. But why are you asking about Bill Murphy?"

"Cate Gaulois had a card with the name and D.C. phone number of a William A. Murphy. If he's Congressman Wheaton's chief of staff, that links Cate to your political enemies. What do you know about Bill Murphy?"

"Not much. I've met him two or three times, but that's about it. He's in the other chamber as well as the other party, so we haven't had occasion to work together."

"All right, I'll ask this Nelson about him. What's the phone number?"

"Oh, no, don't do that! Frank can be very suspicious, especially of people he doesn't know. He'll wonder why you're asking, especially if he finds out you're working for me."

"But—"

"Listen, I don't want Frank in on this thing—he'd run straight to my father with it."

"I'm going to have to talk to him sometime. He's in an excellent position to know who might be out to get you."

"Wait, let me think." Lisa was silent for several seconds. "Okay, I've got an idea. The Virginia State Society is having a cocktail party tomorrow night—basically a networking thing. I'll be there, and Frank probably will be too. Bill Murphy might show up. Why don't you come as my guest, meet Frank, maybe Murphy, and talk to them more casually?"

"I—you, rather—can't wait that long to check on Murphy, not with Friday staring us in the face. If his name is actually William A. Murphy, I'm going to try to see him this afternoon. But it probably would be helpful for me to go to the party. Can you get me on the guest list?"

"Sure, I'll call about it this morning."

I promised to phone when I had more news. I hoped it would be good news for a change.

CHAPTER NINE

I spent a couple of minutes mulling over my conversation with Lisa. Then I turned to my computer and logged on to the information database to which the firm subscribed.

I found a listing of House members and their key aides. William A. Murphy was shown as Representative Albert Ridley Wheaton's chief of staff, and his telephone number matched the one on the card.

I skimmed Wheaton's bio and printed it for the file. There was no bio for Murphy.

Next I found several newspaper and magazine articles that quoted or discussed Wheaton and a few, mostly in D.C.-based publications, that mentioned Murphy.

I printed the articles from the past year, highlighted certain phrases, and jotted a few notes in the margins. Wheaton appeared to be a smart, capable politician who took good care of his constituents and had little trouble being re-elected every two years. He also seemed to be a forceful proponent of his party's stance on most issues. I thought Wheaton sounded tough enough to exploit the weakness of a political rival, especially one competing for contributions from the same state.

The articles didn't tell me much about Murphy except the predictable information that he shared his boss's political philosophy.

I ran similar searches for Frank Nelson and got similar results. The only significant difference was that Nelson seemed more outspoken—at least the media quoted him more often.

Then I checked on Osborn and learned that a Thomas J. Osborn from New York had served two terms in the House of Representatives before going through Washington's famous—or infamous—revolving door to become lobbyist. A big-time lobbyist who represented mostly large companies, usually successfully and always making a lot of money from it. His most recent triumph had been batting down a bill that would have forced tobacco companies to create a fund for the families of smokers who'd died of lung cancer.

The articles gave me some potentially useful background but that was all. I made more notes, then phoned a friend who did legislative work for a big D.C. law firm. I got the receptionist, who put me through.

"Sarah Goldstein."

"Hi, Sarah, it's Robert Shipley."

"Hello, Robert! How *are* you?"

"Fine. What's new in the world of tassel-loafered lobbyists?"

She laughed. "My God, where did you hear that one?"

"I think I read it in the *Post*."

"And you believe that rag? *The Washington 'Compost'*?"

"What? You mean everything in the *Post* isn't true?"

"Yeah, I know: you're shocked to find there's gambling in the casino. Well, the way it works is that if a story is favorable to one of our clients, it's probably true. But if the story is unfavorable, especially to a big client, it's our job to point out how inaccurate or at least slanted it is."

"Still going to bat for the fat cats, huh?"

"Sure. Have you ever seen a cat, fat or thin, that could bat for itself?"

"Good point. Hey, Sarah, I need a favor."

"I figured. You haven't called in a while, so I didn't think you were after my sculpted body."

"Well, I am but I'm trying to be subtle about it."

"Then you're succeeding. You know, pal, there's such a thing as being *too* subtle."

I remembered the night Sarah Ruth Goldstein, Esquire, had made dinner for the two of us. Afterward, as we sat listening to Chet Baker's mournful trumpet and finishing the bottle of middling wine I'd brought, she'd let me know in a ladylike manner that she wouldn't mind also making breakfast for me. Although I'd been tempted, I knew the strongest emotion I'd ever feel for Sarah would be warm friendship, and I'd been careful ever since not imply otherwise.

"I'll keep that in mind, but right now I need any information you can give me concerning William A. Murphy. He's Congressman Al Wheaton's chief of staff."

He heard her sigh. "Robert, sometimes I wish you were the kind of man my mother warned me about." She paused. "William

Murphy? Sure, he goes by 'Bill'. Originally from Richmond, same as his boss. He's been on the Hill quite a while. Kind of a throwback to the old school."

"The old school?"

"You know, good ol' boys drinking bourbon in a smoke-filled room and making decisions without bothering to consult the voters. They're gone now, mostly, but Murphy reminds me of them. He's blunt and opinionated, especially when looking out for his political friends. He has a lot of them, especially in the tobacco industry."

"I assume he knows Senator Lindstrom."

"Murphy knows just about everybody worth knowing in this town. Probably a lot of little fish too—for example, I met him once at a cocktail party. He almost spilled his drink trying to look down my dress. But I doubt Murphy knows the senator really well."

"Why not? They're from the same state. I'd think that would throw them together pretty often."

"They're in different parties and different houses of Congress, so they wouldn't have much to do with one another. Including socially."

"Are they enemies?"

"Enemies? That's probably too strong. I'd call them determined opponents."

"Which means what to someone like me who doesn't work the Hill?"

"They're on opposite sides in a company town where the fights—or debates, if you will—are becoming increasingly partisan. Plus I imagine Murphy's very frustrated about the success of Lindstrom's party over the past several years. When Murphy came here—I think he was a committee staffer a few years and then went home to help Wheaton get elected to his first term—the situation was just the reverse, and his party was in power."

"But that's politics."

"Well, sure, but personalities play a big part too. I happen to know Wheaton doesn't care for Lindstrom on a personal level, so I doubt Murphy has much affection for him either, especially since Lindstrom's the kind who implies that his party has all the virtue and the other has all the vice. And they're completely different types of people—Lindstrom can be rather sanctimonious and Murphy likes to have a good time. Social partying as opposed to just the political kind. I think they might actually enjoy disagreeing with each other."

"Does Murphy have political ambitions—for himself, I mean?"

"I've heard he does. Of course, he's waited a long time to do something about them. Most staffers who want to run for office move back home after a few years, get a job in local politics, and then make their move when a seat opens up or the opposition seems beatable."

"But Murphy's still here."

"He's probably stayed because he's an unusually powerful chief of staff. Wheaton defers to his judgment on most issues. Also, Murphy has a gift for keeping people in line, maintaining party discipline, that sort of thing. I imagine the party leaders have told him to be a good soldier and eventually they'll reward him, either by supporting a campaign of his own or by enabling him to make a lot of money quickly and retire rich."

"He must be quite persuasive, especially considering the big egos up there on the Hill. How does he do it? Not by spreading sweetness and light, I'm sure."

Sarah didn't answer right away. "Strictly off the record?"

"Yep, and subject to attorney-client privilege, if that helps."

"Oh? A client matter? Well, then you owe me dinner—at the very least."

"You got it. Now what's his secret?"

"It's ironic you use that word. Remember I said Murphy knows a lot of people? Well, he knows a lot of their secrets too. He even pays for that kind of information, mostly with political favors but sometimes with soft money—contributions to a political party, not a particular campaign. Then he uses the information as leverage to get people, including members of Congress, to do what he wants. Or what his party wants, which is the same thing, at least theoretically."

"So it's 'support this bill or else'?"

"That's what I've been told."

"By people who've been squeezed?"

"In a couple of cases."

"Sounds even more corrupt than I imagined."

She laughed. "Robert, I know you're a straight arrow, but I didn't think you were that naïve. Murphy's no choir boy, but he's certainly not the only one on the Hill applying pressure when necessary. He's just better at it than most."

"I see."

"What's all this about? If you can say."

"I'm afraid I can't. Sorry, especially after you've been so forthcoming, but . . . well, you know the drill. I've got someone else to ask you about, a lobbyist named Thomas Osborn."

"Thomas Osborn? Sure, I know him—everybody knows Tommy. That's what he always says: 'Call me Tommy.' Used to be in the House but left to make big money. Represents the tobacco companies, last I heard. Could be someone else this week."

"Do you know anything else about him?"

"Well . . ."

"What?"

"I don't like to repeat rumors."

"I understand, but this is important, and anything might help."

"Okay. I've heard—from a couple of people, actually—that he has mob connections going way back to when he was a state legislator."

"Interesting."

"Yes, isn't it? I was told he knows whom to call if one of his clients needs a little muscle. I recall the phrase 'strong-arm stuff'."

"Hmm, that's some rumor. Got his phone number?"

"I should. Let's see . . ." I heard her tapping computer keys. "Yes, here it is." She read the number to me, and I jotted it in my notes.

"Thanks, Sarah, you've been a big help, as always."

"You're welcome. Now about that dinner—"

"You've got it, any time after this week. Pick a place and give me a call."

"Don't think I won't."

"I'll look forward to it—and start saving my money."

"With the restaurant I have in mind, you should've started last week."

I laughed. "That's what I like about you, Goldstein, that lightning wit."

"Really? I thought it was my big brown eyes."

"Those too. Thanks again."

"'Bye, Robert."

CHAPTER TEN

I got a dial tone and punched in Osborn's number.

"Mr. Osborn's office." The woman's voice was crisply professional.

"This is Robert Shipley. Is he available?"

"I'll see. May I say what this is concerning?"

"It's an important private matter." I thought that would probably get Osborn on the phone.

"Hold please."

I listened to saccharine music a while before the receptionist came back on the line and said, "I'll connect you now."

There was a quick buzz and then a man with a strong New York accent said, "Tommy Osborn. How may I help you, Mr. Shipley?"

"I'm a lawyer working on a case. I need to talk to you in person—today."

"That sounds rather urgent. Is your case the 'private matter' you want to discuss?"

"It is. I understand you know Lisa Lindstrom."

"Yes, of course—Senator Talbot Lindstrom's daughter. Why?"

"Did you know she was good friends with a woman named Cate Gaulois?"

"Cate . . . who?"

Over the phone I couldn't tell whether he was sincere or acting. That was why I needed to see him in person.

"Cate Gaulois."

"I don't think I know her."

I caught his use of the present tense. "That's odd—you were there when the two of them met."

"I was?"

"Yes, at some place called Majority Whip or just the Whip."

He didn't answer right away. Then he said, "I may have been there a few times, but there's nothing illegal about that."

"I didn't say there was. I just want to ask you some questions about that night."

"I'm a very busy man, Mr. Shipley, and, not to brag, but my time is rather valuable. Why should I talk to you?"

"There's nothing illegal about going to a gay nightclub, but you might not want your more conservative clients to know about it. Or your wife—especially the part about taking Lisa Lindstrom there."

"Damn it, Shipley, are you threatening me?"

"No. But every reporter in Washington would love to know what I'm working on, and if you're not involved, talking to me is the best way to keep them from shining a spotlight on you."

"All right, all right. Three o'clock today. My office."

He gave me the address and hung up brusquely. I thought I'd done all I usefully could before talking to Murphy, so I dialed the number on his card.

This receptionist told me that Murphy was out at a meeting but would return that afternoon, and I said I'd call back later.

I hung up, feeling frustrated. Time was slipping away, and I wasn't making much progress.

Georgia knocked lightly on the open door and brought in the mail. "Nothing hot. Once again you didn't win the sweepstakes."

I flipped through the mail, throwing away the junk and dropping the remainder on my desk. "Thanks. Say, are you going out for some lunch?"

"If you mean will I go out and pick something up for you, the answer is yes. Jack's already gone—he said he set up a lunch meeting with a potential client."

Shit. Now I couldn't talk to Jack about Lisa Lindstrom's case until the afternoon.

An hour later, having shared Chinese carryout with Georgia, I tried Murphy again.

"Robert Shipley calling for Mr. Murphy."

"Will he know what this call is in reference to?"

"No. I'm an attorney calling on behalf of a client."

"Please wait and I'll see if Mr. Murphy is available."

I thought that even though Murphy didn't know me, he would probably take the call. Seasoned Hill staffers generally tried to avoid offending anyone about whom they knew nothing.

Based on the length of time Murphy had been in the game, I suspected he was a careful man even though I'd obtained his card in a strip club.

Maybe one of the advantages of being from the old school is that you don't have to worry about certain indiscretions. Especially if you know about other people's and they know you know.

After a minute or two the line clicked. "This is Bill Murphy. What can I do for you?"

"Mr. Murphy, my name is Robert Shipley. I'm a local lawyer, and I'd like to talk to you about a matter I'm working on."

"What sort of matter?"

"It's confidential, and I'd rather discuss it in person."

"Well, Mr. Shipley, I'd have to know what it's about before I could agree to make an appointment with you."

"It's about Cate Gaulois."

Murphy took so long to reply that I began to wonder if I'd been disconnected. Finally he said, "Cate Gaulois." A statement, not a question.

"Do you know her?" I was careful to use the present tense.

"Yes, I did, but what business is it of yours? Or of your client?"

Did. "You're aware she's dead?"

There was another long silence. "It was in the newspaper this morning."

"Then you know she was murdered."

"Yes, damn it, I know she . . ." Murphy paused, then continued more calmly, "I mean, yes, the paper said the police think it was murder, not suicide."

"That's why I want to talk to you. I have some information about her murder."

"And you think you should share it with me instead of the police?"

"Oh, I've no objection to talking to the police." I hoped I was bluffing better than I did at poker. "I just thought that, for whatever reason, you might want me to talk to you first."

The silence was considerably shorter this time. "All right. Be at my office at four-thirty this afternoon. You know which building and which office?"

"Yes." My research had told me that.

"Don't be late." He hung up without saying goodbye.

I jotted *Murphy—4:30 p.m.* on the pad and underlined it twice. I liked that conversation. He hadn't denied knowing Cate, had taken the time to read the newspaper story, and hadn't simply referred me to the police. Best of all, he'd agreed to see me.

Maybe I was getting somewhere after all.

I wrote down several questions to ask him. I studied the list and decided the rest of my questions would depend on his answers. Then I went to see if Jack had returned from lunch.

He had but was on the telephone. He held up an index finger in the military "wait one" sign and continued his conversation.

I went downstairs for coffee. Georgia was watering the plants in the reception area. When she saw me, she put down the watering pot and went to her desk. "Here's the Melman brief. I put in Jack's comments and printed it in case you want to make any final changes."

"Knowing that I'm certain to make more changes, isn't that what you mean?"

"Well, yes, but I was trying to be diplomatic."

"You succeeded. Now I know how the North Vietnamese were able to give us such a hard time during the Paris peace talks. Good thing you don't want to negotiate the shape of the conference room table like they did."

"Maybe I'd like to but am too busy doing your work. Speaking of work, don't you have to do something out of the office later? Anything I can do to help you get ready for that?"

I marveled at how Georgia so often seemed to know what I was doing without my telling her. "No, thanks, I'm good. Did Jack sign up that new client?"

"Well, he seemed happy when he got back, but I think his lunch was as much personal as professional." She smiled. "It turns out the 'potential client' is one of Jack's lady friends—that nice woman with the chocolate Lab. I like her."

Jack had been divorced for several years, and Georgia obviously wanted him to find a wife. "So he won't be lonely," she'd said, making me wonder how anyone with as many friends and interests as Jack could ever be lonely. Perhaps she meant so that Jack wouldn't be without romantic love—but in that case I could tell her that the pleasure might not be worth the pain.

"Better watch out, Ms. Nguyen, or you'll turn into a real yenta."

"'Yenta'?" she asked sharply. "What's that? Some bad Navy word?"

"Ask Jack. He'll get a laugh out of it."

As I went back to my office, I smiled at the thought of our young Vietnamese American legal assistant acting like an elderly Jewish matchmaker.

CHAPTER ELEVEN

At two o'clock I left for my appointment with Tommy Osborn. I drove to Arlington's Crystal City Metro station, left my car in one of the parking garages for the underground shopping mall, and stopped at a newsstand for a copy of *The Washington Times*.

The turnstile sucked in my fare card and spat it back, the gate grinding open to let me walk out onto the Blue Line platform. I got lucky—the next train arrived less than a minute later.

I boarded but didn't attempt to find a seat in the crowded car. I leaned against one of the metal poles near the door and read the newspaper. The *Times* was on the opposite side of the political spectrum from the *Post*, and I liked to get both viewpoints before making up my mind about issues. I don't understand people who listen to or read only those political opinions they already hold.

I rode through several stops to the Farragut West station. I exited the train and hiked up the broken escalator—one of Metro's most common but least attractive features—then walked the few blocks to the building on K Street where Murphy had his office.

K Street was nicknamed "Gucci Gulch" for all the well-paid lobbyists who worked there. Some people questioned the accuracy of the word "work"—is backslapping members of Congress really work?—but the lobbyists countered by saying there was nothing wrong with doing well while doing good. They had a point although their profession, not the world's oldest but, as Lisa had noted, similar to it, was one of the reasons Washington could aptly be characterized as Babylon on the Potomac.

And I'm part of it—especially now, doing this dirty job for Lisa. Rolling around in the mud like a typical Beltway bandit.

The thought didn't make me feel any better about myself.

I went inside the office building at 2:55 and rode the elevator to the tenth floor. That was a high floor in Washington, where no building can be taller than the dome of the Capitol.

Osborn and his partners had spent a lot of money to make their office suite look tastefully rich. I walked across the thick blue carpet to a polished oak desk large enough to double as a dining room table.

If she got tired of her current job, the young woman sitting at the desk could switch to fashion model. She looked up from her computer screen and gave me a medium-bright smile that suggested the wattage could go up or down, depending on the value of my business to the firm.

"Hi. Robert Shipley to see Mr. Osborn. I have an appointment."

"Very well. I'll let him know you're here."

Osborn kept me waiting for five minutes. Any shorter would have shown he wasn't busy, and any longer would have been rude. When he walked into the reception area he had the sort of appearance I'd expected. He had a golfer's tan, a Rolex, and a suit that cost more than any three of mine.

He gave a firm handshake, looking me over with shrewd but slightly bloodshot eyes. I couldn't tell what he thought he saw, but I figured the redness—along with his soft waistline—was probably an occupational hazard for someone whose job required a lot of wining and dining.

"Thanks for agreeing to see me on short notice, Mr Osborn."

"Under the circumstances I didn't have much choice."

He kept his voice low so the receptionist couldn't hear him. I didn't reply, and he led the way to his office. He waved me toward a chair and closed the door, making sure it was shut completely.

You can tell a lot about a person by his or her office. Osborn's was impressively large with a good view of K Street. The walls were crowded with framed photos of Osborn with presidents, senators, House members, CEOs, and what appeared to be kings and princes, mostly from Middle Eastern nations. There weren't many photos of Osborn and women, and besides the one with Margaret Thatcher they showed him with a few TV journalists and two or three movie stars.

Behind his desk, placed so that a visitor could see it, he had a photo of his family—his wife and two sons. It was a professional shot, taken at a beach with all four of them wearing white clothes that were almost as bright as the perfect teeth in their posed smiles. Yes, you can tell a lot about a person from an office.

But Osborn wasn't smiling now. He sat behind his desk and looked at me again with those shrewd eyes. "What's this all about, Mr. Shipley?"

"That's what I'd like to know. You're friends with Lisa Lindstrom—

"

"Yes, of course. There's her picture, her with her dad. I know him too."

I looked where he pointed and saw a photo of the three of them, Lisa in the middle wearing a formal gown at some black-tie affair. Based on their appearance, I thought the photo had been taken fairly recently.

"And you also said you don't know Cate Gaulois."

"No, I don't. In my business you have to have a good memory for names and faces, and I don't know a Cate Gaulois."

"But you did meet her once. That night, when you took Lisa to Majority Whip. She was the woman who asked Lisa to dance— short, brown hair, athletic-looking."

"Yes, I remember that—vaguely. But she didn't tell me her name. She was interested in Lisa, not me."

He gave me a little smile that told me what he was imagining about the two women, and I wanted to wipe it off his face. "You never saw her again?"

"No."

"Never went to the 1776 Club to see her dance? That was her job, dancing there."

"Interesting." The little smile persisted, and I had to force myself not to curl my fingers into a fist. "But, no, I've never been there."

"Did you know that Lisa started seeing her? That the two women became close?"

That got rid of his smile. "I, uh—why are you asking me all these questions? I have a right to know. You said you're a lawyer—you're not with the FBI, are you?"

I wondered if he had some reason for thinking the FBI might come calling. "No, I'm in private practice. I'm not a law-enforcement official of any sort."

"Then what's your interest in the Gaulois woman?"

"I'm trying to find out who killed her."

"She's . . . been murdered?"

"Yes, it's in the news today. Someone shot her."

"But I—I—that is, I don't know anything about that."

"You didn't answer my question earlier: you didn't say whether you knew Lisa had started seeing someone, another woman."

"No, I didn't answer it. If Lisa had told me something like that, it would be between the two of us. I'm not in the habit of repeating

all over town what friends—or clients—have told me in confidence."
*But you might if there's a buck in it for you—or something else you
want.* "Maybe not, but this is important. A woman is dead."

"And I'm sure the police will try to find the murderer. What
business is it of yours?"

"A client hired me to do an investigation, and Cate Gaulois is—
was—part of it."

"Which client? Not Lisa?"

I shook my head. "I can't say, Mr. Osborn. That's confidential—and
I protect confidences too."

"Well, that's all I can tell you. I saw the Gaulois woman only once,
that night at the club, and I know nothing about her."

"Do you know Bill Murphy?"

He frowned. "Yes, of course. I know all the senior Congressional
staffers. Why"

"Did he know Cate Gaulois?"

"I have no idea. Why don't you ask him?"

I didn't tell him I already had. "I suppose you know Frank Nelson
too."

"Certainly."

"Same question: did he know her?"

"Goddamn it! How should I know! You'd have to ask *him*, not me."

"Who would want to keep Lisa Lindstrom from running for the
Senate?"

That stopped him cold. He looked at me, then picked up a pen and
toyed with it for several seconds before answering. "I heard she
might be considering that—her father's poor health is no secret.
Does she plan to run?"

"As you said to me, you'd have to ask her. But suppose she does.
Who'd want to stop her?"

"Oh, probably lots of people—people opposed to her politics,
people who might want to run themselves. All politicians have
opponents, even enemies. I certainly did when I was in the House."

"Do you still?"

He smiled again but not smutty like before. "Sure. Lobbyists
aren't well liked, generally speaking. Fortunately, it's not my job to
be liked."

"Who'd want to stop her badly enough to do something about it—
I mean, pressure her into dropping the idea?"

"What sort of pressure?"

"Hard. Even illegal."

"Well, it wouldn't be the first time in this town. I could tell you stories you wouldn't believe."

"Do you know who might want to stop her badly enough to kill someone?"

"Someone? You mean Cate Gaulois."

I noticed he'd used her full name this time. "Yes."

He paused before answering. "Mr. Shipley, I've told you all I can about the Gaulois woman. It wasn't much, but it's all I know. I'm not going to speculate about who might have committed a serious crime like blackmail or murder."

"I didn't mention blackmail."

His face reddened to match his eyes. "Yes, you did—you asked who'd blackmail her to keep her from running."

"I just said 'pressure'."

"You also said 'illegal', so I, uh, just assumed . . ." His voice trailed off, but I didn't say anything. "I mean, that's what it sounded like."

"What do you know about any blackmail attempt against Lisa Lindstrom?"

"Nothing! I have no knowledge of that—if there even is such a thing." He stood, glaring at me. "Look, I've said all I'm going to say. You're not law enforcement, and I don't have to talk to you."

"But you should talk to me. It's better for you than talking to reporters—or the police."

"Don't try to scare me, Shipley. I can play rough when I have to."

"What the hell does that mean?"

"It means just what it sounds like. Now get out of my office."

"Calm down. If you're not involved with what I'm investigating, you've got nothing to hide."

"I don't have anything to hide, but I'm done talking to you, and I want you out of here. If you don't leave right now, I'll call security, and they can help you leave."

I got out of the chair and looked at him. "All right, I'll go. But I think you are hiding something. I don't know what, but I'll find out."

He reached for the phone, and I held up a hand. "No need for that."

I walked out of his office and down the hall to the reception area. The receptionist looked surprised to see me without Osborn. I gave her a little wave and left the office.

Riding down in the elevator, I replayed what Osborn had told me and tried to make sense of it. *He'd seemed genuinely surprised to hear about Cate's death. That might rule him out as the murderer—or it might simply mean he was a good actor.*

If he had killed her, what was his motive? Money? Maybe—that's why he'd become a lobbyist—but he didn't seem like someone who'd kill for a paycheck.

Then I remembered what Sarah had said about his background. He might know someone who'd commit murder for hire. And hiring it done was the same thing as doing it himself.

In either case he might well know more about Cate than he'd told me. And more about Lisa—perhaps including the blackmail ploy.

But given the way the conversation had ended, I didn't think Osborn would talk to me again. That meant I'd have to figure out another way to get to the bottom of things.

I'd begin by talking to Bill Murphy. Maybe Osborn hadn't known Cate Gaulois, but there was no doubt Murphy had. So that was my next stop.

CHAPTER TWELVE

I took the Metro to the Capitol South station, where the escalator—surprise!—was working. After reaching street level I walked toward the manicured grounds of the House office buildings.

Gray clouds were gathering low in the west, but cotton bolls floated in the deep blue over the Capitol dome, and trees swayed in the breeze as though their still-green leaves could ward off winter. The trees on the Blue Ridge Mountains west of Washington weren't supposed to display fall colors for at least two more weeks, so I guessed the leaves in the city wouldn't begin turning for a month or more.

I walked up the marble steps of Wheaton's building. Just as I reached the front doors, three intense-looking people in suits came out. I recognized one as the speaker of the House and was sure I'd seen the other two on Sunday-morning talk shows. Several aides and assistants swam in their wake.

Such encounters were common in Washington. Still, I had never become blasé about running into D.C.'s powerful people and thought I probably never would, no matter how long I lived in the area.

Inside I passed through security and at the appointed time was standing in front of Wheaton's office. I pressed the button next to the door and heard the muffled sound of the buzzer.

When the lock clicked, I pushed the door open. I told the receptionist I was there to see Murphy, and she asked me to have a seat.

I looked around the empty waiting room, sat in a large leather chair facing the receptionist, picked up a copy of *Time* and began reading about the political scandal of the week.

A few minutes later a pair of nylon-clad legs came into view above the magazine. I glanced up and saw an intelligent-looking young woman gazing at me.

"Mr. Murphy can see you now. Please come this way."

I followed as she walked past the receptionist's desk, turned in front of a conference room that looked out over Capitol Hill, and then went down a hallway lined with several tiny secretarial bays and a few small offices. Having learned from my research that 100 senators have three office buildings but 435 representatives and their staffs are crammed into only four, I wasn't surprised to find the office suite crowded.

The hallway terminated in a large, dark-paneled office that I guessed was Wheaton's. My guide stopped at the last office before her boss's and knocked lightly on the closed door.

"Come in." A deep voice came clearly through the dark oak. The woman opened the door and stood aside.

The office's sole occupant was sitting behind a large desk cluttered with letters, memos, file folders, spreadsheets, press releases, and newspapers. His thick, dark hair was going gray. A pair of tortoise-shell glasses looked fragile on his strong face. The man removed his glasses and stood, showing muscular arms beneath twice-rolled sleeves.

"Mr. Shipley." The man's tone was polite, but he didn't come from behind his desk or offer to shake hands. He was about my height and solidly built. Something about the man reminded me of a boxer I'd known in the Navy—a fighter who won most of his bouts.

"Good afternoon, Mr. Murphy. Thank you for taking time to see me." As I laid one of my business cards on his desk, I heard the door softly click shut.

"Please." He waved toward a close relative of the chairs in the waiting room. After we were seated, he picked up my card and examined it closely. "Shipley. Just like the guy in *Sands of Iwo Jima.*"

"How's that?"

"A movie about the Marines in World War II. Shipley's the guy who charges the Japanese machine-gun bunker. He says, 'I want to get at 'em,' or something like that."

"What happens to him?"

"He's killed. Of course, that gives Sergeant Stryker, played by John Wayne, the motivation to charge the bunker himself, and he blows it up."

"Hmm. Given the characters' names, I would've written the scene the other way round."

"No doubt. But Shipley had to do it—lead the way, I mean."

"Although Wayne is the guy everybody remembers."

"True, but people seldom know the names of the men who charge the guns—just the name of whoever gives the order." Murphy paused. "Now, what can I do for you? Or, more precisely, for your client?"

"As I said on the phone, I want to talk to you about Cate Gaulois."

"Why? And who is your client?"

"I'm afraid I can't identify the client right now. I can tell you that Ms. Gaulois was involved in a blackmail attempt, perhaps unwittingly, and that her involvement may have led to her death."

His eyes widened. Instead of replying, he turned toward the windows, which looked out over Capitol Hill. The western clouds were now thicker and grayer.

After several seconds he said, "Blackmail? That wasn't in the paper. It just said she died from gunshot in a probable murder."

"I'm sure the police will know more soon."

He turned back to me, but his face was now a mask. "Maybe, maybe not, depending on how careful the killer was."

"With today's DNA tests and other forensic evidence, it's almost impossible to leave no trace."

"Well, I wouldn't know. Being a lawyer, you're probably well versed in that sort of thing. I just try to run this office and keep the constituents happy."

"That doesn't sound easy, especially if you have other things to do . . . such as keeping some of your colleagues in line."

Murphy looked closely at me, but the mask didn't slip. "Not many people are aware that I knew Cate. How did you find out?"

"One of her coworkers told me."

"What else were you told?"

"About you? Mostly that you used to go to the 1776 Club to watch Cate dance."

"I went there to see her, not to watch her dance."

"What does that mean? That you looked the other way whenever she was on stage?"

"Save your sarcasm, young man. I meant exactly what I said: I used to go there but not to watch her dance. I went to the club to talk to her, be with her."

"Why?"

"That's my business."

"The police will likely to make it theirs. What'll you tell them?"

"That I cared for Cate. That I wanted to be her . . . friend, help her if I could."

"Just a friend? Cate Gaulois was a good-looking young woman who made her living by dancing naked. Do you expect me to believe your relationship with her was strictly platonic?"

"I don't give a damn what you believe. It happens to be the truth. Maybe in your line of work you hear the truth so seldom you have trouble recognizing it."

"Well, I can sure recognize bullshit when I hear it. How were you trying to help her?"

"I was trying to protect her."

"From what?"

He paused. "Everything. This town. People who might try to take advantage of her, use her."

"And who's that?"

"A lot of people. Certainly whoever killed her."

"Do you know who did?"

"No, do you?"

I leaned forward in the chair. "Look, this is going nowhere, and I don't have time to play games."

"Nor do I, but I seem to be doing most of the talking. Why should I tell you more than I already have? Especially when you've told me nothing, either about your client or this supposed blackmail."

"Because I might be able to protect Cate's reputation. That is, if she wasn't a willing participant in the blackmail scheme."

"This supposed scheme—you've given me no evidence that it actually exists."

"It exists, all right, or I wouldn't be here. Come on, Mr. Murphy, who had a reason to kill Cate?"

"I told you: I don't know. No one—unless maybe some creep she met at the club."

"I need a name. Was she seeing anyone?"

"No one in particular, as far as I know. Just different guys."

"Any women?"

He froze. "Women? Cate had lots of female friends. Girls who worked at the club, other girls."

"That's not what I mean. Did she have romantic relationships with other women?"

"Cate wasn't a lesbian!"

He got up and went over to the windows. A dark blanket was spreading over much of the sky, and a few lights had winked on along the streets, making the unlit places look black by contrast. "A little experimentation wouldn't make her a lesbian," I said to his back. "And what if she was? She'd still have been the same person you cared about."

He turned to face me. "Well, I don't think she was. She seemed perfectly normal to me. Of course, we never talked about . . . that sort of thing."

I waited but he didn't elaborate. "There was something between you two. I don't know what it was, but there was something between you."

"If there was, it was our business, not yours or anyone else's."

"Did Cate have any family in the area?"

"No." His tone was flat.

"What was she to you?" The words sounded harsh even to me.

Anger glittered in Murphy's dark eyes. "Fuck you." His didn't raise his voice, but it was rough with gravel. "Get the hell out of my office. Don't ever ask me about her again."

☐ ☐ ☐

Heading down the parkway toward Old Town, the Tuesday evening traffic was unusually light, and I was able to drive faster than I'd expected. From distraction or obstinacy I'd left the MGB's top down, and wind whipped over and around the bug-streaked windshield, strong enough to ruffle even my short hair. The sky was now completely clouded over, and the temperature had dropped noticeably. I caught the sharp scent of rain on the way.

As I drove, I thought about what Murphy had told me. *Not much, certainly not as much as he seems to know. His relationship with Cate had to be more than casual, but what was it exactly? Sexual, despite his denial? Was he in on the blackmail? Or could it have been something else?*

I got to Old Town just before the rain began. I pulled over to put up the top, then drove the remaining distance to the office, the three short wipers beating time as they slicked water from the windshield.

Walking into the building, I remembered coming in with Lisa the day before, which now seemed like a week ago. I said hello to Georgia and poured a cup of burnt, end-of-the-day coffee.

"How did it go?" Georgia gave me what I thought of as her "supportive" smile, the one she used when she sensed things weren't going well.

"Great. The first guy told me almost nothing, and the second one didn't tell me anything useful, but he did tell me to go fuck myself."

"Really? That's rude."

"I agree." I drank some of the coffee and wished I hadn't.

"What can I do to help?"

I started to say there was nothing she could do, but then I remembered she was better with computer research than I was.

"In the morning you can double-check my database searches on a few people. Maybe you can find something I didn't."

"All right. What else?"

"I can't think of anything right now. And don't you have class tonight?"

"No, not on Tuesdays."

"That's right—I forgot. Well, I'm going to get some dinner later. Want to join me?" To lighten the invitation, I added, "Maybe that'll help make up for Jack and me keeping you late so often."

"It would be a good start, but I'll have to take a rain check. I don't have class, but I do have plans."

"Oh." I was more disappointed than I'd have imagined. "Sorry you can't make it. Maybe another time."

"I'd like that—I'd like it very much." She smiled as she turned back to her work.

I went upstairs. Jack was on the phone, talking loudly and gesturing. He waved absently when he saw me walking past and then almost shouted, "No, goddamn it! Don't admit or concede anything. Just tell them that you're discussing the situation with your lawyers and that one of us will get back to them in a few days."

At my desk I looked at the work that was beginning to pile up while I chased whomever was after Lisa Lindstrom. Or chased my tail—I wasn't sure which. I picked up a document and started to read but found myself scanning the same paragraph over and over. I kept thinking of Cate's dead body, the synthetic joy of the 1776 Club, Osborn's gangster connections, and Murphy's threatening growl.

Around 6:30 I looked up to see Georgia in the doorway. I sensed she'd been there for a while, watching.

"I think I'll go now, unless you need me for something," she said. "Jack said he's about done for the day."

"Got a hot date?" I admired her figure as she stood there, one knee slightly bent, a hand on the doorjamb.

"Well, I'm going to dinner with a friend, and, yes, it's a male friend."

"Hey, I didn't mean to pry. Have a great time, and kiss him once for me."

She raised her delicate eyebrows. "Just once? I was hoping to do better than that."

I tried to think of a clever reply but couldn't, and Georgia seemed surprised at my silence.

"Actually, I'll probably make it an early night. I've got some studying to do."

"Well, have fun. I know I did at your age."

"Still do, from what I hear."

"If you heard it from Jack, he's only trying to cover his trail."

Georgia chuckled and then turned and left, moving with her usual grace.

I looked back at the snowdrift of papers, then tossed the unread document on top of the pile. I picked up my scuffed leather briefcase, said goodnight to Jack, and headed out the door.

CHAPTER THIRTEEN

I trotted in the rain, dodging puddles, to the little Italian place down the street and ate dinner at the bar while I watched the news on the wall-mounted TV. The bartender knew me and my habits and made just enough conversation to be friendly but not so much as to be intrusive.

I declined his offer of dessert on the house but lingered over a second glass of red wine, thinking about Lisa's case and wondering if there was anything more I could do about it that night. I couldn't think of anything, so I decided to go home and start fresh in the morning.

By the time I came out of the restaurant, the rain had stopped but the trees were still dripping. The rain seemed to have driven almost everyone indoors, and beneath the streetlights the empty pavement shone like a gray satin ribbon.

I went back to the office for my car and started for home. I had just turned off Washington Street when I noticed that a pair of headlights seemed to be following me. The brightness grew until I had to cant the rear-view mirror.

That cut the glare somewhat but seemed to signal the other car to follow more closely. Suddenly the car accelerated, sped past me—it was a big, black sedan—and swerved to block the narrow street.

I braked as hard as I could without locking up, and the car slid to a stop on the wet pavement. I wished I had my gun, a .357 Magnum that I took to a shooting range about once a month. But the revolver, a Dan Wesson make, was where I usually kept it: locked in my desk at the office.

My adrenaline surged the way it had in Navy SERE school, where the instructors in Survival, Evasion, Resistance, and Escape techniques had taken great delight in making us students feel like hunted rabbits. I hadn't needed to draw on my SERE training since then, but I remembered a key lesson: once spotted by the hunter, rabbits run . . . or die.

A lanky man in dark clothing scrambled out of the sedan and pointed something at me. I couldn't see it well, but I was pretty sure what it was.

I ground the gearshift into reverse and floored the accelerator. As the car jerked backward, something flashed in the darkness, and I heard a hard, flat noise like a two-by-four slamming down on concrete. A bullet drilled through the windshield, leaving a spider web in the safety glass. Dust and stuffing poofed from the passenger's seat.

My heart raced. *Better scared than shot.* I kept backing up as fast as the old car would go.

The gunman put a second shot through the windshield a few inches from the first, making the spider web bigger. The bullet zipped past my ear.

No lights sprang on in houses, no one screamed, no dogs barked. I was on my own.

I cranked the wheel hard to the right to swing the car's rear end toward the sidewalk. When the wheels hit the curb, abruptly stopping the MGB, I slammed the car into first gear and pumped the accelerator. The little car shuddered and began to move.

As I gathered momentum, I bent low over the wheel and speed-shifted into second. The MGB lurched forward, tires squealing, as I began a sharp left turn.

The evasive action may have confused the gunman but only for a moment. A third bullet punched through the convertible top and buried itself somewhere in the dashboard.

The lanky man's aim was good enough to make me grateful it wasn't better. As my car continued to accelerate, I straightened it out with white-knuckled hands and sped down the street.

I glanced in the rear view and saw a pair of headlights slant my way, then point directly at me and grow brighter. As the tailing car began to gain, I screeched around a corner, dashed down the block, and took another corner. Halfway down that block I braked hard, swerved to the right, and squeezed through an alley with blank brick walls.

Now there were no headlights in the mirror. At the end of the alley I turned onto the street, quickly drove two blocks, and headed for a ramp that led into an underground garage. I was about to go down the ramp when a police cruiser appeared behind me, roof rack flashing.

The cop closed in and gave a quick blast on the siren. I slowed to a crawl and pulled into a metered space.

I sat with both hands on the wheel while the officer called in my tag number, and I stayed that way until he tapped on my window. Then I rolled it down and looked at the cop. I knew several Alexandria police officers but didn't recognize this one.

"Good evening, sir. Do you know why I stopped you?"

I knew better than to admit I'd been speeding. "Did I do something wrong?"

"You were going over the speed limit, sir."

"I was?"

"Yes, sir. The speed limit in this area is twenty-five miles per hour. You were going close to fifty. May I see your license and registration, please?"

I dug them out and handed them to the officer, who checked the photo against my face before walking back to the cruiser.

In a couple of minutes he returned. "Any particular reason you were speeding, sir?"

"Someone was shooting at me."

I saw in the policeman's face that he'd never heard that excuse before and didn't believe it this time.

He cleared his throat. "Someone was shooting at you?"

"That's what I said. Take a look at the windshield on the other side."

The officer stared at me, then walked around the rear of the car to the passenger's side. He shone his flashlight on the windshield, bending to examine the small, starred holes.

"When did this happen and where?"

I could hear him clearly through the convertible top. "Right here in Old Town, less than five minutes ago."

"Who was shooting at you?"

"I don't know, but I'm going to find out."

The policeman me a disapproving look. "Wait here."

In the rear view I saw the cop talking on his cruiser's radio. After a short conversation he came back. "Lieutenant Lytle says to bring you in. Also says he knows you."

"We're acquainted."

"For your sake I hope you mean socially. Okay, please get out of your car and come with me."

I locked the MGB and followed the policeman, relieved that he didn't reach for his handcuffs. I climbed into the cruiser's back seat, knowing that my long day was about to get longer.

CHAPTER FOURTEEN

Half an hour later I was sitting in an uncomfortable chair in Lieutenant John Lytle's office at Alexandria police headquarters. "Little John" had supposedly gotten his nickname from the last-name-first, first-name-last roll calls in police basic training. I thought the nickname probably had more to do with the fact that, like Robin Hood's lieutenant, Little John was big—six-four with a chest like an oil barrel and arms like oak limbs.

"Well, Robert, what you got yourself into this time?" Lytle's voice was soft for a big man, but there was a hint of steel in it. His worn chair creaked as he leaned back and propped a foot on a half-opened bottom drawer of his desk.

I didn't have to guess whether he was annoyed. His ebony face wore a scowl that would've been frightening if I hadn't known him better.

"It's been a bitch of a day," Lytle said, loosening his necktie further below the open collar of his wilted white shirt. "Now, instead of going home to my wife and a good dinner, I got to deal with you."

"Did the arresting officer tell you someone shot at me?"

"Yeah. Hell, I've wanted to take a shot at you myself a time or two."

"That's only when I win your money at one of Jack's poker games."

"No, it's mostly when you remind me how much I've lost. At least you take Jack's money too. Shit, I can't believe two Marines can't beat a sorry-ass, no-account squid at poker."

He reached down into the open drawer and pulled out a bottle of Early Times. He emptied a coffee cup onto a dying plant and poured a stiff shot into the cup. He moved as if to cap the bottle, then looked at me.

"That's because you don't know how to bluff," I said, looking steadily back at him.

Lytle frowned and reached into the drawer for a second cup. He blew out the dust, splashed in some whiskey, and passed the cup across the stacks of files on his desk.

He propped his foot on the drawer again and took a drink. "Now, tell me true. Why would someone want to close your account, permanent-like?"

"I don't know. I haven't offended anyone any more than usual, as far as I know."

He snorted. "In that case it's probably some woman looking to even the score—and no jury would convict her."

"Thanks for that vote of confidence, but the shooter looked like a man."

"Then I'm guessing you're mixed up with what my mama calls the wrong sort of people."

"Your mother sounds like a wise woman."

"Yeah, well, she's smart enough not to get shot at." Lytle took another drink. I drank some myself, waiting.

"Come on, Robert, what're you into? A client who's dealing? Pimping? Both? Or maybe what you counselors call white-collar crime, like washing money and hanging it out to dry?"

I knew I had to tell him at least part of the truth. "Nothing like that. I'm working on a blackmail case."

Blackmail, huh? Don't you think that's a matter for us 'pue-lease'? Or maybe you still think we're too dumb to handle shit like that?"

I knew he was referring to my *pro bono* defense, three months earlier, of a drug dealer whom the police had wrongly suspected of murder. One cop was so determined to get the dealer that he planted evidence. After I proved what the cop had done, the judge dismissed the case.

"You know that's not true!"

"I do? How do I know that? You didn't come to me first, give me a chance to fire that cop's sorry ass and have the prosecutor let your guy go. No, you had to wait until the case was in court. You had to make the whole damn police department seem corrupt because of what one fool did. The papers may have loved you for it, but I sure didn't."

"I've told you before that I didn't have all the evidence before the trial started."

"Well, you had enough to come to me, and you should've. Even Jack thinks you were wrong on that one."

"He does? He never told me that."

"Maybe you ought to do less talking, more listening. You're smart, but no one knows everything, not even Robert Edward Shipley,

Esquire. And something else: there's nothing wrong with asking for help when you need it."

I thought for a moment. "I still think I did the right thing. I'm sorry if it made you and the rest of the department look bad."

"Yeah, like that makes everything okay." Lytle dropped his foot to the scuffed tile floor, and the chair creaked again as he leaned forward. "Now let's talk about your latest mess. You're working on a blackmail case and someone's shooting at you. Who's your client, what's the blackmail angle, and who's the shooter?"

"I have no idea who shot at me. The blackmail involves a sexual indiscretion—that's all I can say right now. I can't tell you who the client is because of attorney-client privilege."

"Oh, I see. Somebody's shooting up my streets, but you can't tell me jack because it's privileged."

"That's the best I can do. I'll tell you what I can about any criminal activity I uncover."

He banged his cup down on the desk so hard I thought the porcelain might break. "Well, that's just fine! You'll tell us what you can when you can. I sure do feel better now."

He paused for a moment, glaring at me. "Listen here, Robert. I don't give a damn what the Virginia State Bar would think about it. I want to know everything you know about this case, right now. If you don't tell me, you're going to wish you had."

"I'm sorry, Lieutenant. I can't tell you. I can't disclose anything my client has said or given to me in confidence, and I have nothing to say about the shooting incident except what I already told the patrolman."

Lytle looked as though he would explode. "Then you can just sit in jail, goddamn it!"

Then I understood why Jack said Lytle's fellow Marines had been almost as afraid of him as the North Vietnamese troops he'd fought. He stamped out of the office, his heavy tread making the floor vibrate. I knew better than to follow him or even get out of the chair.

After a couple of minutes a uniformed officer appeared in the doorway. She had a blank expression and said in that robotic tone cops often use when dealing with civilians. "Come with me, sir."

I'd expected to be booked and taken to a cell, but she escorted me to an interrogation room and left me there with the door locked. For almost two hours I sat with nothing to eat or drink and, worse, nothing to read. I reminded myself that at least no one was singing in my ear, puking on my shoes, or trying to make me his bitch.

Eventually I began wondering how much trouble I'd get into if I took a leak in the trash can. I decided I was in enough trouble already and would wait until I had no choice but to use the can—literally.

I'd just about reached that point when the lock clicked, the door banged open, and Lytle strode in. I straightened but otherwise remained still while he glowered at me.

"You gonna talk now?"

"Sorry, I can't."

"You can, but you won't."

"All right, I won't. Not yet."

"You're making a big mistake, Robert."

"Maybe. If so, it isn't my first one."

He didn't reply right away. Clearly angry, he made a fist but was too good a cop to hit me, so instead he pounded it into his open palm.

"Then I guess I'll have to have to let you go. I've got nothing to hold you on but that speeding crap and—according to you—being shot at. Unfortunately, that's not enough. You understand me, don't you?"

"I understand your job is to enforce the law. I also understand there's no evidence to suggest I've broken any laws."

A muscle twitched near Lytle's mouth. "We'll see. I hope Jack Benton knows as much law as he pretends to—I think you're going to need a good attorney. And you know what they say about a lawyer who represents himself."

He started to go but turned back. "Robert, before you're done with this, you'll wish you'd talked to me about this thing. I guarantee it. Now get the hell out of here."

Lytle left. When the sound of his footsteps had faded, I walked out, detouring through the men's room along the way. No one tried to stop me from leaving the building.

Hailing a cab after 11 p.m. took a while. When the cab dropped me off at my car, I climbed wearily inside and called Lisa.

She picked up after two rings. "Yes?"

"It's me. Bad news."

"What's that?"

"Someone doesn't want me looking into this."

"Really? How do you know?"

"Because that someone—or somebody he hired—tried to kill me tonight."

I heard her suck in her breath. "How?"

"The usual way, with a gun."

"You're not hurt, are you?"

"Just my pride. The police picked me up as I was getting away. They're not too happy with me."

"You didn't tell them about me, did you?"

I frowned. "Thanks for your compassion. No, I didn't tell them about you, but I may have to if this thing gets out of hand."

"What do you mean, 'out of hand'?"

"I mean, if people keep shooting at me. Remember I'm withholding evidence of at least two crimes, blackmail and murder."

"Isn't that covered by attorney-client privilege?"

"Yes, but you can waive the privilege anytime you want to."

"I can't do that, Robert. It would kill my chances for election."

"No, God forbid we should do anything that would hurt your career. Maybe you should have thought about that before you had an affair with a stripper."

"You bastard! Who are you to talk that way to me?"

"Maybe the only person who's ever told you the truth about yourself!"

The remark seemed to catch her off guard. She paused before saying in a more even tone, "Perhaps you're right. But who's told you the truth about yourself?"

"Jack, once in a while. And Georgia—even though she usually disguises it as a joke."

"Haven't I ever told you the truth? About you or . . . about us?"

"I'd have to think about it." I looked out at the empty street, remembering. "Maybe. Yeah, maybe you did, and I just had a little trouble recognizing it."

She paused again. "Robert, I never wanted to hurt you. I really did care—I mean, I *do* care for you. It's just that at the time, well, I think I got caught up in the situation and may have misled you about some things."

"I see. Well, it doesn't matter. I don't think we'll be in that particular situation again."

"Maybe not. But you never know. Remember how we got there to begin with?"

"I think you stopped me after an evening class and said you had some questions about civil procedure."

That's right. We talked about them—and some other things—over drinks."

"Several drinks."

So many that I'd finally taken her keys and driven her home. After I helped her up the steps, she'd turned to kiss me goodnight. At least I thought it was goodnight. One long, deep kiss led to another, then still another, and soon there was a trail of clothing across the floor of her living room and into her bedroom.

"Yes, we had a few. And when we got to my place . . . well, your procedure wasn't all that civil, but it was effective."

"So was yours. I was sore the next morning."

"But I brought you a pizza that evening so we could have dinner and then study."

"We didn't get much studying done."

"No"—she drew it out like a cat purring—"not *that* kind of studying."

I savored the memory for a moment before getting back to business. "I went to see Bill Murphy."

"Good. Did he tell you anything useful?"

"Not really. He admits knowing Cate Gaulois but won't say much about their relationship. He claims it wasn't sexual."

"I'll bet he's lying."

"Nice implication about your former lover."

"Sorry, darling, but we didn't have an exclusive relationship. At least I didn't, and I didn't expect her to. You should know that."

"Yes, and I guess I should. Well, we'll probably never know how she felt about it. In any case Murphy claims not to know about the blackmail."

"And you didn't mention my name to him?"

"Of course not. Bottom line: there's no smoking gun in the blackmail thing." Suddenly remembering how Cate died, I regretted my choice of words, but Lisa didn't react, at least not enough to detect over the phone. "Just the coincidence of the attack on me, which is certainly suspicious but doesn't prove Murphy's involved."

"So where does that leave us? I've only got three more days!"

"I know. I'll try Murphy again tomorrow, see what he says about my little adventure tonight. Maybe the police will turn up something on the shooter. I'll call you with any news. Otherwise, I'll see you tomorrow evening at the state society event."

"Umm . . . okay. Good night, Robert."

"'Night."

As I drove home, tired, hungry, and in need of a drink, my brain buzzed with confusion. Thoughts about the case, Lytle, and Lisa whirled through my head. The mysterious relationship between Cate and Murphy, the surprising one between Cate and Lisa, Lytle's anger and frustration with me.

And my past with Lisa. Her combination of beauty, wit, and self-assurance made her attractive to most men. Her family background and money and, of course, her uninhibited attitude toward sex made her more so. I remembered how she'd looked in bed—that tousled blonde hair, her face shiny with sweat, her mouth open and breathing hard. . . .

I knew I could tell myself that I was just trying to help a client, but I also knew that things were different with this particular client, that I wanted to do a good job for more than just professional reasons.

Maybe to prove to both of us that I'm capable of playing in the same league as a senator's daughter who's now a millionaire's wife. That I can cut it after all.

That might not be the right answer, but it was an answer, and I was willing to let the matter rest there, at least for the moment. I decided to focus on the case and not my motives for taking it.

When I got home, I walked straight to the shower, stripping as I went. I stood under the stinging spray for a long time, trying to wash the day's events from my pores. When I finally got out, I rubbed myself with a towel, wrapped it around my waist, and went down to the kitchen.

I was still hungry but felt too tired to eat. Instead I splashed two fingers of bourbon into a glass and drank the whiskey in three gulps. It burned.

I stumbled upstairs, dropped the towel on the floor, and fell into bed. Sleep came quickly.

CHAPTER FIFTEEN

Morning sunshine woke me, cutting through the half-closed blinds and slanting in golden bars across the bed. The pattern of shadows made me remember the previous night—the gunman, my escape, jail.

I knew I'd poked a stick into a hornets' nest.

Downstairs I made coffee, inhaling its aroma as I poured a cup. I had one sip, then another, and felt warmth beginning to spread through my body. I reminded myself to retrieve the gun from my office desk. I knew I'd been lucky to have gotten away the night before at the expense of some auto glass and a royal ass-chewing by Lieutenant Lytle.

I refilled the cup and took it to my bedroom, replaying my late-night conversation with Lisa. I was struck by how little the murder of Cate Gaulois seemed to have affected her.

Maybe it's just a tough-girl act and she really cared more for Cate than she shows. Or maybe she doesn't realize the blackmailer might be willing to do anything. Like kill me or anyone else who gets in his way.

When I got to the office, Georgia was at her desk as usual. Jack was away at a deposition. I re-read my notes on Lisa's case, made a few new ones, and spent some time thinking about what Osborn and Murphy had told me—and wondering what they hadn't. I still had more questions than answers, but I hoped that talking to Murphy again and going to the state society event would result in some progress.

I put the database printouts I wanted Georgia to check into a file folder and went downstairs, where she was eagerly taking photographs and papers from a cardboard box and spreading them on her desk.

"What have you got there? Something from a client?"

"*Không.*"

I recognized "no," one of a few Vietnamese words I'd learned from her.

"This box came in today's mail—it's from one of my aunts in

Vietnam. There's a letter too, but I haven't read it all yet."

Georgia's excitement made her accent more pronounced. "She's sent me some photos of my family in Vietnam and a few letters my mother wrote to her. Even some of my mother's scarves and jewelry."

"That's good. Family history is always interesting."

"Yes, especially when you don't have much."

I heard the sad note and watched as Georgia passed her hands over the photographs and letters, touching them lightly with her fingers. Suddenly I felt ashamed that I'd never asked Georgia about her childhood.

"Was it hard growing up in that orphanage in Saigon?"

"Ho Chi Minh City. That's what they changed it to when I was little although many people still call it Saigon." She paused. "Yes, it was hard. The orphanage itself wasn't great, but the worst thing was being ridiculed as a *Việt kiều*, a Vietnamese with an American father. Someone who's not really Vietnamese."

Her sadness gave way to bitterness. "That's why they kept me in the orphanage all those years. That, plus the way my mother had lived, hanging around bars and American soldiers."

"I'm sure it was hard. But at least you finally got out."

"Yes, I'm lucky a Vietnamese American family was willing to take me in as a teenager. I'll always be grateful for that even if I'll probably never think of myself as . . . belonging to them."

Georgia picked up one of the pictures and looked at it closely, turning it over to read the handwritten notation. "This is my mother and a serviceman in 1970, the year before I was born."

She held the photo out to me. The color had faded almost to black and white, but I could make out an attractive young Vietnamese woman in a short, Western-style dress. She was standing close to a man wearing dark-green fatigue trousers and a light-colored T-shirt. "DOGS" was written on the shirt in large reddish letters. A bush hat shaded the man's tanned face, making his features unrecognizable.

He had one arm around the woman, who was smiling into the camera, and the other arm cocked on his hip. Something about the careless stance made Shipley think of a cowboy who'd been paid off in Dodge City on a Saturday night.

I handed the picture back to her. "Your mother's lovely. Reminds me of her daughter."

Georgia blushed. "Right. Why don't you try being serious for once?"

"I am. You definitely inherited her good looks. Who's the guy with her?"

"*Tôi không biết*—I mean, I don't know. I suspect there are a lot of photos like that."

Her gaze lingered on the picture before she placed it on her desk. She sifted through the photos left in the box and held up another one. It showed Georgia's mother sitting at an outdoor cafe with an even younger Vietnamese woman and three laughing Americans. The tabletop was littered with empty bottles of "33" brand beer, crushed cigarette packs, and an overflowing ashtray.

"That's my aunt, the one who sent me the box. She was just a schoolgirl then and shouldn't have been at a bar, much less drinking. I guess she looked up to my mother and wanted to do whatever her big sister did."

Georgia cradled the picture in her hands. "If she and my mother were so close, I wonder why, when she was older, she never came to take me away from that place." The last few words were so soft that I had to strain to hear.

"I'm sure she would've if she could. She may have tried, but the government wouldn't let you leave it. Not to stay in Vietnam."

"Maybe you're right—I'd like to think so anyway. I guess I'm naïve, but I don't see how someone could abandon a child."

I had no answer for that. I didn't want her to be sad, so I tried to steer the conversation in a different direction. "Well, your aunt's certainly pretty, just like your mother. It seems to run in the family."

The trace of a smile crossed her face. "What's this, Robert, setting me up to work late tonight?" Her tone was warm despite the words, and I could see that the compliment pleased her.

She turned the photo over. "There's a note on the back. 'Your mother and me with some Americans, February 1970'."

I watched as Georgia stared at the picture again. Then she looked up at me. "One of them might be my father."

"Maybe. I'm sure your father would've liked to have known you."

"I would've liked to have known him. But I don't even know his name, and now I suppose I never will."

She blinked and wiped her eyes. I moved close to her and put an arm around her waist. She turned to me and began to cry, putting her hands on my shoulders and hiding her face against my chest. I stood awkwardly, not knowing what to say. Her sobs slowed after a minute, then gradually stopped. Georgia pulled herself away and sat down. She yanked a tissue from the box on her desk and dried her eyes.

"Sorry—didn't mean to get all emotional on you. Sometimes I just get sad about . . . things."

"I understand, Georgie. What's that phrase you used? *Việt* . . . what?"

She balled the tissue and dropped it into the wicker wastepaper basket. "*Việt kiều*. A Vietnamese born of the war. Like me."

Georgia put her hands in her lap and looked away, staring at nothing—or rather at something I couldn't see, obscured by the years. "Have I ever told you about my earliest memory?"

"No."

"I remember the day Saigon fell to the North Vietnamese. It was in the spring, and we wanted to play outside but they wouldn't let us. They made us take our naps early, but we couldn't sleep because of all the shooting and people shouting in the streets. Then we heard a sound like the flapping of giant bird wings. Later I learned it was the helicopters taking the Americans and a few Vietnamese away."

She paused, then looked at me. "We were left behind."

Even though I'd been in junior high at the time—April of '75—her words made me feel guilty. I nodded. "I know. Jack's still angry that we didn't do anything about it. He hasn't forgotten the buddies he lost in the war. Or what the war did to South Vietnam."

"Well, that fund Jack and his Marine friends set up sure helped me with college. I'm still amazed at how they found me, looking in Vietnam, then here."

"They must've thought a great deal of your mother."

"That's what Jack says. And it was nice of him to hire me so I could go to law school at night. I owe him a lot."

"So do I. Jack is generous that way. He was willing to give me a chance after . . . you know."

For a moment I thought Georgia was going to say something, but she simply reached out to squeeze my hand and then began putting the photos and letters back in the box.

I left the file folder with her and returned to my office, where I worked up an outline of the questions I wanted to ask Bill Murphy.

A little after noon I stood and stretched. I put his card in my wallet and some stale news magazines—emergency reading material—in my briefcase. Then I headed downstairs.

"I'm going out, Georgie."

She was too good at her job to ask where I was going and too good not to ask, "Do you know when you'll be back?"

"Probably not today. Just leave a voice message if you or Jack need me for anything."

"All right. See you tomorrow." She turned back to her computer, and as I walked out I could hear the keys clicking like a dozen knitting needles.

□   □   □

I slid into the convertible and pushed a homemade Elmore James cassette into the tape deck. As the electric blues of "Dust My Broom" surged from the speakers, I rolled onto the street.

I drove downtown to the vicinity of Farragut Square. A few blocks off K Street I pulled into a parking garage near the Armed Forces Club.

In the less formal of the club's two dining rooms I picked up *The Wall Street Journal* from a table near the door and scanned the headlines while the hostess, a stately, middle-aged woman, seated another party. She smiled at me as she walked back to her lectern.

"Hello, Commander Shipley. How are you today?"

"Hi, Nancy." I folded the paper and smiled back. "I'm fine, how are you?"

"Very well, thank you, sir. It's good to see you again. Table for one today?"

"Yes, please."

As I followed her to a quiet table I suddenly realized the club's employees, a few of whom had been there since I was in elementary school, now treated me exactly as they had my father, "Captain Shipley," years before. I remembered coming to the club when he was stationed at the Pentagon. The staff had fussed over me, saying I looked like a future admiral. My father had just laughed and told Nancy—a young woman then—and the others that they were spoiling me.

I also remembered that those outings stopped abruptly after my mother died in a car crash as she and my father returned from the club late one night. Dad, who'd had more than a few drinks before driving home, still blamed himself.

I was nine then. What I recalled most clearly about my mother was her quick smile and gentle hands, especially because my father wasn't known for gentleness. Sometimes when I was on the verge of sleep, I would hear her voice, the soft Southern cadence as soothing as cool water. But the words were always indistinct.

I ate a light lunch of soup and salad and read through the newspaper. Afterward I was tempted to spend a few minutes in the club's large library, where I almost always found something, usually a volume of history or biography, that I wanted to read. But I knew that a few minutes in the library usually turned into at least half an hour.

Promising myself a quiet drink and a chapter of a good book in the club bar that evening before I went to the state society event, I went to a tiny room off the lobby, took Bill Murphy's card out of my wallet, and punched his number into the telephone sitting on an antique desk.

The receptionist answered, and we went through the usual routine. I had to wait considerably longer than the day before, but eventually Murphy came on the line.

"What do you want now?"

"I want to find out who tried to kill me last night."

There was silence, then Murphy cleared his throat. "Someone tried to kill you?"

"Yes, tried pretty hard. My mother taught me not to hold grudges, but that sort of thing isn't easy to forgive and forget."

"Well, I know nothing about the matter, if that's the reason for your call."

"The reason is there has to be a connection between the attack on me and the murder of Cate Gaulois."

"I've said all I have to say about her. I thought I made that clear."

"You were very clear you don't want to talk about her. Beyond that not much is clear except she's dead."

"Damn it, Shipley, why are you meddling in this? The police are investigating her death—let them do their job."

"Like I told you yesterday, I'm working on a client matter that involves Ms. Gaulois. And it would be better for you to talk to me, Mr. Murphy. It might save you from having to talk to the police later."

I heard harsh breathing for a few seconds. Then Murphy said, "All right, come by my office right now. I'll give you a few minutes, but that's it."

Then I phoned Alexandria police headquarters and asked for Lieutenant Lytle. He wasn't in, but I left a message asking him to call me if he'd learned anything about my attacker.

I went outside and the doorman hailed a cab for me. Half an hour later I was standing in front of Wheaton's receptionist again. "Mr. Murphy's expecting me."

In a cooler tone than she'd used the day before, she told me to sit. After a few minutes a staffer—male this time—escorted me to Murphy's office.

The door was open, and Murphy glanced up as we arrived. Light glinted off his glasses, and I couldn't see his eyes.

Without standing, Murphy waved me to yesterday's chair. Then he turned back to his paperwork and kept me waiting a full minute while he read, or pretended to read, some sort of bound report.

Finally he put it down. He seemed annoyed that I was still there. "All right, let's get to it. Ask your damn questions."

"There's really only one, Mr. Murphy. Who murdered Cate Gaulois? I think you can help me answer it."

"Does your asking me for help—again—mean I'm off the list of suspects?"

"No, but you're the best lead I have right now."

"Well, I didn't kill her, so I hope you won't conclude I did."

"It's what the police think that counts. If I don't give them someone else soon, the cops are going to come knocking on your door."

Murphy gave me an angry look. "All right, but I don't have much to tell you. As I said yesterday, I don't even know who might've wanted to kill her."

"Well, someone wanted to. And shot her in the heart to do it."

CHAPTER SIXTEEN

The room became so quiet I could hear his desk clock ticking.

"How do you know that? It hasn't been in the news."

"I saw her body."

"At the morgue?"

"No, in her apartment. I'm the one who called the police. But apparently you already knew the details of the shooting. How?"

Murphy sat still. He continued to stare across the desk, but his gaze had become less hostile. "Through certain connections I was able to get a copy of the preliminary autopsy report."

"That proves you had an interest in Cate—and in her death."

"Perhaps, but it doesn't prove I killed her."

"If you didn't, who did? Given your interest in her, you must have some idea."

"If I did, young man, I'd be out looking for that person, not sitting here."

"You wouldn't care what that might do to you politically? I mean, depending on where the trail led?" I couldn't help sounding skeptical.

"Some things are more important than a job or even a career. Don't you know that, counselor?"

"Yes, I do." *I learned it the hard way.* "What's important to me is to find out who killed Cate."

"'Cate'? You never even met her."

"No, but I'd much rather have found her alive than dead."

Murphy didn't say anything. He took off his glasses and rubbed his eyes. After a few moments he said, "It was probably some guy who saw her at the club—some creep who became obsessed with her."

"That wouldn't explain someone coming after me. The motive must have been something else."

"Like what? You mentioned blackmail yesterday—that's ludicrous. Robbery? I doubt she owned anything worth stealing, much less killing for."

"Suppose she *knew* something?"

He replaced the glasses and shook his head. "I don't think so. I can't imagine what it would've been."

"What if she really was mixed up in a blackmail attempt? Say, one involving a politician?"

"Now you're circling back to me. I don't know anything about a blackmail plot. You're just fishing."

"I'm trying to help Cate, and you can help her too."

He looked away. "No, I can't—she's past help now. Past pain too."

"Okay, help yourself. If I can prove that someone else killed her, that means you didn't do it."

"I don't care what you can or can't prove. I know I'm innocent."

"If you're really innocent, you'll help me find the murderer."

"Goddamn it! Things aren't that simple! Leave this to the police and let them do their job." Beads of sweat had popped out on Murphy's forehead. He pulled a crumpled handkerchief from his pocket and mopped his face. "I don't want you or anyone else trying to dig up dirt on Cate, her life, her friends. I don't want to see any truth like that in the news."

"I understand your concern, but it's too late for you to try to protect her." I hesitated, then decided to say it. "Maybe you should have done something earlier, gotten her off that stage. But I guess watching her dance naked was just too much fun."

Murphy's face reddened and a vein bulged in his neck. "You don't know what the hell you're talking about! It wasn't like that." He took a deep breath, visibly trying to regain control. "I hated to see her dance, but I promised. . ."

"What?"

He didn't reply. His face was ugly, dark and drawn, jaw clenched beneath the stubbled skin.

"Promised *what*?"

"I made . . . I made a promise to help Cate. To look after her."

"And why did you make that promise?"

"I knew a relative of hers. A long time ago."

"You told me Cate didn't have any family."

"That's right. She was an only child. Her mother died when she was little."

"Who was this relative? Her father? Someone else?"

He didn't speak for several seconds. Finally he said, "I don't know why I've told you anything about Cate and me, but the truth is I had nothing to do with her death, and I don't know anyone who might've. Naturally, I hope her killer is caught and punished."

"Mr. Murphy—"

"Young man, you'll have to excuse me. I'm afraid I have nothing else to tell you, and I have a lot of work to do."

"Okay, just one more thing. Senator Talbot Lindstrom and his daughter Lisa—do they have any enemies?"

"What the hell does that have to do with ... oh, I see. Is somebody trying to get to one of them? The blackmailer maybe?"

"I didn't say that. I just asked if they have any enemies."

He barked out a laugh. "What a stupid question! And I'd begun to think you might be rather bright. Everyone in politics has enemies, lots of them."

"So you have enemies too?"

"Of course. Some of them I know, some I don't."

"Would any of them have killed Cate? Maybe as revenge against you?"

His eyes narrowed. "Revenge for what?"

"I'm asking you."

"This can be a dirty business—often is—but a political murder? I can't see it. Besides, nobody knew that Cate and I were ... friends. No one outside the 1776 Club anyway."

"Could Cate have had a relationship with someone else in politics? Or someone closely related to a politician?"

"Someone in politics, maybe someone named Talbot Lindstrom, eh?" When I didn't answer, he continued, "Maybe she was having a 'relationship' with Lindstrom? Or someone close to him, maybe someone on his staff?"

"I'm just considering possibilities."

Murphy shook his head. "Seems too unlikely. As I said, it was probably someone she met at the club. Some weirdo, some sick guy who watched her dance and then followed her home."

"What about the man who attacked me?"

"I have no idea, but there doesn't have to be a connection. Maybe it was a disgruntled client—that sort of thing has happened, you know."

"Yes, it has. Well, if your theory's right, I'll probably never find Cate's killer. But I'll keep working on the supposition that there was some rational motive behind the murder, that someone killed her for a reason other than lust or jealousy or hate."

"Aren't they all pretty much the same thing?"

There didn't seem to be anything else to ask, so I stood to go. "Well, thanks for your time."

Murphy didn't say, "You're welcome," but he did manage a graceless "Sure."

Neither of us offered to shake hands. As I reached the door, he said, "There is one thing."

I stopped with my hand on the knob. "Yes?"

"It probably doesn't mean anything."

"What?"

"I saw someone in the club one night."

"Who?"

"Frank Nelson, Senator Lindstrom's chief of staff."

"What was he doing there—besides the obvious?"

"I don't know. He didn't talk to Cate while I was there, but I wasn't there very long. Maybe he said something to her before I got there or after I left."

"Or maybe he didn't talk to her at all."

"Maybe, but it seems odd a man in his position would go to a place like that." He didn't seem to be aware of the irony of his remark.

"But he was there."

Murphy nodded.

"You think there's some significance to that?"

"Like I said, probably not. But haven't you made this your job? To find out?"

"Yes, I have." I waited a moment, but he didn't say anything further. I closed the door softly behind me.

□ □ □

Back in a taxi I thought about what Murphy had said and, perhaps more important, hadn't said. Obviously, the man had some connection to Cate beyond the 1776 Club. Maybe he'd been friends with someone in her family, or maybe he owed one of them something and looking out for Cate, however poorly he did it, was his way of fulfilling the obligation.

Murphy said everyone in politics has enemies—that sure doesn't make things easier. What was Nelson doing in that club? Washington has several strip joints—it seems like too much of a coincidence for him to have picked that one at random.

As the cab pulled into the semicircular driveway of the Armed Forces Club, I thought, *Well, I can look into that tonight, assuming he shows up.*

As I'd promised myself, I went to the library and browsed through the stacks, finally choosing a book on World War I. The book made me think of a photograph of my great-grandfather taken in France in 1918. He was standing in the mud, holding a mule by its bridle, a service pistol strapped to the waist of his Army overcoat. He'd been raised on a farm and seemed to be clinging to the mule as an anchor in the strange and terrifying sea of war.

I went down to the gym and found the locker I'd kept from when I worked downtown. Three-quarters of an hour later I was covered with sweat from using the treadmill and weights. Showering afterward, I thought of Lisa.

I remembered how she'd liked to get into the shower with me, pinning me against the tile while we kissed. Those showers usually turned into slippery love-making sessions that lasted as long as the hot water. Then we'd go to bed, dripping, and finish as the sheets dried us.

When I noticed the effect the memory was having, I yanked the lever to "Cold" and let the frigid water wash away the image of Lisa's naked body pressed against mine.

As I knotted my tie, I glanced in the mirror at my reverse image. Facing myself that way I couldn't help thinking, *Don't you know better than to get mixed up with her again, especially in something like this?* I had the answer but didn't like it.

I took the elevator to the second floor and walked into the main bar. The bartender saw me and began fixing my bourbon on the rocks. I sat at my usual table, one near the floor-length windows that looked out on the park across the street.

The bartender brought the drink over and put the glass on a paper napkin with a club chit beside it. I thanked him, took a sip of the drink, and picked up the book. But I couldn't concentrate, so after a couple of minutes I went to the end of the bar, where I dialed Lisa's number on the telephone next to the cigar humidor. The bartender busied himself with some glasses, making just enough noise to give me privacy.

I listened to Lisa's phone ring once, twice, three times. Just as I was composing a voice-mail message, she answered.

"Hello?" Her voice was cool and unhurried as if nothing as ugly as murder had ever entered her perfect world.

"It's me. I've got news."

"Do you? Good. What is it?"

I heard the slight slurring. "Have you been drinking?"

"Yes, Sherlock, just enough to face the state society matrons tonight. Or maybe not quite enough—I'm not sure which."

I was surprised she was nervous about going to a typical Washington social event—that is, work masquerading as fun. Then I realized how much strain the blackmail threat must be putting on her.

"Look, this is important. Bill Murphy told me some interesting things."

"Interesting as in helpful?" She paused, and I heard ice rattle in a glass.

"Could be—I'm not sure yet. When can we talk?"

"At the party."

"No, somewhere private."

"Oh, trying to get me alone, are you? Maybe you want to do more than just talk."

She laughed, and I heard liquor in it. *Yes, pressure's getting to her.* "Goddamn it, Lisa, I'm serious."

"Yes, you are, my friend. You're not joking, so I can tell. You've been that way ever since I've known you."

I knew it didn't matter, not anymore, but I couldn't help asking, "What do you mean?"

"You like to joke around but not when you're focused on something. Like studying for an exam. Or working on this case. Or even . . . taking my clothes off." She laughed again, softly this time. "Remember?"

I tried to keep the irritation out of my voice. "I wish I could get *you* to focus. And I hope you'll be in better shape later tonight."

"I hope so too." She seemed to sober somewhat. "Oh, don't worry about me, Mr. Shipley, I've had lots of practice at this. I'll be fine at the party—I always am."

I wasn't sure whether to believe her, but I didn't have much choice. "Okay, what time are you and your father arriving? I doubt that Frank Nelson will show up much before his boss."

"*We* are not arriving—I'm meeting them there. Frank said they're going straight from the office—no time to come all the way out to the suburbs and pick me up."

"Are you okay to drive?"

"Yes, yes. Don't be such a mother hen, Robert, I'm fine. I'll see you in the hotel ballroom at seven. We can talk then."

She hung up and I returned to my chair. I took a long swallow of the drink, then another. The whiskey had acquired a bitter taste. Still, I drained the glass.

The bartender appeared by the table like a genie swirling from a bottle. "Would you like anything, Commander?"

As I scrawled my name and club number on the chit, I thought about what the literal answer to that question would be. A long list of things, starting with the identity of Lisa's blackmailer.

But I simply said, "No, thanks," and left.

CHAPTER SEVENTEEN

I threaded the MGB through traffic to the hotel where the Virginia State Society was holding its cocktail reception. The elevator from the underground garage opened into a large, dark-green, marbled-floored lobby that, despite the decorator touches of wood and brass, failed to look like anything but new money. I went down a wide, carpeted hallway toward the ballrooms. Along the way I passed male and female conventioneers wearing nametags so they could pretend to know each other and vague smiles to indicate they were in "business-social" mode.

I found the maze of ballrooms almost as confusing as the layout of a suburban mall but finally came to the right one. There were two busy bars, one near the door and a second at the far end of the room. A long buffet table, almost as crowded, was on one side of the room, and a lectern with a microphone was on the other.

A couple hundred people filled the room. Except for a few black-clad artsy types who looked as if they belonged in New York, the attendees were dressed in the Washington uniform: blue or gray business suits for the men and most of the women, with some women in purple or red. A few of the younger women, probably those labeled "creative" in high school, were wearing cocktail dresses—most conservatively tailored but some a bit more daring— or interesting outfits thrown together from the better items in a Junior League thrift shop.

The sound system was playing New Age jazz apparently intended to mark time before whatever program there was got underway. An alto sax weighing heavily on the scales made me wish for some Sinatra to add a little class to the mix.

I didn't see Lisa or Murphy. Nor did I spot Senator Lindstrom.

What I did see was a pert little brunette coming toward me with a drink in each hand. She would have been a welcome sight even without the extra drink.

She came close and stopped. "Hi, I'm Roberta Carver. I'm on the membership committee. Are you a new member? I know most of the people here."

"No, I'm not a member, but it certainly seems like a friendly group." I nodded at the drinks. "One of those for me?"

"Oh, sure. Actually I got it for Charles, my boyfriend, but he seems to have left me on my own."

I took the glass she held out to me. "Doesn't he worry about leaving such an attractive woman alone with all these men?"

"No, damn it, but I wish you'd tell him he should. And you are—?"

"Robert Shipley."

"Oh, what a coincidence! Robert and Roberta." She laughed pleasantly and sipped her drink. Her slight flush told me the drink wasn't her first one of the evening.

"Yes, quite a coincidence. Say, do you know Senator Lindstrom?"

"Sure." She looked around the room. "I know the whole Virginia delegation. He's not here yet, but he may stop by later."

"Do you know his daughter?"

Her smile vanished. "Lisa? Yes, I know her but probably not as well as some people here. Some of the men, I mean."

I knew what she meant all right and was trying to think of a way to steer the conversation in some other direction when she added, "Are you one of them?"

"Who's 'them'?"

"One of the men who know her well."

"We went to school together."

"How nice." She had some more of her drink. "Then you've known her for a long time."

"Yes, I guess so. Do you know whether she's here?"

"No, but then I don't pay as much attention to her as you men do. Charles included, unfortunately." Her manner had grown chilly, and I could practically feel the temperature drop. She started to continue but then seemed to notice someone behind me, so instead of speaking, she gave me a disdainful look and moved away through the crowd.

She hadn't gone six feet before someone squeezed my left buttock and whispered in my ear, "You son of a bitch. I just can't trust you with other women, can I?"

I turned and looked at Lisa. She was wearing a little black dress made to measure and cut to keep a man's interest without offending his wife. She gave me a bright smile, kissed my cheek just hard enough to leave a trace of lipstick, and linked her arm through mine.

It's good to see you, Robert. I always know a lot of people at these things but never feel like I have any real friends in the room."

"Are we still friends? I thought I was just your lawyer now."

She laughed. "Don't be silly. I wouldn't have come to you if I didn't think we were friends—we have too much history not to be."

"Then maybe you should try being straight about things."

She pulled away and looked at me in surprise. "Why, what do you mean?"

"Come on, Lisa, you know exactly what I mean. You know more than you've told me, a lot more. I can't help you unless I know everything you know."

Anger flashed in her eyes, and she seemed about to speak sharply. But then she hissed, "Shh, we'll have to talk later. Here come my father and Frank. I'll introduce you as an old law school friend."

"Old?" I murmured as the two men walked up.

"Good evening, my dear."

Senator Lindstrom was a tall, silver-haired man whose suit hung on him as though he'd lost weight. He was handsome, with the distinguished look of a successful politician, but his face was pale and deeply lined. He looked tired, and I could see why his doctor had warned him to start taking things easy.

"Father, this is one of my law school classmates, Robert Shipley. He practices in Alexandria."

The senator gave me a weak smile and a practiced handshake. "Good evening, Mr. Shipley. I hope you're enjoying our state society gathering. Are you a native of Virginia?"

"I was a military brat, so I grew up all over, but I'm from Virginia as much as anywhere."

"I see. Well, Frank here, my chief of staff, is as Virginian as they come. The Nelsons are one of the FFV."

The man with the senator must have noticed my puzzled look. "FFV—First Families of Virginia. What the senator didn't tell you is that I'm from a minor branch of the family tree."

I liked that he could joke about being from a distinguished family. "I'm pleased to meet you, Mr. Nelson." We shook hands, his grip stronger than the senator's.

Nelson was tall, a couple of inches over my height, and built like a runner—lean but muscular. He wore his black hair swept back from his angular face and a bit long, covering the tops of his ears and touching the collar of his suit coat. Apparently in his early 40s, he had an intelligent, serious look.

Judging from the man's appearance, the position he held, and what I'd heard about him, I guessed Nelson was clever, capable, and ambitious. One thing I didn't have to guess at was his curiosity.

"So, Mr. Shipley, you know Lisa from law school?"

I sensed more than mere politeness in the question. "Yes, she pulled me through, in fact. We used to study together."

Lisa laughed. "Don't believe a word of it. Robert pulled *me* through, and I only interfered with his studying."

Nelson smiled politely, but I could almost see the wheels turning. He looked as if he were about to speak, but the senator beat him to it.

"Frank, isn't that Skip Tunstall, the bank president, over there? I think that he and some of his friends might be willing to help Lisa."

I know enough about politics to realize that by "help" Senator Lindstrom meant "donate money." He was experienced enough to be genteel about having to do what all politicians do: grub for campaign contributions.

"Come on, Lisa," the senator said, "I want you to meet Skip. Frank, why don't you get Lisa a drink? We'll be right back."

Nelson watched with a stony expression as Lindstrom took Lisa by the arm and guided her across the room to where a middle-aged man who looked like a former college football player beginning to go to fat was holding forth to a semicircle of attentive listeners. Then he swiveled back toward me. "I guess I'll get Lisa that drink. Would you like something, Mr. Shipley?"

"Not right now, thanks. Maybe I'll get a refill later."

He nodded and walked off toward the less crowded of the two bars. I gazed at the various groupings of people in the room, looking for Bill Murphy or a man who resembled the pictures I'd seen of Congressman Wheaton. I didn't see either one.

Then I looked at Nelson, who had his back to me as he stood in line at the bar. I had the feeling something important was drifting right below my consciousness. Right there, where I could almost touch it. But what was it?

CHAPTER EIGHTEEN

As I tried to figure out what my subconscious was trying to tell me, Roberta and a young man appeared at my side.

"Obviously you found Lisa Lindstrom," she said "Or was it more like she found you?"

"I think she spotted me first."

"That figures. Well, Charles wanted to meet you."

We went through the usual greeting ritual. Then Charles said, "You must be well connected, Mr. Shipley. I saw you talking to the Lindstroms and Frank Nelson."

"If I'm well connected, it's news to me. I knew Lisa Lindstrom before she married."

"Oh, I see. Well, Lindstrom's generally regarded as our better senator. The word around the Capitol—I work for a joint committee he serves on—is that Frank Nelson is a big reason. He's one of the best chiefs of staff in the whole Senate."

"Maybe Nelson's the power behind the throne then." I smiled to take the edge off the words.

"That's what Charles is always saying. He thinks Nelson really runs the office and the senator just gets the credit."

"Roberta! Don't be telling tales out of school." Charles looked at me anxiously. "I wouldn't want anything like that getting back to the senator."

I decided to apply the leverage they'd given me. "Hmm, no, you wouldn't want that. Say, just between us, Charles, does Nelson have political ambitions?"

"Huh? I mean, why do you ask?"

"No special reason. I suppose it's only natural that he might."

"Well, sure, lots of people in his position do. But I never heard that about him. I think someone told me once that Nelson plans to go into business, use his contacts to finally make some money."

"Some people prefer money to power but not many in this town," I said. "You know what they say: New York's a city about money, Los Angeles is about glamour, and Washington's about power."

Charles nodded and seemed to relax as though he'd decided I

probably wouldn't tell Senator Lindstrom what he'd said.

"There's a lot of truth in that." He finished his drink and looked around for somewhere to put the glass. "Say, we're going to leave soon and meet some people at a club in Georgetown. Hear some live music. Want to join us?"

Given our short acquaintance, I thought he was simply trying to ensure I wouldn't relay any part of their conversation. "Sorry, I can't. I have a prior engagement."

Roberta glanced over at Lisa and then looked back at me. "I see. One you want to keep, I'm sure."

"One I need to."

Charles said, "Well, maybe some other time?"

"Sure, that would be great."

They said goodnight and left, Roberta walking slowly and carefully on her high heels. I turned back toward the bar and saw Nelson headed my way with two drinks.

"Here you are, Mr. Shipley. I thought you might need a little something after being trapped by Roberta Carver. She does great things for the state society but she can go on."

"Thanks." I took the drink, honey-colored with a faint aroma of vanilla. "Either you're a bourbon drinker or you figured I am."

"Many Virginians are, and as the senator might say, the ones who aren't, should be. Cheers."

I noticed Nelson studying me over the rim of his glass. "This society is a friendly group," I said. "You're the second person to hand me a drink tonight. By the way, Ms. Carver and her boyfriend certainly speak highly of you."

He didn't visibly react. "I think Charles is doing a good job for the committee. My dealings with him have been pleasant so far."

So he's careful as well as smart . . . a powerful combination. No wonder he impresses people. Trying to catch him off guard, I changed the subject abruptly. "Did you know a young woman named Cate Gaulois? She lived here in the city."

"Cate Gaulois? I can't recall anyone by that name. What's your interest in her?"

"I needed to talk to her on behalf of a client, but she died—very suddenly."

"Died how? Sounds like it wasn't from natural causes."

"It's natural to die if you're shot in the right place, and she was."

"I see. Then I assume the police are on the case?"

"Yes, but there's an unusual aspect to it."

Nelson swirled his drink, waiting.

"It's possible the killer has some connection to politics."

"What makes you think so?"

"Because of something the murdered woman was mixed up in."

"What was that?"

"I'm afraid I can't say. Attorney-client privilege."

"And you thought I might know something about her or her death or this . . . thing she was involved with. Why?"

"Well, politics is Washington's main industry, and you've crossed paths with a lot of people in that industry."

He gave me a cool look. "I don't know who might have killed Ms.— the woman you're speaking of."

"Cate Gaulois. You seem pretty sure."

"I am."

"Bill Murphy told me the same thing although he admitted knowing her."

"Bill Murphy?" Nelson looked out over the crowd as though the man's name might conjure up his appearance.

"Yes. And I've looked too, but I don't think he's here," I said.

Nelson frowned. "Sounds like you're asking everyone in town about this Gaulois woman. Who's your client?"

"Sorry, I can't even tell you that. Actually, Mr. Murphy was one of the first people I talked to. I found out he knew Cate—pretty well, in fact."

"Then why aren't you focusing on him? I doubt he murdered her, but Murphy's certainly no saint. It's an open secret he drinks a lot and runs after women. I've heard rumors about stag parties and strip clubs and . . . other things."

He paused, looking at me. "I'm no prude, but there are some things people in public life just shouldn't do. There's too great a chance they'll be used against you. Frankly, I'm surprised Representative Wheaton's kept Murphy on all this time."

"Do you really think he'd get involved with anything that would lead to murder?"

"How would I know? Listen, Mr. Shipley, I don't know you and I didn't know Cate Gaulois. I don't know what all this is about, but I really don't care as long as none of it affects me—or Senator Lindstrom, of course. If Bill Murphy knew the girl, I suggest you talk to him and leave me and my boss alone."

Nelson glanced at his watch. "Now if you'll excuse me, the senator has a plane to catch." Without waiting for an answer, he strode away, shoving his empty glass at a passing waiter.

I watched as Nelson found Lindstrom and Lisa in the crowd. Standing in the middle of a group of people, the senator and his daughter smiled and nodded at the eager faces who seemed to be speaking all at once. Nelson approached Lindstrom from behind and slightly to the left, worked his way through the cordon to touch the senator's elbow, and whispered into his ear.

Lindstrom turned to glance at him, apparently annoyed at the interruption. Nelson tapped his watch and whispered again. After a moment the senator jerked his head up and down. He patted Lisa on the back in what seemed to be a practiced signal, spoke briefly to the people around them, and began shaking hands. Lisa embraced the two women in the group and allowed the faded football star to kiss her cheek.

She walked with her father toward the door, Nelson a step behind. On the way she glanced around the room, and I saw her look at me.

At the door Lisa stopped and spoke to her father. Nelson tried to interrupt but she wouldn't let him. After a few seconds the senator smiled indulgently and nodded. Then he put an arm around Nelson's shoulder and steered him out of the ballroom.

I thought that at the last moment Nelson turned to glance back at Lisa, then at me, but I couldn't be sure at that distance and with several people between us. Lisa was walking toward me, and the way she looked coming across the floor made me remember the first time I'd seen her.

She'd been coming down the hall in law school, walking in that same slow, hip-rolling way that always made me think of a young lioness on the prowl. I'd thought she'd pass me by, but she'd stopped, touched my arm, and looked into my eyes before asking me some simple question I'd long since forgotten. In fact, with her standing close enough for me to get a whiff of her perfume and even sense the warmth of her skin, I'd had trouble answering her.

And this evening she touched me and looked at me exactly as she had that first time. "Well, it's just you and me now." There was that purr again and the familiar flick of tongue over crimson lips.

If she wasn't already lit, I thought, she was well on her way. "Oh, goody, that sounds like fun."

"Fuck you." Despite the words she was smiling. Then, as if she'd just thought of it, she said, "Gosh, maybe I will. Daniel's in California on business, so I'm all alone. What are you doing later, Robert? If you're not busy, want to do me?"

Her laugh was loud enough to make two or three nearby people turn to look. I took her by the arm and led her to a corner of the room.

"Better watch it. You don't want people spreading rumors about you, especially now." That seemed to sober her a bit.

"Okay, okay, counselor, I hear you."

"Good."

In a lower voice she said, "Maybe you're right—I've got to start fundraising soon, and I don't want any idle talk to interfere."

"No, you don't."

"That's about all members of Congress do now, you know, raise money for the next election."

"That's why I never went into politics—plus I'm not very good at kissing babies."

"At least not until they're old enough to vote." She winked and casually let the back of her hand brush my fly. "I don't think that's a gun, so you must be glad to see me." She laughed again but not as loudly as before. "Okay, enough witty repartee for one night. Let's get out of here. How about we go to your place and you show me your etchings?"

"That's an old line, the man is supposed to say it, and I've only got one etching."

"Well, one is better than none, I guess. Especially if it's the right one." She moved closer, and just as I had years ago, I felt the heat of her body and smelled the musk of her perfume. "Are you ready?"

"All right, if you promise to tell me everything you know about this business. It's murder now, not just blackmail, and I've put my ass on the line for you. Plus you've only got two days left."

"It's my ass that's really on the line, not yours!" Despite the heat in her tone she kept her voice low. "Okay, I promise."

I remembered what some of her promises had been worth in the past, but I figured I was in too deep to back out now. I thought of the long odds against everything coming out all right for either of us, much less both.

She tapped a spike heel on the hardwood floor. "So, are we going or what?"

I squared my shoulders and looked at her. "We're going."

CHAPTER NINETEEN

I drove down the G.W. Parkway faster than was prudent after drinking. Nevertheless, Lisa, who'd drunk considerably more than I had, shot out ahead, the taillights of her Mercedes dancing away from me. I fast-forwarded through the cassette to the Robert Johnson song that seemed like an appropriate soundtrack—"Me and the Devil Blues."

Lisa had never been to my place, but she did a surprisingly good job of leading me off the parkway and through Old Town toward the address I'd given her as we left the party. She pulled away on the last straight section and lost me around the corner. When I rolled up to the house, the Mercedes was by the curb, and Lisa was sitting in it, smoking a cigarette.

She got out, slamming the door and flicking the butt into the gutter. We met at the bottom of the steps.

"Hi, darlin'," she said. "How the hell are you this fine evenin'?"

Lisa's mid-Atlantic accent seemed to have moved south. I wondered briefly if, like some other politicians, she tried to "talk Southern" around rural voters.

"I'm fine. But then no one's blackmailing me."

"Hey, Bobby?"

She knew how much I disliked that nickname. "Yes?"

"Fuck you and the horse you rode in on, if you know how to ride." She laughed. "But of course you know—you've ridden me a few times. Not a bad jockey either. Just don't forget that people pay to see the horse, not the rider."

The liquor had made her aggressive as well as amorous. I took her arm. "Yeah, but only if the horse is a winner. Now come in and I'll make you some coffee."

"No, no coffee." She shook her head, making a blonde swirl. "I will have another drink. Just one, if you have some scotch. You do have some scotch, don't you, my love?"

She leaned on me, laughed again, and breathed in my face. She smelled of alcohol, cigarettes, and, underneath, that expensive perfume.

"Let's go inside, and you can lie down for a while."

"That's right, let's lie down. Some good lovin' is just what I need right now. I bet you do too."

I don't argue with someone who's drunk. I led Lisa up the steps, letting her lean on me while I unlocked the door. Then I half-carried her to the sofa.

As I turned on some lights, she kicked off her shoes and curled up like a cat. Then she looked at me, lips slightly parted, breathing as if she'd done all the work.

"I'll be right back." I emptied my pockets onto the little table in the hall and hung my suit coat in the closet. I pulled a blanket off the top shelf and returned to the living room.

All the lights but one were off again. Lisa was lying on her side, her head resting on a pillow at one end of the sofa. She watched me through half-closed eyes and said nothing while I draped the blanket over her. When I tucked it around her shoulders, she reached up to pull my face down close to hers.

"Robert, you may be the only decent man left in this rotten town."

I thought it sounded like a line from a play, maybe one Tallulah Bankhead had done on Broadway long before either of us was born. Lisa's voice had that throaty sound I remembered from our late nights together.

"I'm not as decent as you think."

"See, that proves it. You won't even let me compliment you."

I looked into her eyes, inches away from mine, and felt as though I were falling into a bottomless blue pool. I resisted the strong temptation to kiss her.

She brushed my cheek with her fingertips. "How does it feel to be gallant when chivalry is dead?"

If she could come up with that, maybe she wasn't as drunk as I'd thought. "More like 'strong back, weak mind'."

She smiled and pushed herself up to kiss me. I didn't cooperate but I didn't pull away either.

After a moment she lay back against the cushions. "We'll try that again when you're more relaxed. But first we need a drink. How about some cognac? Don't you like that late at night?"

"I thought you wanted scotch. In any case I think you've had enough to drink."

"Robert, *I'll* decide what I want to drink and when I've had enough."

"You're the senator's daughter, all right. But you're in my house now, so if you get sick, you have to clean it up."

"That's a deal. You've obviously forgotten how well I hold my liquor. Daddy taught me that."

"I'm sure he taught you a lot of things."

Her head jerked as though I'd slapped her, and she gave me an angry look. I thought she might speak angrily too, but after several seconds she said in a voice that was almost normal, "Never mind that. I want some cognac—now, with you."

"Well, that's too bad, because I don't have any, and even if I did, you're getting coffee. We've got to talk about your case."

"Later. We have other things to do first—just as important and a lot more fun."

"No, damn it! No, Lisa, we don't."

I shoved myself away from the sofa. I went into the kitchen and set up the machine to make three cups of coffee. I thought one or two would sober her up enough to discuss business, and I needed one myself.

While the coffee was brewing, I went into my little office and found a notepad and a pen. As I was doing that, jazz began coming softly from the stereo in the den. Miles Davis, *Kind of Blue*, which Lisa must have remembered was one of my favorites.

Back in the kitchen I jotted down some questions to ask Lisa. I finished when the coffee maker did and put my notes and everything for two cups on a tray.

As I walked into the living room, I saw that Lisa was still covered by the blanket but her clothes were jumbled on the floor, wispy black panties on top of the pile.

She watched me as I crossed the room. I bent to put the tray on the coffee table next to the bottle of scotch and two glasses she'd found when she went to switch on the stereo.

"Just like old times, eh, Robert?"

"Not quite. I seem to recall you're married now."

"A mere technicality, counselor. Daniel has his life—he had it a long time before he met me—and I have mine."

"Good for both of you, but it's not a mere technicality to me."

"Oh, don't be so stuffy. You weren't always, I remember." She patted the sofa cushion. "Come sit here."

I answered by handing her a cup of coffee and sinking into an armchair next to the sofa.

She put the cup back on the tray and poured herself a generous glass of scotch, almost losing the blanket. She laughed and looked at me as if waiting to see what I'd say or do.

I was angry but didn't react. I reached out for the other coffee cup, and she clasped my wrist. I wondered if she felt my pulse as strongly as I did. She looked at me again as though trying to read my mind.

After a long moment she let go of my wrist, and I leaned back in the chair. I thought she would speak then, but she didn't.

I sipped the coffee, and she had some of the scotch. For a couple of minutes we sat there silently, the jazz flowing in from the next room seeming to take the place of conversation.

Then I put down the cup and picked up the pad and pen. I looked at her. "Okay, now do you want to talk about it?"

"No." She drank more scotch. "Not tonight—in the morning."

"What about your promise?"

"I said we'd talk about it. I didn't say tonight."

I threw the pad at the table. It bumped the tray, sloshing coffee from her cup, and slid onto the floor. I threw the pen after it.

"I should have figured something like this would happen!"

She gave me a look that tried but failed to be innocent. "What do you mean?"

I didn't bother to answer. "Neither of us is in any shape to drive, but I'll call a cab for you while you get dressed. We'll deal with your case tomorrow."

"I don't want a cab." The scotch seemed to have worked in her, because she thrust out her lower lip and pouted as well as any five-year-old. "And I don't want to get dressed—I just want you. See?"

Lisa got to her feet, letting the blanket slide to the floor, and stood there nude. Swaying slightly, she spread her arms and giggled. "See? Ready, willing, and very able. Come here and I'll show you."

I stood and took the two steps to her but dodged her outstretched arms and bent to pick up the blanket. I wrapped it around her, not staring but not looking away.

"You can sleep in the guest room." I tried to ignore the surging in my veins. "I suppose you can think of something to tell your husband in the morning."

"No, no, no." She pressed her face into my chest and wrapped her arms around my neck. "I want to sleep with you. Don't worry about Daniel, he doesn't care. Just hold me tight—the way you used to."

I sighed. I bent, put one arm under her knees, and picked her up. Lisa closed her eyes and smiled as she snuggled into me.

I carried her up the stairs and into a bedroom. I set her gently on the end of the bed and pulled back the spread and sheet. "Okay, get in."

She grinned in triumph. She tossed the blanket aside and slid under the covers, a flash of white and a patch of dark against the pastel sheets. As she reached for me, I stood back, folding the blanket.

"That'll wait." She ran the words together but her tone was commanding. "Now get undressed—I want to watch. If you need help, I'm good with buttons and buckles." She laughed.

"I know you are, but I think I can handle it." I laid the folded blanket on the foot of the bed and turned toward the door. "Goodnight."

"Wait! Where are you going?"

"To my own room. To sleep. We'll talk in the morning."

"*No!* I want you here with me."

"Sorry, Lisa. Things are different now. You and your husband may not care, but I do. If that weren't enough, you're my client, and the Virginia State Bar frowns on lawyers sleeping with their clients."

"When did you become so prudish? Or care about what some stupid rule says?"

"Maybe I've grown up some." I paused. "Maybe you—what happened to us—helped me do that."

Her eyes became slits and her face grew dark. "Or maybe you're just afraid you'll like it too much—the way you used to, when you couldn't get enough of me."

I gave her a bleak smile. "Yes, maybe that's it." I left the room, closing the door softly.

In my own room I undressed, dropping my clothes on the armchair in the corner. I turned off all the lights except the reading lamp and crawled into bed. I picked up the novel I was reading— *The Drowning Pool*—but the words didn't seem to make sense. After I'd gone through the same paragraph twice without understanding it, I snapped off the light.

The image of Lisa's body floated above me in the dark, and sleep didn't come quickly.

□ □ □

Sometime in the early morning, when the color of the sky was between black and blue, Lisa came to me. She quietly opened the unlocked door and slipped into my bed, pressing her naked body against mine.

The warmth of her skin stirred something buried within me. Still half asleep, I reached for her and drew her to me, holding her close, her breath warm on my chest.

Swimming slowly toward the light of wakefulness, I moved my hand from her shoulder to her breast to her belly and felt her respond to my touch. Then, emerging into full consciousness, I realized that what I'd thought was a dream wasn't a dream at all.

"Hello," I said softly into her ear.

"Hello." She cuddled even closer.

"I don't recall inviting you into my bed."

"No, you didn't, but I came anyway." She laughed softly. "Well, not just yet, but soon, I hope."

She pressed my hand against her and spread open like a flower wet with morning dew. I hesitated, thinking of what I'd said to her earlier. But then I decided—or biology decided for me.

I caressed her, gently at first and then harder as her breath came faster and she began to moan. I threw the covers back and ran my fingers over her as though she were an instrument I could play by ear, the music swelling up from somewhere inside her.

Toward the end of the long, long song she raised her hips to meet me and dug her nails into my shoulder. Then she arched her back, every muscle tensing, and let out a deep, shuddering breath.

She took my hand in hers then and held it while we rested. After a few minutes she said, "My turn," and rolled over so that she was almost on top of me. With her eyes closed she surveyed my body with her mouth, beginning at my face and then working her way down, retracing the familiar route.

By the time she reached her goal, my muscles were tense and I was sensitive to her lightest touch. She worked on me with an enthusiasm that partially disguised her practiced technique. When I felt myself surging toward release, I gently pulled her head away and lifted her back up to me.

In response to her look of surprise and the unspoken question, I kissed her lips and ears and eyes. Then I rolled her onto her back and moved on top of her.

She smiled. Her whispered "Oh, yes" sounded like a promise. She closed her eyes and hooked her legs on top of mine.

I entered her like a diver simultaneously parting and becoming one with the water. We moved together rhythmically, rising and falling as though we were stroking through the sea toward some sensed but unseen beach. Twice I felt myself getting ahead of her and slowed down until she pulled even with me again.

Then I couldn't wait any longer and spent myself in one long, last thrust. Seconds later she arched again as if electrified and clung to me while her breath sobbed in her throat.

When finally her grip loosened and her breathing slowed, I eased myself off and lay beside her, my own breathing gradually becoming normal again. The ceiling fan dried the sweat on both of us. The intensity of our lovemaking had left me feeling drained yet fully alive.

Lisa turned toward me and draped her arm across my chest, her fingertips lightly caressing my shoulder. "Well, you haven't lost a thing, Robert. I'd tell you that you're still the best, but I know it'd go to your head."

"Maybe it's just that you were a good teacher."

She kissed my cheek. "You're sweet."

"I seem to remember your calling me something else at the boat."

"Did I? Well, that's just sometimes, when you're stubborn and don't do what I want you to."

"I never claimed to be the answer to a mother's prayer."

"You're not—at least not one concerning her daughter."

She moved her hand slowly on my chest, stopping it over my heart as though to check whether my pulse was in synch with her own. "Now tell me what you've found out."

"Shh." I placed a finger on her lips. "I don't want to spoil the afterglow or whatever the magazines are calling it these days, but we need to get some sleep. Besides, blackmail and murder aren't good topics for pillow talk. I'll update you over breakfast."

She frowned. "Robert, it's Wednesday night—no, Thursday morning. I've got today and tomorrow to find out who's after me or my whole life is ruined."

"I know, but we can't do anything about that at five a.m. Let's go to sleep and then start fresh."

"But—"

"Hush! I'm too tired to discuss it now, and you'd be too, if I were really as good as you say."

Her frown deepened to a look of anger, and I thought she'd continue to press me. But after a moment she seemed to reconsider, smoothing out her face and making a sound somewhere between a growl and a chuckle.

"Yes, sir, Commander, but remember your promise when you wake up." She kissed me lightly on the lips, rolled onto her back, exhaled deeply, and was soon asleep.

I pulled the covers back up and gently spread them over her. I lay awake for a long time, thinking about what had just happened and all that had happened since she'd appeared at the marina only two—now three—days ago.

I tried to fit a few more pieces into the jigsaw puzzle beginning to take shape in my mind, but there were still too many missing shapes for it make sense.

I watched the sky gradually lighten from navy to royal blue and fell asleep again about sunrise.

CHAPTER TWENTY

I woke to the smell of coffee. Savoring the aroma, I yawned and stretched, debating whether to get up or stay in bed another five minutes. Then I remembered how the night had ended and a wave of guilt hit me.

Sleeping with a married woman . . . one who's my client. Shit. Why I don't I just tear up my law license now and save the state bar the trouble?

Not having a good answer to what I thought was a good question, I rolled out of bed. I reached for my robe, but it was missing from its place on the bedpost. I pulled on sweatpants and a T-shirt and padded downstairs.

Lisa was in the kitchen, sipping coffee, smoking a cigarette, and reading *The Washington Post*. A few bread crumbs were scattered on the saucer next to her cup. Wrapped in my robe, she seemed smaller than she had the night before.

She smiled when she saw me. "Morning, Robert. Hope you slept well."

I gave her the best smile I could under the circumstances and reached for my usual Navy cup. "Not bad. You?"

She watched as I dumped in sweetener and poured coffee. "Fine, once we . . . worked things out. Sorry if I made it hard for you."

"So to speak." I put the cup on the table and sat next to her. "What's this strange power you seem to have over men? And some women?"

She tapped ash from her cigarette—hard—on the edge of the saucer. "You know, Robert, it's not like I've fucked everybody in Washington. Sure, I've been with a number of people and, yes, one was a woman. What's that to you? I'm certain you're no saint."

"No, far from it. Look, I'm sorry. I didn't mean that the way it sounded."

Lisa continued to glare at me. Finally she said, "Okay, I accept your apology."

"Thanks."

"Now, what have you learned? What son of a bitch is after me?"

"I don't know yet, but I think I'm making progress." I drank some coffee while I mentally tallied what I'd learned so far. "Tommy Osborn is probably hiding something to do with Cate Gaulois, Bill Murphy definitely is, and apparently Frank Nelson knew her. One of them must have some information that will lead to the blackmailer."

"Frank knew Cate? That doesn't seem likely, and anyway he couldn't have anything to do with this thing."

"Maybe not, but he's connected to Cate, and I'm sure her death is related to the blackmail."

"Do you have any evidence of that?"

"No, but the timing's too coincidental otherwise. The two things must be linked."

"Well, they could be, of course, but I'm sure they're not. The way she lived, who she was—anyone could have done it."

That surprised me. "Even if there isn't any connection, don't you want to know who killed Cate?"

"Well, sure, if you know. Do you?"

"Not yet, but I will. I feel. . ." I paused, not sure what I wanted to say.

"What?"

"I feel it's something I have to do."

"Robert, don't waste time trying to figure out who shot Cate. I hired you to find the blackmailer and stop him."

"Goddamn it, Lisa, I'm not a lawn service! It's not like you say, 'Cut the grass but don't trim the shrubs.' I do what I think I need to, and I give you the best professional advice I can. You may not like some of it, but that's how I work."

"I wish you'd told me this when I hired you."

"Most of my clients are smart enough to figure it out on their own. You're not a fool, so I assumed you knew you were hiring a lawyer, not some guy with a weed whacker."

"What I assumed was that after all we've been to each other, you'd help me. That means doing what I want you to do when and how I want you to do it. And I want you to focus on finding out who's after me, not on solving Cate's murder. Her death's unfortunate, but it's not the important thing right now."

When I didn't reply, she added, "I'm sorry if I sound like a heartless bitch, but that's just how it is."

"You're wrong. The police may have found forensic evidence in her apartment that will lead to the blackmailer. That's another reason you should go to them, as I suggested in the beginning."

"I can't, Robert. One of the first things they'd do is talk to Daniel, and I can't risk that. I don't want to lose my husband—our marriage—as well as the election."

"Well, if you want my help, you have to let me do my job my way. That's the only way I can work."

By unspoken agreement we paused to let things cool down. Lisa busied herself with lighting another cigarette, and I got both of us more coffee.

When I was seated at the table again, I said, "Want me to tell you more?"

"Yes, of course."

"Okay. Murphy admitted knowing Cate but didn't want to discuss details. For what it's worth, he seemed genuinely saddened by her death. That doesn't mean he didn't kill her, of course. Maybe he's just a very good liar. Maybe you have to be if you're in politics."

"It certainly helps," she said with no irony in her tone. "I'll bet Murphy's the blackmailer. He's in the other party, hates my father, and likes to play rough. Plus I've heard he wants to run for office himself. Who else would have so much to gain by it?"

"I don't know. But he did mention that he'd seen Nelson once in the club where Cate worked."

"*Frank* Nelson? I seriously doubt it. Frank's very careful about what he says and does in public. He has to be, working for Dad. He certainly never said anything to me about going to that club—or seeing Bill Murphy there."

"Was there any reason he would have?"

"Well, Frank and I are pretty close. We talk a lot, mostly about people we know in politics." When I didn't say anything, she added in an annoyed tone, "To help my father, of course. So I think he probably would've told me something like that."

"'Pretty close?'" Sounds like you've slept with him."

"That's none of your business!"

"It is if it affects your case."

She stabbed the half-smoked cigarette out in the saucer. "I think he may be in love with me."

"Do you love him?"

"Let's just say that I care for him a great deal."

I wonder if she's capable of really loving anyone . . . or, for that matter, if I am. "You think what Murphy said about seeing Nelson is true?"

"I doubt it. I just can't imagine Frank in a place like that."

"Imagination is a funny thing. A couple of days ago I would've said I couldn't imagine seeing you on video making love to another woman."

"Asshole. I knew you'd throw it in my face eventually."

"What? That you've been to bed with a woman? I don't care. You can sleep with anybody you like, singly or in groups. It's your business, and I won't interfere with it even though this time I'm stuck with the clean-up."

"How good of you."

Lisa surged from her chair and stamped out of the room. In a few minutes she returned, wearing the black dress. The evening elegance was gone, replaced by a tawdriness I'd never seen in her.

"I'm leaving." Her cold, flat voice was far different from the half-gasp, half-cry with which she'd called my name the night before. "You better got somewhere with this investigation—and fast. Begin by forgetting about Frank Nelson because I don't think he had anything to do with it."

"And nothing to do with Cate's death?"

"No, but although as I keep telling you, Cate is not the issue."

"How can she not be? I have to investigate the murder to find the blackmailer."

Lisa paused as though considering her reply. Then she said in that same wintry tone, "Okay, Robert, as of right now you're fired. I don't want you poking around on this anymore."

I shrugged and stood. "Fine. I've been fired before. But I can still keep looking for the truth."

"I'm ordering you to stop working on this case!"

"You can't—you fired me, remember? Besides, as a lawyer I'm an officer of the court, and so are you, counselor. We've got an obligation to prevent crimes if we can. Do you think what happened to Cate can't happen to someone else mixed up in this? You, for instance?"

"I'm not afraid."

"Well, you damn well should be. I know I am—someone tried to kill me and may try again."

"I can take care of myself. Don't forget you're the one who taught me how to shoot."

"And don't you forget that shooting on a range in broad daylight isn't the same as defending yourself on a dark street."

"I said I can take care of myself! You just stay out of my way while I'm doing it."

"Okay, but I'm not going to stop working on this case."

She gave me a hard look. "All right—maybe I can't stop you. But I'll say this: don't do anything either of us will regret."

"Such as?"

"You may not know until after you've done it."

"Well, I've learned to live with regret, so I guess we'll just have to see where things lead."

"And don't think our . . . friendship will stop me from doing whatever I have to do to protect my interests. It won't."

I paused. "I know. And I understand."

"If whoever sent that tape contacts me again . . . well, like I said, you're the one who taught me to shoot."

"I remember." I paused. "That was a fun day—you were pretty good out there."

"Thanks." She paused too, then reached up to take my face in her hands. She kissed me hard and long as though she wanted both of us to remember it.

Eventually she pulled back and looked into my eyes. She gave me a brief, enigmatic smile, slapped me lightly on the cheek, and walked out of the house.

CHAPTER TWENTY-ONE

After the echo of Lisa's footsteps faded, I sat in the kitchen for a full minute, replaying what she'd said and staring at the harsh shadows the morning sun threw on the white wall. Then I shaved, showered, and dressed, jerking a knot in my necktie when I remembered how coldly she'd said, "You're fired."

I headed for the office, top down, making rolling stops at intersections. Halfway there the back of my neck began to prickle. I turned and saw a large, dark-blue car that looked like an unmarked police cruiser.

The car veered off after a couple of blocks, and nothing else appeared close behind me the rest of the way to the office.

"Morning, Georgie." She sat at her desk in a tailored suit the bright red of a Chinese firecracker. "Nice outfit. New?"

She smiled. "Yes, it is. Thanks, Robert. I didn't think you noticed such things."

"Well, I did this time. Say, is Jack in?"

"Yes, and he wants to see you."

"Does that mean I'm in trouble?"

"Probably no more than usual. He's in his office."

I gave her a wink and headed upstairs. I paused in Jack's doorway, watching him mark changes on a document with the red fountain pen, an antique Parker Duofold, that Georgia had given him for his birthday.

I glanced around the office, seeing the familiar photos of Jack in his dress uniform, wearing jungle fatigues in 'Nam, and graduating from law school. His Bronze Star hung in a shadow box that stood next to the black-and-red bulldog figurine—"Uga," his university's mascot—that I gave him last Christmas. There were also pictures of Jack shaking hands with various politicians, including President Reagan, and going deep-sea fishing on several boats.

Jack didn't display any photos of his first wife—she'd died from cancer a few years after they were married—although once, after we'd done some drinking, he'd shown me an album filled with pictures of her. He didn't display any photos of his second wife either, but I knew he'd thrown those away after the bitter divorce that ended their short marriage. Neither marriage had produced children, and I thought he regretted that even though he never spoke of it.

I knocked lightly on the doorframe.

Jack looked up. "Come on in." He laid the Duofold on the page he'd been revising and took off his reading glasses. "We're so damn busy these days that you and I never seem to have a chance to talk."

"Well, better too busy than not enough." I sat in one of the two chairs across from Jack's desk.

"Sure, but you must really be swamped. I've hardly seen you at all lately. Georgia says you're working on something for one of your law school classmates, that woman who was here on Monday looking for you. Is that right?"

"Yes and no. I went to law school with Lisa Lindstrom, but that's not why I took her case. She's just a client like anyone else." I mentally crossed my fingers at the use of present tense.

"I see. Did we get a retainer from her?"

"Uh, no. She offered to give us one, but I didn't think it necessary."

"Hmm. If you two used to do more than study together, that wouldn't make any difference, would it?" Before I could answer, Jack continued. "Well, you're probably right, considering her position—a senator's daughter who's planning to replace her father when he retires."

I couldn't conceal my surprise. "You know—"

"Yeah, I know who Lisa Lindstrom is. In fact, I've met her father. Even played poker with him once when my boss at the Federal Trade Commission, a regular in the senator's monthly game, was out of town."

"I met him yesterday, but he's worn out and sick now. What was he like in his prime?"

"Smart, charming when he wanted to be, and ambitious as all hell. Maybe even ruthless—certainly not afraid to go after what he wanted."

"Then his daughter's just like him."

"She is, huh? You'd think she wouldn't want to be like him. Wouldn't even like him very much."

That surprised me too. "Why is that?"

"Well, she was in high school when I met her—the senator's only child. I could tell he was very protective of her."

"What are you getting at? What do you know about the two of them?"

"I don't *know* anything. I've heard some things."

"Like what?"

Jack rolled the fountain pen from side to side. "Sure you want me to tell you? I mean, in view of your relationship with her, personal as well as professional?"

"Yes, go on."

"Well, my FTC boss told me that Senator Lindstrom had an eye for young women, college-age women. That his friendships with some of them weren't strictly platonic. I understand it got to the point where his wife would only let him have male interns."

"Like Frank Nelson."

"Who?"

"Senator Lindstrom's chief of staff. He started as an intern."

"Oh. Anyway, there were also rumors that the senator's relationship with his daughter was . . . closer than it should have been."

Instantly I knew what he was implying. "That's bullshit! I don't believe it!"

But as my hot words hung in the air I remembered what Lisa had said as we were leaving that orphanage during law school. She'd brushed away a couple of tears and told me that knowing the children would have to lose their innocence one day made her sad. "It's a hard world, and they'll have to learn that one day." She'd glanced at me, then looked away. "Just like I did."

Maybe that explained a lot about her.

Jack seemed surprised at how sharply I spoke. "Look, I don't know whether those rumors were true. I hope not. But I do think it's true Senator Lindstrom dated, in effect, some of Lisa's friends, some of her college classmates. And that Lisa knew about it—maybe even introduced some of the girls to her dad before . . . well, whatever happened between the two of them."

He paused, looking at me as though to gauge my reaction. "Supposedly, someone had evidence of one or more of those flings and threatened to expose him."

"For what reason?"

"Who knows? Money, power, votes? Or maybe something else we can only guess at."

"So what happened? The evidence never came out."

"No, it didn't. Maybe the person who had it got what he wanted in return for not going public with it."

"Any idea who that might have been?"

"At the time there were whispers about a younger guy who worked on the Hill. The story was he'd met Senator Lindstrom through work, they'd hit it off for some reason even though their politics were different, and the two of them used to go out drinking and chasing girls together. Lindstrom may have bragged about some of his conquests and given the guy the idea to put the squeeze on him."

I felt a surge of excitement. "What was this fellow's name?"

"Hmm, Martin, Morton, something like that."

"Could it have been Murphy, Bill Murphy?"

"Maybe. I really don't remember—hell, it was at least fifteen, sixteen years ago." Jack slowly spun his pen on the paper. "In any event nothing ever came of those rumors."

I considered what Jack had told me. How much of the story was true and not, as Jack had cautioned, merely rumor? And how might whatever part was true help me to unravel the death of Cate Gaulois and the blackmail attempt against Lisa? I'd have to think about it.

"But let's get back to Lisa Lindstrom," Jack said. "What's the deal?"

"Just what I told you—she's a classmate of mine who asked me to handle something for her."

"Such as?"

"Conducting an investigation."

"Damn it, Robert, don't make me drag it out of you. Investigating what?"

"Who's trying to blackmail her."

"*Blackmail* her?"

"Yes, with a sexual indiscretion. There's a videotape of Lisa in bed with another woman."

Jack's eyes widened. "Talk about the sins of the father. But that's a matter for the police, not us."

"I know, and I've told her that a couple of times. She won't go to the police."

"Why not?"

I told Jack everything that had happened since Lisa appeared at the marina late Monday afternoon, including my finding the body of Cate Gaulois and making an anonymous report to the police. One thing I left out was sleeping with Lisa, and I justified the omission by rationalizing that because *she* had seduced *me*, the incident shouldn't count. I knew the excuse was feeble even as I made it to myself.

Another thing I left out was that Lisa had fired me. I didn't mention that because I was going to keep working on the case until I found Cate's killer or the blackmailer—or both, if, as seemed likely, they were one and the same. I was going to keep going, and I didn't want Jack to try to stop me.

When I finished, Jack shook his head. "Lord, what a mess! Too bad you made such an impression on her in law school. Otherwise she might have dumped this on some other poor sap—and his partner, the guy I really feel sorry for. The police are going to be very unhappy with you, Robert."

"They already are."

"Attorney-client privilege will help you some, but I don't know if it will be enough. If not, John Lytle might be willing to put in a word with the D.C. cops, but there's only so much he can do."

"I think I've used up my credit with him."

"Well, I should have a little left. We'll see. Meanwhile, what's your next step? Try Osborn again? Keep squeezing Murphy's and Nelson's nuts?"

"I guess so. I'm hoping one of them will confess or give me another lead. I figure if they're starting to point fingers at each other, I must be doing something right."

"Well, just remember everybody's got something to hide, and with these political guys it's not necessarily blackmail or murder." Jack waited until I nodded in agreement. Then he added in a colder tone, "One more thing, counselor."

"What's that?"

"Don't let your dick do all the thinking on this case. Got it?"

"Where did *that* come from?"

"I ran into Lisa Lindstrom at a fundraiser for her father a couple of years ago. She's a damn good-looking woman—the kind you don't forget—and I know you too well to think the only thing you ever slipped her was a set of class notes."

My face grew hot. "You know, Jack, your name's not on my birth certificate anywhere."

He laughed derisively. "What the hell does that mean?"

"It means you must think you're my father, the way you try to tell me what to do sometimes."

"Well, I do think I'm your business partner, your *senior* partner, and therefore entitled to advise you about business matters."

"There's more to this thing than just business!"

"I know. That's why I want you to be careful not to step over the line."

"I will be."

"Assuming, of course, you know where the line is, which remains to be seen. I guess I'll find out soon enough if you don't."

"Look, I don't blame you for being concerned. Georgia also warned me about my 'thinking' with regard to Lisa. But I am being careful, really—or as careful as I know how to be."

"I damn sure hope so!" Jack paused, his expression softening a little. "Look, Robert, I'm sure you're trying to do the right thing. But let me know if I can help. Deal?"

"Sure, Jack, I will. Thanks."

"A good lawyer knows he doesn't know everything."

I nodded and got up from the chair.

"Okay, see you later," Jack said, turning back to his document.

I went to my office and shut the door. I took out the legal pad with my notes on Lisa's case and summarized what Jack had told me about Senator Lindstrom. Then I wrote down the few facts I'd gotten from Murphy: *Cate had no family. Murphy promised someone to look after her. Murphy saw Frank Nelson at the 1776 Club.*

I read through all my notes but couldn't find a common thread. Maybe there was one, but if so, I just couldn't spot it.

I decided to have one more run at Murphy and called his office. The receptionist said he had meetings out of the office for the rest of the day. Mentally cursing the way time was going by, I told her I'd call back tomorrow.

I dialed Information, got the number for Senator Lindstrom's office, and dialed that. A perky woman who sounded something like the one in Murphy's office answered.

I worked through the layers of staff personnel employed to keep the boss and his chief assistant from wasting time talking to people who couldn't or wouldn't donate money to Senator Lindstrom or otherwise help him apart from giving him their votes. Finally, through perseverance and the closest thing I had to

Irish charm, I was able to talk to the man who worked directly for the Great Man.

"Mr. Nelson, this is Robert Shipley. We met last night at the Virginia State Society cocktail party."

"Yes, I remember. What can I do for you?" The words were polite but his tone was cold.

"I'd like to talk to you."

"About what? Not that woman who died? I told you last night I didn't know her."

"No, it's not about Cate Gaulois's death, at least not directly. Something else."

"What?"

"Blackmail."

"Blackmail?"

I could tell that got Nelson's full attention. "Yes, involving Senator Lindstrom, at least indirectly."

After a pause so long I thought he might have hung up, Nelson said, "All right. I can see you at seven o'clock this evening. But just you, understand?"

"I'll be alone. Where?"

"Not here—somewhere else."

The suggestion seemed odd, but I played along. "Okay, where?"

Nelson named a tavern on the outskirts of Capitol Hill, one I'd been to but not in a while. I remembered it as a dark, quiet place frequented more by people who lived on Capitol Hill than by the politicians, lobbyists, and journalists who worked there.

"Fine, I'll meet you there at seven."

Nelson hung up with a loud click. I did so more softly and sat still for a moment, thinking the world was beginning to seem darker and more dangerous by the hour.

CHAPTER TWENTY-TWO

The weather didn't match my mood. I glanced out the window and saw a fine fall day. It was a good day to be outside. It was a good day to be sailing. It was a good day to be doing anything but trying to solve a murder, foil a blackmail attempt, and get out of trouble with the police, all at the same time and all by tomorrow.

I went downstairs to get coffee. I also wanted the diversion of talking to Georgia but didn't want to interrupt her while she typed the changes Jack had handwritten on a letter. So I stood there, sipping coffee and waiting until she finished.

I could tell she sensed I was watching her, but she said nothing until she'd finished and hit "save," then "print."

"That's rather annoying."

"What?"

"You know."

"Watching you work?"

"Yes. How'd you like it if I stood in your office and watched you work? Supposing you did any, which requires some imagination."

"I did some once. Ask Jack. It was a couple of weeks ago, I think."

"Oh, is that what the malpractice suit is about?"

I turned toward the stairway. "Better watch yourself, young lady. Someone might shoot a rubber band at you. It's been known to happen."

"And someone with better aim might shoot it back and hit her target. That's been known to happen too."

"Lucky shot." I looked back at her from the bottom of the stairs. "Now, if you'll excuse me, I have to go make an entry in a certain employee's file."

"If you can find the file you're looking for without any help, which would be highly unusual, make sure you spell 'stellar performer' correctly. 'Stellar' has two l's, you know."

"I'll do my best."

She sighed theatrically. "I guess that's all we can ask."

"Touché." Feeling a little better, I went back to my office. I re-read my notes on Lisa's case. Still nothing.

I leaned back in the chair. I stared at the ceiling for a while, running over the facts to see how they might relate to each other. Mostly they didn't—or if they did, I couldn't discern a pattern. After a while Georgia brought me a turkey-on-wheat from the deli down the block and iced tea that she'd made in our kitchen.

"Thanks, Georgie, I didn't realize it was lunchtime already. Here, let me give you some money for the sandwich." I pulled out my wallet but found only three dollars in it. "Well, looks like I have to go to the bank first."

"Right, that'll happen. I'll just put it on your tab."

"Fine. By the way, how much am I into you for?"

"Let's just say that one day pretty soon you're going to be making my car payment."

"Does that mean I get to drive your car when the MGB's in the shop?"

"No, it's there too often, and anyway I've seen how you drive. Now eat your lunch and get back to work."

I chuckled and bit into the sandwich as Georgia walked away. I noticed how her new suit showed off her trim figure, and I was surprised to find myself thinking that way.

That afternoon I forced myself to spend some time preparing bills for several of our biggest clients. I knew that I had to keep money coming into the firm—especially given that apparently I was working on Lisa's case for free—and I also knew that clients scrutinized our invoices much more closely than they did any of the legal documents we sent to them. Jack left for a client meeting about two o'clock and didn't come back until four-thirty. By that time I had finished the bills and stacked them up to give to Georgia.

Jack appeared in my doorway with one large hand wrapped around a bottle of Jim Beam and the fingers of his other hand thrust inside three squat glasses etched with different varieties of game birds. He put the glasses on my desk, twisted the top off the bottle, and poured himself a generous drink.

"Buzz Georgia. Tell her it's happy hour, and ask her to bring some ice for any fussy Navy boys on the premises."

Conscious of my impending meeting with Frank Nelson and the ever-tightening Friday deadline, I wondered if I could afford the luxury of a short break. Then I figured I might be able to make more sense of the few facts I'd gathered if I relaxed some—being tense didn't seem to have produced much progress in the case.

As I reached for the phone, I said, "Unlike the so-called 'devil dogs' of the Marine Corps, the gentlemen of the Navy appreciate the refinements of life."

Jack made a rude noise while I called Georgia on the inside line. "Shut down your computer and come up here. Jack's getting obstreperous and I need your help keeping him in line. Oh, and please bring some ice."

Even the tinny telephone speaker couldn't mar the pleasant sound of her laughter. Soon she appeared, carrying an ice bucket and a bottle of spring water. She pushed back some papers to perch on the edge of my desk while Jack plinked cubes in a glass and poured her a drink half the size of his own. He splashed water on top of the whiskey, swirled it gently, and handed it to her with surprising grace. "Here you are, *mademoiselle.*"

"*Merci, monsieur,*" she said in the well-accented French that was another legacy of her childhood in Vietnam. She took a small sip. "Perfect."

"Good."

"One for Georgia but not me? That's what we call sexism," I said as I fixed myself a drink.

"That's what we call manners," Jack said, "and I'm hoping one day you'll learn some."

"Well, in the words of the poet, 'hope springs eternal'." I held up his glass. "A toast to the best legal assistant and future lawyer in Old Town."

"The best in the whole Washington area." Jack clinked his glass on mine.

Georgia smiled. "Well, at least better than you deserve." She raised her own glass. "Here's to the best bosses in the world." Jack and I grinned at each other until she added, "And here's to hoping I find them soon."

Jack and Georgia chatted while I mostly just listened, brooding on Lisa's case. Georgia glanced at me a few times, probably curious about why I wasn't saying more, but I was thankful that she didn't comment on it.

Jack was the first to finish his drink. "I don't know about you two, but I'll sail again. Ms. Nguyen, would you please do the honors? I'll be right back."

Knowing I had to meet Nelson later, I declined another drink, but she fixed one for Jack. She was recapping the whiskey when he reappeared, holding three cigars. "Here we are. Care to sample these with me?"

Jack liked to smoke cigars around the office once in a while, usually after he'd won a case or gotten a favorable settlement. I'd joined him a few times, but Georgia had never expressed any desire to try one. This time she surprised me by saying, "Sure, why not?"

Jack seemed surprised too—he'd probably brought in three cigars just to be polite—but he unwrapped one, clipped its end, and handed it to her. Georgia placed it delicately between her lips as he lit a wooden match.

When the tip glowed dull red, she drew deeply on the cigar. Then she leaned her head back and sent a gray cloud sailing toward the ceiling. She coughed a little, looked at us, and chuckled.

"Well, I'm not sure smoking cigars will become a habit with me, but I'm glad I tried it once, just to see the expression on your faces."

"Why?" Jack said. "Do we look shocked?"

"I don't think it fits your mental picture of me. I don't think you've ever imagined your little girl smoking anything, much less sharing a cigar with the boys."

"Well, actually, no, I never—"

"Oh, hell, Jack, she's a grown woman. She can do as she likes."

He frowned. "She may be grown, but I still have a responsibility. I mean, I—we—should look out for her."

"Hey, guys, I'm still here." She sounded annoyed. "Maybe you should have this little debate when I'm not around, or better yet, let me take care of myself. God knows I've had a lot of practice taking care of you."

"That's right, Georgie, and we appreciate it," I said. "You know, we don't express our appreciation often enough. Why don't you take the rest of the day off?"

She checked her watch. "Hey, that's a whole seven minutes. Your gratitude is overwhelming."

"Never mind him, Georgia. You know we couldn't run this place without you."

"Yes, I know. I'm just glad you do too. Thanks for the drink and the cigar. I'll go straighten up my desk before I leave." She looked at me. "*After* five, as usual." Then she swept regally out of the room.

"I think I'll go too, Robert. We've all been putting in some long hours lately. Why don't you get out of here? Take a pretty lady to dinner or something? That's what I'm going to do."

"Sounds great, but I can't. I'm meeting Frank Nelson, Lindstrom's chief of staff, to see if he has any useful information about Lisa's case."

"Want me to ride shotgun? I can change my plans, and I'd be glad to help."

"No, thanks, although I appreciate the offer, especially if you'd have to break a date to come along. I can handle it."

"Okay, I hope it doesn't take you too long. See you tomorrow." He headed for the door.

"Good night. Thanks for the drinks and the cigars. And, uh, Jack?"

"Yes?"

"Thanks for the advice too. I appreciate it."

He smiled and gave me a short wave.

I thought about Jack's offer. "Ride shotgun" made me think about the car that might or might not have been following me that morning and the man who'd definitely shot at me Tuesday night. Then I remembered how Cate Gaulois had looked with that bullet hole in her chest.

I unlocked a desk drawer, reached past Lisa's videotape and note, and pulled out a wooden box a little larger than a hardback dictionary. I unlatched the box and took out the .357 Magnum. On my most recent outing to the shooting range I'd tried the two-and-a-half-inch barrel, not the four- or six-inch lengths I normally used, so now I didn't have to put the short one on the gun. I opened a box of cartridges, swung out the cylinder, and loaded the chambers. Then I snapped the cylinder back into place.

I reached into the drawer again, got a small leather holster, and clipped it onto my belt between the front and back pockets. I thought about my three-year stint in a reserve unit that supported the Naval Criminal Investigative Service, the only time in my Navy career I'd had to carry a gun. *Not bad training for this sort of thing,* I thought as I slipped the revolver into the holster.

Although I had a permit to carry a concealed weapon in Virginia, I knew it wasn't legal for me to wear the gun in the District of Columbia. But it wasn't legal for someone to try to kill me either.

I put on my suit coat and left my office. When I got downstairs, Georgia had finished clearing her desk and was putting books into her law-school briefcase.

"Going home early for once, Robert? Good for you. You work too much."

"Like you don't. As Jack says, we've all been pushing pretty hard lately, but things will get back to normal eventually."

"That'll be great as long as they don't ease up too much." She smiled. "I've got tuition to pay."

"I don't think we have to worry about not having enough to do." I walked over to her desk. "When it is a little less hectic, Jack and I should take you somewhere nice for lunch."

"I'd like that."

"All right, then it's a date. Well, I've got to go—have an appointment."

I saw her glance at my empty hands and the slight bulge on my right side.

"I don't like the looks of this. Why do you need your gun?"

"Jesus, I hope it's not that obvious to everyone. I was hoping for a little subtlety."

"No, it's not obvious. I guess I just notice things, maybe more than some people."

"More than most people, I'd say. The revolver's just a precaution. I'm sure I won't need it."

"I certainly hope not. Please be careful, Robert."

"I always am, except when it comes to women."

"Damn it, I'm serious!" She stood and put her hand on my arm. "Look out for yourself for a change."

"Okay, Georgie, I will. Promise." On impulse I gave her a quick hug and kissed her forehead.

She hugged me back. "You better keep that promise."

I looked into her eyes for a moment, gave her what I hoped was a reassuring smile, and headed for my car.

CHAPTER TWENTY-THREE

The drive from Alexandria to Capitol Hill took longer than I'd expected. The main delay came as I neared the Hill, when traffic was held up by the presidential motorcade.

Cops on motorcycles, lights flashing and sirens howling, preceded a couple of black SUVs leading two limousines (one a decoy, I knew), a few more Secret Service vehicles, and an ambulance. The police car at the rear signaled the end of the motorcade, and the whole procession was common enough in Washington that few people stared at it. I'd seen the sight several times, but somehow being that close to someone with so much power still gave me a thrill.

Once the motorcade had passed, I drove to the bar Nelson had mentioned. Finding a nearby parking space took another five minutes, but checking my watch as I walked back to the bar, I saw it was only 6:46. I figured I was still early enough to have beaten Nelson there.

As I entered, a few heads turned, but I seemed to go generally unnoticed in the dark, smoky atmosphere. The bar was about half full, almost all of the patrons falling into that nebulous mid-thirties, early- forties group—the kind of crowd that wants liquor as well as beer and wine and likes music "you can dance to."

I found a stool at the near end of the bar. One of the two bartenders smoothly disengaged himself from three pretty women and ambled over.

I ordered my usual bourbon on the rocks with a splash of water. The bartender smoothly fixed the drink, put a coaster in front of me, and set the short glass on it. Then he looked at me, made a quick evaluation, and didn't tell me how much or ask for a credit card. He slid a bowl of mixed nuts next to the drink and left me alone.

I looked around, glancing from the couples huddled over little tables to the several groups of people telling jokes and laughing. My gaze lingered on each of the four men sitting alone. Two were staring into their glasses, their thoughts obviously far away. One was reading *The Washington Post*, holding the newspaper cocked to the dim blue light of a neon beer sign.

The fourth man was Nelson. Obviously, he'd also wanted to be the first one there. He was sitting at the other end of the curved bar, back to the wall, nursing a drink and lightly tapping the bar in time to the jukebox music.

The casual gesture made him look like a coiled spring. When he saw me looking at him, Nelson nodded slightly, then glanced around the bar as though trying to be sure I had come alone.

I waited, giving him time to decide I was there by myself. I didn't look at him again—I just sat there, not moving except to have some of my drink once in a while. Finally he walked around the bar, leaving his empty glass.

In his elegantly tailored gray suit and with his tall, erect carriage, Nelson stood out from the neighborhood drinkers. He reminded me of a presidential candidate working a New Hampshire diner for primary votes.

He picked a stool that left a vacant seat between us. He looked at the bottles neatly lined up against the mirrored back wall until the bartender came over to him.

"Another single malt, neat."

Guess you're not a bourbon man after all. Must've been trying to charm me the other night.

In a few seconds the bartender delivered the drink. "There you are, sir. I'll add this to your tab." Nelson said nothing.

The bartender looked at him a moment, then glanced toward me, raising an eyebrow. I shrugged, and the bartender smiled slightly. Then the bartender pointed an index finger at my glass, and I nodded. He fixed me another drink, accepted my quiet thanks, and returned to the three women.

Nelson glanced at his Rolex. "Well, I'm here," he said in a flat tone that could mean anything or nothing. "What do you want?"

I looked at my reflection in the mirror. My face was pale and stiff. I looked as though I needed a vacation, maybe somewhere on a powdered-sugar beach with green palm trees waving against a sapphire sky. But I didn't have a plane ticket in my pocket.

"Somebody doesn't want Lisa Lindstrom to replace her father in the Senate. I mean, *really* doesn't want her to—is trying to stop her, in fact." I was surprised at how tight and low my voice sounded. I was also surprised that Nelson seemed amused.

"Is that what you wanted to discuss? There are always people who don't want a particular politician to run for office. People who don't like him or his policies, want someone else to run, or want to run themselves." He made a dismissive motion. "You're naïve not to know something as basic as that."

"I know politics is hardball—I've been getting a practical education in that lately. But what's going on here, blackmailing someone for political reasons, seems extreme."

"It's unusual but certainly not unknown. In fact, it's probably more common than most people think." He sipped the single malt, holding it in his mouth before swallowing. "So you think someone's blackmailing Lisa? Trying to get her to stay out of the Senate race?"

"I know someone is."

"How do you know?"

"I can't say—yet. But I want to find out who's doing it. Are you saying you didn't know about it?"

"Yes—I mean, no, I didn't, and I'm damn sure the senator would bring me in on something like that. Obviously it affects him too, and one of my primary duties is damage control."

"Does Senator Lindstrom have that much damage to control? Besides this thing with Lisa, I mean."

"You'd be surprised. People in politics are human like anyone else, some more so. Look at Bill Clinton and lots of others—in both parties. Most politicians, elected or aspiring, have something to hide, and there's usually someone around who wants to keep them from hiding it or take advantage of the fact that it's hidden."

"Well, maybe Senator Lindstrom didn't tell you about this because he doesn't know about it."

"How could Lisa be the subject of a blackmail attempt and the senator not be aware of it?"

"Now who's being naïve? You know her as well as I do."

"I wish I could pretend I don't know what you're talking about, but like I said, damage control's one of my main jobs. I don't know how she can be so . . ."

"Reckless?"

"Frankly, yes. Maybe it's because she's beautiful and can be very charming—when she's not being vulgar or conniving. She's also clever although too often she mistakes cleverness for intelligence."

Seeming to catch himself, he said, "But I don't mean to insult my boss's daughter, and I believe she's a friend of yours."

Nice job of not insulting her. "Yes, I've known Lisa quite a while, or more precisely, I knew her well a few years ago. But you're right—she's all those things and more, many of them contradictory. Maybe that's why she's a woman who's not easy to forget."

"No. No, she's not."

It occurred to me that he and I had more in common than just being in this bar, and I wondered if that amused Lisa. I imagined it did.

"You know her," Nelson said. "Do you think she could serve in the Senate? Effectively, I mean? I very much doubt it."

The question surprised me. "Oh, I think so. Her wanting to do good for people might be—hell, probably is—more about getting her elected than helping them. Still, the net effect is that she would help people."

"While helping herself."

"Sure, but that'd hardly make her unique in Congress, would it? And maybe politicians are like fighter pilots: you need a pretty big ego just to get up in the morning and do what they do."

"I hadn't thought of it that way. You may be right." He took another sip of his drink before continuing. "I suppose Lisa hasn't told me about this because she thinks I'd go to the senator with it. But maybe I won't have to—it depends on what she decides. In any case I'll handle this from now on. Thanks for letting me know."

"I wouldn't have except that I thought you might know something about it."

"Logical enough." He drained his glass. As he put it down he said in a casual tone, "By the way, what's the hook?"

"You mean, what's the blackmail about?"

"Yes."

"You'll have to promise me *not* to tell Senator Lindstrom. It's up to Lisa whether she wants him to know."

He paused. "All right. You have my word."

"Your word as a gentleman?"

"Certainly—my word as a gentleman."

I thought I heard a hint of sarcasm, but I let it pass. "It involves Cate Gaulois. Apparently, she and Lisa were . . . very good friends."

"As in *let's be* friends?" Nelson slurred the two words together.

I guess I must have seemed surprised, because he added, "Lucky guess. Lisa told me she'd always wanted to try that. So she finally did?"

"Sounds like you two had some interesting conversations. Just how well do you know her?"

"Mr. Shipley, my relationship with Lisa Lindstrom, personal or professional, is none of your business. In any case, that's not what we're here to discuss."

I almost felt sorry for him. Almost. "The fact that you've slept with her makes it more complicated."

Seeing his look of surprise mixed with anger, I said, "Call it my own lucky guess. Knowing Lisa as I do, I'd be amazed if you two hadn't slept together. But there's no reason to get mad—I'm certainly not in a position to criticize you or her. As you say, your relationship is your business."

Nelson stared at himself in the mirror behind the bar, and I saw that his reflection looked as pale and stiff as my own.

"Better be careful," I said. "Lisa knows what she wants and will do anything to get it. She's very good at manipulating people—she's had lots of practice."

"Thanks for the warning, but I'm well aware of her character. Now returning to the business at hand, I take it that Lisa and the Gaulois woman got together, so to speak."

"Suppose they did. And suppose there's a videotape to prove it."

"That would be very indiscreet—even for her. You've seen the tape? Do you have it?" His voice was low but insistent.

"I've seen *a* tape. The blackmailer has the original, of course, and probably more copies."

"Yes, he—or she or they—would. But you have that tape? Lisa gave it to you after she got it in the mail?"

"The tape I saw is safely put away."

"I'll take that as a yes. So Lisa came to you with this, and now you've come to me. Is that right?"

"Let's just say that if you have any ideas about how to keep the blackmail story—Lisa's relationship with Cate—away from the media, I'd be glad to hear them."

"I'll protect the senator, of course, and even Lisa, but I won't cover up murder, if that's what you mean."

"I didn't ask you to. The police know Cate Gaulois was murdered, so I'm sure they're on the case. I want your help in stopping the blackmailer. The cops aren't working on that—yet."

"So you haven't told them anything? Not about the tape? None of it?"

"No, but I can't keep holding back much longer, especially with Cate dead. The blackmail attempt almost certainly figures in her murder."

"Maybe, maybe not. Who knows? As you said, the police are looking for the murderer or murderers. I'll handle the blackmail—that's my job."

"And mine. That's what I was hired to do and how I got mixed up in all this in the first place."

"Well, let me take it from here. You go practice law, but first I want that tape."

Although he hadn't been actually rude, Nelson's haughty manner annoyed me, and that "go practice law" comment made me angry.

"Let me think about it. You know you don't have to worry that I'll do anything with that tape to threaten Lisa's future."

There was that bleak smile again. "What about your future? Do you really feel safe with that videotape in your possession? Some people would do almost anything to get a seat in the Senate."

"That much I've learned. Someone took a shot, well, a few shots, at me the other night."

"You think it was the blackmailer? Trying to get you out of the picture? Or could it have been someone else, someone who just wants to get the tape from you?"

"I don't know, but I'm going to find out."

Nelson was silent a moment. "Perhaps it was meant as a warning."

"Or perhaps it was just bad shooting. If someone really meant to warn me, it didn't take."

"Well, maybe whoever was doing the shooting will figure you need to be warned again." He paused and cocked an eyebrow at me. "And maybe his aim will improve."

"And maybe I'll start shooting back."

"The modern world is no place for heroes, Mr. Shipley. You should've learned that by now."

I said nothing as I reached for my glass.

"Fine, have it your way, but I still want that tape. Call me when you're ready to discuss turning it over." Nelson stood up and threw some bills onto the bar. "In the meantime I think you should stay away from Senator Lindstrom and Lisa. And from me, for that matter. As far away as you can."

He looked at me again. I saw determination in his eyes but

something else too. Empathy perhaps? At least understanding.

"Otherwise," he said, "I think you'll regret it."

"Thanks for your time, Mr. Nelson. I'll remember what you said, but don't expect me to take the advice—I've never been very good at that."

"Maybe you should practice more."

"Maybe you're right. Other people have told me the same thing."

He opened his mouth to speak, but then closed it, his lips forming a thin line. He turned and headed for the door.

In the mirror I watched him leave. Then I sat thinking and drinking for several minutes until only the ice was left.

The bartender reappeared. "Another one, sir?"

"No, thanks, still got work to do tonight."

"Working late, eh?"

"Yep. Looks like you are too. That's why they pay us the big bucks, right?"

The bartender laughed, enjoying the joke but not giving it more than it deserved. "Right. That's why I've got a Mercedes parked out front."

I glanced at the money Nelson had left, barely enough to pay for his drinks, let alone provide a decent tip. Having stopped at an ATM before driving to the Hill, I took a twenty and a ten from my wallet and slid the bills under the edge of his coaster. "That should cover it."

"Thanks. I'll get your change."

"No, that's okay. Use it to get the Mercedes washed."

He laughed again, a bit more this time. "All right. Next time you're in, the first one's on me."

"That's a deal. Say, the fellow I was talking to—has he been in here before?"

"A few times, three or four maybe. Comes in by himself but usually ends up talking to someone, like with you tonight."

"Anyone in particular?"

"Not really. Nobody I know. One girl, short with dark hair, I think maybe I've seen somewhere else, but I can't place her."

"Was it dancing at the 1776 Club?"

The bartender grinned. "Aw, hell, who looks at their faces?"

I thought of Cate's sad eyes in her self-portrait. "So you don't know who he is?"

"No, he's not a regular. Guys who work on the Hill don't come here much—place isn't fancy enough."

"How do you know he's from Capitol Hill?"

"Friend, I've lived in D.C. all my life, and you get to where you can just spot 'em. Like lawyers or locusts—not that there's much difference."

I smiled as I stood. "Yeah, those damn lawyers—ought to be a bounty on them. Thanks for the drinks. See you around."

CHAPTER TWENTY-FOUR

Leaving the bar, I couldn't decide whether Nelson's parting remark had been a warning or a threat. Resorting to violence seemed unlikely for someone in his position. Still, as I walked toward my car I was consciously alert, holding my arms out slightly and looking from side to side.

When I got to the MGB, I hesitated, then popped the hood and looked at the engine. There didn't appear to be any extra wiring, at least none visible in the glow of the streetlights. I closed the hood and slid into the car.

Then I remembered what Jack had said after someone, probably a client of one of the many lawyers he'd defeated in court, had slashed Jack's tires: "Just because you're paranoid doesn't mean they aren't out to get you." I grimaced and turned the key but heard only the usual coughing as the engine started.

I drove out of the city and headed for home. It was only a little after eight and I was hungry. I knew that, as usual, there wasn't much in my refrigerator besides beer, bread, and milk, and the milk was probably sour by now.

No one was following me—at least I couldn't see that anyone was. Someone might be waiting for me, but that would be at my house, not somewhere else.

I picked up my phone and fumbled for the seldom-used speed-dial number I wanted. The call connected. I counted three rings and was about to hang up to avoid the answering machine when Georgia answered.

"Hello."

"Hi, this is Robert."

"Robert who?" she said in a warm voice. Then she laughed.

"What're you doing?" The question came abruptly, and I realized I sounded a bit nervous.

"I should be asking you the same thing, but I already know the answer. Drinking with a client or maybe driving to or from that."

"Close but no cigar like the one you were smoking this afternoon."

"Surprised you with that, didn't I?"

"Yes. Jack too, I think."

"Good—that's mostly why I did it." She paused. "So what *are* you doing if not drinking with a client?"

"Coming back from drinking with a source of information—at least he was supposed to be one. I think I ended up telling him more than he told me."

"Then it was a waste of time?"

"No, I wouldn't say that. Sometimes you learn a lot from the questions people ask."

"What did you learn?"

"I'm not sure, have to think about it some. But I didn't call you to talk about work."

"You didn't? That's a first."

"Well, I haven't eaten yet, and I was wondering if you'd like to have dinner with me.

"Yes, that would be nice."

I liked how she said it right out, no hesitation.

"But I changed clothes as soon as I got home from school," she added, "so maybe we can go someplace casual."

When she said *go*, it occurred to me that taking Georgia out wasn't the smartest idea—given that someone was apparently trying to kill me. That someone probably knew where I lived, but wasn't likely to know where Georgia lived. She was protective of her privacy and had an unlisted phone number.

"In that case maybe I should pick something up and bring it over."

"Hey, I don't think I look *that* bad."

"I'm sure you don't—you always look great—but I just think tonight is a good night to stay in."

"Hmm, I know you pretty well, Robert. Is there something you're not telling me?"

I paused. "Yes, but I don't want to go into it on the phone. I'll fill you in over dinner, okay?"

"Fine."

"Let's see . . . you like the Gold Rush Café, don't you?" The place bordered on being a dive, but they had good food and a memorable slogan: *Our chili's hot and our beer's cold.* "How 'bout I get something from there?"

"Sure. I haven't had heartburn in a while, and I'm about ready again."

"How's salad, chili, and cornbread?"

"Perfect."

"Okay, I'll be at your place in half an hour."

"Good. Know my address?" Without waiting for an answer, she recited it—an apartment building in Alexandria's West End. "See you soon."

We hung up, and I called the café to place a to-go order. Then I pushed a tape into the deck and drove down the parkway listening to Sonny Boy Williamson—the second one—singing about that "Little Village."

The Gold Rush had the food ready when I got there. I paid, put the bag in the car, and headed for Georgia's. On the way I checked the rear view several times but still didn't see anyone following me.

When I got near her place, I drove into the parking lot of the apartment building next door and chose a visitor's spot as far away from her building as I could. Carrying the bag of food, I walked across that lot and the one for her building.

To the right of the front door was a brass panel with three rows of white buttons. I pressed the button labeled "A.G. Nguyen." At the answering buzz I went inside and found her apartment on the first floor.

The memory of Cate Gaulois's apartment clicked on, and a chill swept over me. I could still see Cate's body crumpled on the floor and feel the icy touch of her skin.

I knocked on the door, and Georgia opened it. She had on a pair of snug jeans, a black leather belt that cinched her slender waist, and a loose white shirt that contrasted with her dark eyes.

Her warm smile helped to drive away the chilly feeling. "Hi," I said. "You look nice."

"Thanks."

I fumbled for something else to say. "Glad we could get together on such short notice."

"Yes, well, I had to disappoint a couple of guys, but maybe they'll get over it."

"Let's hope so anyway."

"Come in. I'm hungry, and I'll bet you are too."

Something make me hesitate the barest instant before saying, "All right."

Georgia's apartment was small but welcoming. She'd decorated it in a surprisingly smooth blend of colonial American and classical Vietnamese styles. Simple, sturdy furniture sat on the hardwood floor, which was largely covered by a dark green rug that complemented the Williamsburg colors of the walls and trim. A beautiful hand-painted paper screen stood in the corner between large front and side windows. I wondered if Georgia had painted the screen.

Two bookcases were crammed with books—novels, several works on Vietnamese history and culture, and recent editions of legal texts I remembered from law school. The only photo in sight was a silver-framed portrait of a young Asian woman I recognized from the snapshots as Georgia's mother.

I could hear the tinkling of wind chimes outside and the gurgling of a small fountain inside. The fountain sat on a lacquered table along with a vase of flowers that faintly scented the air.

As I glanced around the room, Georgia took the bag from me. "Please sit down," she said. "I'll fix us a drink, and then we can eat."

I passed up a comfortable-looking rocking chair by a reading lamp to sit on the sofa, picking the end closest to the side windows. The lights were low enough for me to see out into the courtyard. A man and a woman were sitting on a bench, holding hands under the rising moon.

"I like your apartment. You've made it quite . . . charming, I guess is the word."

"Thank you, Robert. I'm glad you like it."

On her way to the kitchen Georgia stopped by the stereo, and Frank Sinatra began singing "In the Wee Small Hours of the Morning" as though it were still 1955. The bittersweet music spilled out of the speakers, flowed across the floor, and lapped around me like waves on a beach.

I thought of Tony Kornheiser's description of the eternal Sinatra: standing in a trench coat on a late-night New York street, a cigarette in one hand, a glass of scotch in the other, and Kim Novak waiting in the back of a taxi.

The tinkling ice cubes blended perfectly with the music. Georgia soon reappeared, carrying a tray on which sat two short, thick glasses, each half-filled with ice and dark-gold liquid. She bent to offer me the tray. "Here you are."

I chose one and waited while she put the tray on the coffee table and sat on the sofa halfway between the far end and me. When she picked up her glass, I clinked it and smiled. "Cheers."

"How about to the firm of Benton and Shipley?" Her eyes were playful.

"Maybe one day. We'll see." I tried the drink. "Mmm, that tastes like good bourbon with just a splash of water."

"Like you ever drink anything else."

"I've been known to."

"Only when something else was all someone else was buying."

"That could be true, but it's not very ladylike of you to mention it."

"Who says I'm a lady?" She took a small sip of her drink.

I didn't know what to say to that, so I had some more of my drink and she did the same. We finished the drinks as Sinatra finished the song.

CHAPTER TWENTY-FIVE

We ate at the four-person table in the dining area off her living room. Georgia had set two places with silverware, cloth napkins, and delicate-looking china. She'd put the chili into bowls and the salad and cornbread onto small plates. Everything was simple but elegant. *Just like her,* I thought.

I carried out the glasses of iced tea she'd made and held the chair for her as we sat.

"Thank you, Robert."

"No, thank you. I mean, thanks for having me over." I paused. "I wonder why we never thought of this before."

"I don't know why you've never thought of it, but I have."

"You have?"

"Well, yes. We seem to get along all right, and I always thought it'd be nice if we got to know each other better outside the office. Jack and I have dinner once or twice a month, and I'm sure he and I are closer because of that."

"Oh." I knew I sounded surprised and maybe a little jealous. "He never mentioned that?"

"No."

"I assumed he had."

"Not that I recall, but I know how much Jack thinks of you."

She smiled and picked up her salad fork. I took the cue and did likewise. For most of the meal we kept the conversation light, not talking about work but rather discussing books and movies, things like that. It was pleasant to get my mind off Lisa Lindstrom and her case for a while.

But when we were almost finished eating and there was a lull in the conversation, Georgia said, "So, what is it, Robert—the thing you didn't want to get into on the phone?"

For a moment I thought about evading the question and trying to change the subject. But then I realized that talking things out with her might help me to understand what I'd learned about the case—and what I still needed to know.

"You don't mind talking shop, especially here? And now?"

"Not at all. It has something to do with that Lindstrom woman, doesn't it?"

"Yes."

"Well, what is it?"

"Someone—and maybe more than just one person—doesn't want me working on her case."

"How do you know?"

"Someone tried to stop me Tuesday night—with a gun."

I hadn't meant to be dramatic, but she put a hand to her mouth and her ivory skin paled.

"You—you weren't hurt, were you?"

"No, I was lucky. All it cost me was some cracks in my windshield. No worse than driving behind a gravel truck on the Beltway."

"But suppose whoever it is tries again?"

I thought of the car that might have been following me the previous morning. "He—or they—could, but the police know about them now, so it would be riskier." *Not that the risk would stop them,* I added mentally.

Georgia didn't speak for several seconds. Then she said, "I think you better tell me everything you know about this case, everything you've learned."

"I don't want to drag you into it."

"But I may be able to help." She gave me an aggravated look. "That is, if I know what's going on!"

"Okay, okay, let's discuss it."

"Good. See if you can find a pad and a pen in my desk while I clear the table. Then I can take notes while we talk."

I did as she asked, and in a few minutes we were seated in the living room again with her pen poised over the pad.

I started at the beginning and told her about the blackmail scheme, how Lisa planned to run for the Senate and what was on the videotape locked in my desk. Then I told her about the death of Cate Gaulois.

Georgia didn't seem shocked by the first part—in fact, she took notes—but when I described finding Cate's body, she stopped writing and closed her eyes.

When she opened them again she looked at me and said, "So she was in on the blackmail . . . and died because of it."

"I think whoever killed her had to be part of it. I never met Cate Gaulois—alive—but there's no indication she was interested in politics. If Cate was the blackmailer, she'd have asked Lisa for money, not to drop a bid for office."

"She must have known about the video camera in her apartment."

"Not necessarily. Lisa says they were close, at least very good friends and perhaps even in love—at least on Cate's side. It's possible someone else hid the camera and Cate didn't know they were being taped."

"Hmm, I suppose that is a possibility. But it seems more likely she did know, so what then?"

"Then she must've been paid. But by whom? I mean, by which of the many people and groups that stand to gain from someone else holding that Senate seat?"

"It could be almost anyone."

"In this town? With these people? You're right—almost anyone. But I think it's probably someone—or several someones—in one political party or the other. Senator Lindstrom's and Lisa's opponents or their so-called friends."

"Would someone in politics really blackmail a person in his own party?"

"Sure. People have done worse than that. A local woman who ran for the Senate was convicted of trying to poison her husband and his lawyer."

"Yes, I remember that case—it got a lot of coverage in the *Post*. I guess truth is stranger than fiction sometimes."

Next I told her what I'd learned about and from Osborn, Murphy, and Nelson. She listened closely, taking more notes.

When I'd finished, she read over what she'd written. "Lots of connections—almost too many. Maybe they're all in on it."

They weren't all in the same party, but, as the saying goes, politics makes strange bedfellows, and I didn't know enough to eliminate anyone as a suspect. "That could be."

"Probably not though—not all of them. So why do they all seem to be hiding something?"

"Most people have things to hide."

Looking at her, so lovely in the lamplight and so intent on helping me, I thought about my past with Lisa, and I hurried on before Georgia asked me any questions I couldn't answer without upsetting her. "The question is whether they're hiding something to do with the blackmail scheme."

"Well, they all seem to be hiding something about Cate Gaulois.

Don't you think?"

"Yes, but what?"

"I don't know, but maybe Murphy is the key. Apparently he knew her best. And liked her the best."

"Doesn't that mean he'd be the least likely to get her involved in something like blackmailing Lisa?"

"One would think so, but I suppose a blackmailer doesn't have many scruples—or any."

"You're absolutely right, Georgie. This whole thing was a dirty business even before Cate was killed."

"Say, I just thought of something. In the video does Cate ever glance toward the camera, try to get Lisa facing it, anything like that?"

"No, it looks genuine, not staged."

"Hmm, so you have the experience to tell one from the other?" Without waiting for an answer, she said, "I guess that's- another reason you think Cate was unaware of what she was participating in."

"Yes, but it isn't conclusive evidence. Perhaps she did know about the blackmail and I just want to think she didn't."

She laid the notepad on the coffee table. "Why is that?"

I paused. "I'm not sure. I don't know much about her, but what I do know suggests she wouldn't betray a friend, a lover. I like to think she was a better person than that."

Georgia smiled. "Sir Robert Shipley, knight of Virginia."

"If I'm a knight, I'm one in tarnished armor."

"That's no problem—I have a can of polish around here someplace." She stood. "I'll make coffee. Meanwhile think about what I said: maybe Murphy is the key. I think you're right that there has to be a connection between Cate's death and the blackmail scheme."

"Okay."

As she left the room, I thought about what I hadn't told her. I hadn't said that Lisa fired me—I didn't want Georgia to have to keep that secret from Jack the way I was doing.

And I hadn't told her about what had happened between Lisa and me the night before. I rationalized that it had nothing to do with the case, but I knew the real reasons were that, first, I thought it might hurt Georgia, and, second, I was ashamed of myself for letting it happen.

When she came back with the coffee, I moved to the sofa and sat next to her as I added sweetener to my cup. Georgia poured enough milk in hers to make the coffee a light brown and stirred in two spoonfuls of sugar. *That's how the Vietnamese usually drink it,* I thought, *light and sweet.*

"By the way," she said, "I read through the case file you gave me and did some more research."

"Find anything useful?"

"Three or four things, nothing spectacular. The most interesting is a *Post* article that mentions both Representative Wheaton and Senator Lindstrom and has a picture with Murphy in it."

"Okay, I'll take a look at them." I sipped my coffee. "And now let's take a break from Lisa Lindstrom and her problems."

"Sounds good—you probably need it. One final question: have you talked to Jack about all of this?"

"Yep. He probably thinks I'm an idiot for even taking the case."

"I doubt that. He's loyal to his friends, just as you are."

"Thanks, Georgie."

"You are welcome."

She said it in an oddly formal way, as though we didn't know each other well, and looked at me for a long moment. Then she went over to the stereo and put on more slow, beautifully sad Sinatra.

On the way back she dimmed the lights.

CHAPTER TWENTY-SIX

Georgia was curled on the sofa, shoes off, feet tucked beneath her, and she looked even more lovely than she had earlier. Fighting the temptation to lean over and kiss her, I picked up the drink I'd made and had some of it.

"This is nice," she said. "I'm glad you called."

"So am I. I'm lucky you were free. You know how it is: 'Lucky at cards, unlucky in love.'"

"Oh, that's just a saying."

"I think my former girlfriends would disagree."

She was silent a moment. "Suppose I asked them—what would they say?"

"Maybe that . . . well, that I didn't make time for them."

"Didn't you?"

"Honestly? No. Too many late nights, too many working weekends. Of course, then I was trying to get ahead, trying to make partner. But it's tough to sustain a relationship that way."

"Don't blame yourself, Robert. No woman who really cared about you would object to your taking your job seriously."

"Well, there's such a thing as taking it too seriously."

"Yes, but look how you were able to walk away from it. You decided not to sell your soul for money and power."

I looked at her. "How do you know about that?"

"Jack told me. He's very proud of you for what you did."

"Both of you give me more credit than I deserve."

"You underrate yourself. You're a good lawyer or Jack wouldn't have brought you in as his partner. And you're a good man or I wouldn't want to be with you like this."

"Well, thanks. I'm glad you wanted to for whatever reason."

She picked up the drink she'd asked for when I'd made mine. She had some of it, maybe a little too much at once, and coughed.

"You okay?"

"Yes, yes, I'm fine." She put the glass down. "You know, Robert . . ."

"What?"

"I'm not some good little girl who knows her place. If I want to have some whiskey with you, I'll do it."

"Okay."

She looked at me. "I hope you're not mad, but—what was it you told Jack? I'm a grown woman, and I can do as I like."

"Yes, and as he said, we're just trying to look out for you. You know, I think of you as my little sister sometimes, and you're almost like a daughter to Jack."

"Well, I'm *not* your sister, and Jack . . . well, I don't think he'd know what to do with a daughter if he had one. Or a son, for that matter."

"Really? I bet Jack would be a good father."

"Anything's possible, I suppose. But at this point he's probably missed his chance."

"Yes, probably."

I had some more bourbon, and she did likewise, being careful not to drink too much at once.

"I just need a little practice," she said.

I laughed. "Well, you can try drinking with Jack and me some more before you hit the big leagues."

"Maybe I should."

"Jack will be pleased—he never minds practicing."

"Nor do you, I think."

"No, I guess not. Probably been practicing too much since . . . well, since I stopped working downtown."

"I wish you could get past what happened. You need something else to think about."

"I do?"

"Yes."

"Like what?"

She paused, looking at me. "We'll think of something." She sat up, leaned toward me, and put her hand on my arm. Her lips parted slightly, and she closed her eyes.

I didn't need an engraved invitation. I kissed her, and she kissed me back. We stayed that way for a few seconds. Then I pulled back and saw her looking at me again.

"Uh, sorry. I didn't mean to get carried away."

"Don't apologize—I liked it."

"Well, we've both had a good bit to drink."

She flushed. "Hey, Robert?"

"Yes?"

"Being grown up means I can kiss anybody I want to, okay?"

"Even an old man like me, huh?"

"Old? You're only eight years older than I am. That's not much."

"Sometimes I feel older—like this week. But, okay, I get it."

"Good."

Georgia picked up her drink and finished it. When she put the glass down she didn't cough. Instead put her face up next to mine and I kissed her, making it last and hoping she liked it as much as I did.

She must have—she put her arms around my neck, drawing me so close that it seemed as though we melted into each other. Time seemed to stop.

When I finally drew back to catch my breath, my head felt light. Looking into her bright-dark eyes, I thought I saw amusement mixed with desire. Then I kissed her again, long and hard, tasting the wet saltiness of her hungry mouth.

She caressed me as though she'd dreamed about it, and I caressed her in return, tentatively at first but quickly becoming more sure. We fumbled with buttons and belts and zippers until we were half-undressed and the situation was becoming ridiculous.

"Don't you think we'd be more comfortable in the bedroom?" she asked quietly.

"Yes, probably. But I don't know if that's a good idea."

As I spoke, an image flashed through my mind: Lisa, drunk, naked, seducing me—but not without some cooperation. I felt a flash of anger that was quickly drowned by shame.

"Georgie, about Lisa . . . she and I . . . uh—"

She put a slim finger against my lips. "Hush, Robert. I know, and I don't care."

"You know?"

"I could tell from the first there'd been something between you two. Maybe she thinks—or thought—there might still be. But I sense it's over. Am I right?"

"It's been over for years. I see now what Lisa was doing. She didn't want to go to the police with this blackmail thing, and she thought she'd be able to manipulate me, control the way I'd conduct the investigation."

I paused, looked at Georgia, then looked away, thinking about what had happened the previous night. "When she finally figured out she was wrong, she fired me."

Georgia flushed again. "Why, that bitch! I wish I hadn't been so polite to her. What did you ever see in her?"

"I don't know. I was a law student with no money and only a few friends in Washington. Lisa was pretty and smart and rich—a senator's daughter who introduced me to important people. She even told me I should go into politics one day."

"Obviously she didn't know you don't suffer fools gladly."

"Or at all, if I can help it. All I can say is that being with Lisa Lindstrom seemed right at the time."

"But not now?"

"God, no. Now she's just a client—or was. Letting her talk me into taking her case was a mistake—but not one I'll repeat."

"I'm glad to hear that." She kissed me again, and it was even better than before. "Now where were we? Oh, yes, I remember: about to get more comfortable."

"You sure? I mean, I want to, but does it feel right?"

"I'm sure it's what I want. About whether it's right—well, I think it's right to love someone if you want to."

She took my hand and interlaced our fingers. "And I think it's wrong to manipulate someone to get what you want. I know you'd never do that—unlike your former client."

"Lisa's . . . well, she is who she is. I guess I've always known that but didn't want to face up to it." I squeezed her hand. "I appreciate your faith in me, Georgie, but I certainly haven't lived a faultless life."

"Who has? But you do the best you can. That's what's important."

"I'm glad you think so." We kissed again, still taking our time. "You're sure about tonight?"

"Yes, I've been sure for quite a while. It's not like predicting the weather—it's just listening to your heart."

"You're obviously better at that than I am."

"Oh, I don't know. We might never have met if you hadn't listened to your heart and come to work with Jack. I'm glad you did—for several reasons."

The truth of what she said struck me like sunlight breaking through fog. Suddenly I felt more clear-headed than I had in a long time.

I stood, gathered her in my arms, and found the way to the bedroom.

CHAPTER TWENTY-SEVEN

Later, much later, feeling pleasantly tired, I got out of bed. I pulled on my boxers and went into the living room. I switched on the stereo and was surprised to find that Georgia had the radio tuned to the jazz station I liked. I turned up the volume until the music was just loud enough to be heard in the bedroom.

In the kitchen I found two glasses, put some ice into each, and topped them off with water. I drank one glass and refilled it.

Moving carefully in the dim light, I put a glass on the table next to Georgia's side of the bed. I thought she was asleep—curled on her side, black hair tumbled across her face, covers tucked beneath her chin—but at the slight sound she opened her eyes.

"Hi, you." She smiled. "How'd you know I'm thirsty?"

"I didn't, just knew I was."

"Well, I am too. Thanks." She sat up, letting the covers slip to her waist, and drank deeply.

For a moment I couldn't move. I thought I'd never seen anything more beautiful—her elegant neck, shapely arms and shoulders, and small, firm breasts.

I wondered if Georgia could see my expression. To stop myself from staring, I went to the other side of the bed and crawled under the covers.

Georgia rolled over to kiss me and then spoon herself into my side. "Goodnight, Robert."

"'Night, Georgie." I pulled her to me so that her head was on my chest, and she soon fell asleep. Holding her close and feeling the warm, slow pulse of her breathing, I closed my eyes and drifted into darkness.

□ □ □

A faint noise like an icicle breaking woke me. I lay in bed with Georgia next to me and thought lazily about taking her skiing. I imagined the two of us flying down steep, white hills and making love in the yellow-red flicker of a fire.

Then I remembered it was barely autumn and there were no

icicles to break.

I slid silently out of bed, went to the dresser, and felt for my belt holster. When I found it, I eased the gun out and stood still, listening intently.

I heard a strange, hushed sibilance. After a moment I recognized it as wood sliding slowly on polished metal. I moved quietly toward the living room.

No lights were on, but even in the dimness I could see that the window closest to the front door had been pushed up and the curtain shoved aside. What looked like shards of glass lay on the carpet, and the screen had apparently been cut and pulled out of its frame.

A dark figure was standing outside the window, holding something darker still. I thought that if not for the black backdrop of the low brick wall between the building and the street, I would see the silhouette of a pistol.

I dropped to the floor just as the figure pointed the gun at me and fired. A bullet smashed into the wall directly above my head. The booming report sounded as though it came from a powerful gun, maybe a .44.

I hugged the floor even closer and brought up my gun, left hand supporting the right as my Marine drill instructor had taught me. I fired without cocking the double-action revolver.

Even before my ears stopped ringing, I knew I'd hurried the shot and missed. The dark figure dropped out of sight below the window.

"Robert!" Georgia sounded scared but not hysterical. "What is it? Are you all right?"

"Stay in the bedroom—get on the floor!" I hissed as I kept staring at the window.

The shooter's head and shoulders popped back into view, this time on one side of the window. The figure aimed and fired quickly.

Thunder came again, and the bullet plowed into the floor inches from my face, throwing dust in my eyes. Half-blinded, I snapped a shot at the place where I'd seen the figure, knew I'd missed once more, and rolled to move away from my previous position.

I waited a moment, blinking rapidly to clear the dust from my eyes. Then I crawled cautiously toward the window. Halfway there I heard someone running.

I sprang to the window in time to see someone dash through the circle of light cast by the street lamp. Dressed in black, the runner had a man's height and gait. He flew down the sidewalk to a black sedan parked nearby.

The car looked like the one that had ambushed me Tuesday night. Parking at the building next door hadn't been enough to keep this guy from finding me. He—or they—must have been doing some research too.

I ducked my head and leaned awkwardly out the window. I cocked, aimed quickly, then fired, one-handed this time, as the runner jerked the driver's door open.

I was pretty sure I'd hit the car, which meant I had missed the shooter again. Apparently I'd gotten him angry, though, because right then the man made a mistake.

Instead of climbing into the car and getting away, he hesitated a few seconds. Then he tried another shot, stepping clear of the door and its window.

I'd climbed outside and sprinted to the sidewalk, partly to make my own shooting easier and partly to keep any more shots away from Georgia's apartment. Standing there on the edge of the circle of light and wearing nothing but white shorts, I knew I made a big, inviting target.

But apparently not big enough. The man missed again although I heard the whiz as the bullet whipped by not far from my head.

I planted my feet and brought the revolver up into the target, using both hands again. I pulled the hammer back, sighted carefully—all too aware of the stubby barrel's limitations—and squeezed the trigger.

The sound of my shot rang loudly between the rows of apartment buildings. For a moment I thought the bullet had gone wide, but then the dark figure staggered back a few feet, half-turned, and fell.

Keeping my gun pointed at the man on the ground, I walked slowly toward the car. Halfway there I heard faint sirens. The man on the ground didn't move.

When I was less than ten feet from the car, I heard Georgia say, "Be careful, Robert! Wait for the police!" Her voice, higher-pitched than normal, came from the sidewalk behind me.

I didn't take my eyes off the man or the big, black pistol that lay a few inches from the man's outstretched fingers. "Go back inside!" I said over my shoulder. Then I advanced the final few steps.

There'd been more blood under Cate's body—or maybe the rug she'd bled on had made it look that way—but this man was just as dead.

I relaxed my grip and lowered the revolver to my side. Then I looked down at the first person I'd killed.

Although I had aimed for the center of the man's chest, adrenaline had caused me to shoot high. The bullet had gone in above the man's left eye, probably killing him almost instantly.

The man, a stranger to me, was white but had blackened the planes of his face for night work. Tall and lean, he appeared to be in his early forties.

Well, he won't get any older, I thought.

I wanted to feel remorse, but it was hard after the man had tried to kill me. Still, I didn't feel proud—not even of having made that final, difficult shot, which I knew was largely luck. Mostly, as the sirens grew louder and the adrenaline rush faded, I felt tired, not in the good way I'd felt earlier but rather drained of energy as well as emotion.

While I stood there numb, Georgia rushed up to me. Dressed in a bathrobe and slippers, she clutched my trousers and shirt in one hand and my shoes in the other. As I took the clothing, she looked at the body and gasped. "Is he—"

"Yes." I stepped into the trousers and stuffed the gun in a pocket.

She stared at the body a moment longer, then turned to look at me. "I don't know him. Do you?"

"No." Another key question was how the guy had found me. Maybe he or someone else had been following me after all. Or maybe the shooter had just spotted the MGB in the parking lot next door and figured I must be with Georgia—it might not be easy to learn her address, but it wasn't impossible.

Regardless, the man had tracked me down, and now he was dead. The stakes in this crazy game—one that seemed to have no rules—kept getting higher.

As I buttoned my shirt, two police cars roared into the block, sirens howling and roof racks blazing. I was sliding my bare feet into the shoes when the police killed the sirens and sprang out of their cars, service pistols drawn.

"All right, you two! Get over here and put your hands on the car!" The speaker, a solidly muscled man in his mid-thirties, appeared to be the senior officer.

I bent over a fender and Georgia followed suit as two other officers, one man and one woman, quickly closed on us from opposite sides. The female officer called out, "Hey, Mike, there's a citizen on the ground. Looks dead." The words were matter-of-fact, but her tone had an edge.

"Get an ambulance," the senior officer called over his shoulder to the fourth cop, who was monitoring the radio in one of the cruisers.

"And backup?" that cop asked.

"No, just the Homicide squad. I think I know this guy here. He's a local lawyer who likes to give police a hard time."

I didn't recognize the senior officer although obviously he recognized me. I winced at his last remark but let it go. I said quietly to the male officer, who was closest to me, "Gun in my right front trousers pocket."

He immediately shoved his pistol, hard, into the small of my back. "Okay, mister, freeze. Don't even breathe until I tell you." He reached carefully into my pocket and pulled out the revolver. "Got a gun here!"

"Cuff 'em," the senior officer said, taking the weapon.

The cop behind me holstered his pistol. Then he yanked my arms behind my back, snapped handcuffs on my wrists, and patted me down. The female cop did the same to Georgia.

The whole thing made me angry, but I kept my mouth shut. *Play it cool. Get Georgie out of this mess.*

"Nothing but the gun," my cop said.

"Nothing on her at all," said Georgia's.

"Of course not," I said. "Ms. Nguyen had nothing to do with it. She—"

"Wait!" the senior officer said, "If you're going to do any talking, we got to read you your rights. You should know that."

He pulled out a small laminated card and in a fast monotone recited the *Miranda* warnings. I noticed he didn't need to refer to the card.

"Now, do you understand your rights?"

"Yes, damn it! I'm trying to tell you this woman had nothing to do with the shooting. She just brought me my clothes after it was all over. I know I'm going to the station, but leave her here."

"Why? Isn't she a witness?"

"Not to the shooting. Look, I'll explain everything to Lieutenant Lytle. You can leave Ms. Nguyen here until the lieutenant says he wants to talk to her. She works in my office, she's not going anywhere."

"She works in your office, huh? So what's this? A little overtime?"

The cop behind me chuckled at his boss's sarcasm, but the female officer frowned.

The senior cop sobered when he saw my expression. "Okay, buddy, no need to get pissed. What happened? Since you're willing to talk."

I nodded toward the body. "This guy tried to get in the apartment."

The senior officer played a flashlight over the body, lingering on the face. He grunted, snapped off the light, and turned back to me. "Her place or yours?"

"Hers."

He waited, but I didn't add anything. Why I was there was none of his business—even police business.

"Did you know him?"

"No, not even without the shoe polish on his face."

"How 'bout her?"

Georgia glanced at the body, then looked away, shaking her head.

"You sure? Burglary's unlikely in an apartment complex—there's always somebody around. So is rape although it's been known to happen."

I knew why he was asking—most shootings are between people known to each other. "Yes, I'm sure," I said. "I don't know who he was, but I think I know what he was."

"And what's that?"

"A man hired to do a job. He was told where he might find me, or maybe he just figured it out—in a town this size it could be done. And someone's been following my car. Maybe it was this guy."

The cop thought about that. "Well, given the way he looks and the way he's armed, yeah, maybe he could be a hired gun. You say he broke in—how?"

"Pulled the screen out of a front window and cut out the glass in front of the lock. That's what woke me. Then he raised the window and was about to climb through when I surprised him. He took a shot at me, I shot back, and things went from there."

"Went bad for him, I'd say."

I had to force myself to look at the corpse. "Yes, it did."

"You say the woman brought you some clothes. So you weren't even dressed when you came out here after the guy?"

"Guess I got caught up in it."

"Yeah, that can happen." The senior officer's expression became less hostile. "You stopped him with one round?"

"Well, I fired four, but only one hit him. Lucky shot."

He looked at the short barrel on the .357. "Yeah, you had some luck, but it wasn't just luck. Tough to hit anything with this at more than a few feet."

"Military training and some practice since then."

"Uh huh. That explains your shooting but not why you were carrying the gun in the first place."

"Let's just say I had a premonition."

"Let's say a little more than that. Let's say you knew someone might have a reason to hire this guy and send him after you. Why?"

"Not here. No offense. Let's go to the station, and I'll talk to Lieutenant Lytle."

The hostile look returned—patrol cops hate being edged aside by detectives. "Okay, but he won't like your story any more than I do."

"What about the woman? Come on, give her a break."

He chewed his lip. "Well, he'll probably want to talk to her in the morning. It'll be Homicide's call, but maybe they'll let her stay after forensics is done."

The man turned to the officer who'd frisked Georgia. "Take her cuffs off and get her info." Then he turned back to me. "Let's go."

I looked at Georgia. "It'll be okay, Georgie. After they've finished with your apartment, try to get some sleep. I'll call you from the police station when I can."

"Shut up and get in the car," the senior officer growled. My cop opened the back door and pushed my head down so I didn't hit the car's roof. The ambulance arrived as he slammed the door.

Georgia stood to one side, looking small and vulnerable in her robe and slippers. She hugged herself tightly even though the fall night wasn't chilly. I saw her eyes searching for me, but I knew she couldn't see much in the car's dark interior.

I also saw the ambulance crew and the police officers clustered around the body of the man I'd killed. They were looking down at the dead man as though he might tell them something.

I looked at him too. He'd be there a while longer as first the forensics techs and then the Homicide detectives processed the scene. But eventually the ambulance would take his body away and the techs would scrub at the blood.

In the darkness they probably wouldn't get it all. A hard rain would have to come to wash away the rest.

CHAPTER TWENTY-EIGHT

I'd thought they would put me in a holding cell, and they started to, but apparently Lieutenant Lytle told them to bring me to his office. So once again I found myself in the familiarly uncomfortable chair in front of his desk. The bored officer who'd escorted me through the maze of hallways had removed the handcuffs but warned me in a flat cop voice not to go anywhere.

So I sat, listening to the rasp of the ventilation fan and smelling the stale odor of the little room. Nothing in the office seemed to have changed in the last forty-eight hours. The desk was just as cluttered, the furniture just as shabby. And the accumulated fear and hopelessness on my side of the desk were as palpable as the cigar butts ground into the ashtray.

Finally Lieutenant Lytle banged into the office and slammed the door shut. Wearing a rumpled suit with no tie, he dropped into his desk chair, which complained loudly. He stared at me across the piles of paper.

"Told you you'd be back, didn't I?"

I was surprised at the heat in Lytle's voice but didn't react to it. "Yes, you did. I guess they told you I was shot at again and—"

"You *shut up* and stay shut up! I swear to God, I'll throw the fucking book at you and enjoy doing it!"

I shut up.

"Yeah, that's right, you better not mess with me this time. Why is it wherever you go, trouble follows? Huh? Or do *you* just follow *it?*"

The needling irritated me. I hated that I'd killed a man, but it was self-defense and too late to undo now. "I'm just—"

"No, don't talk! I don't want you to say nothing. You just sit there quiet as a mouse, and maybe I'll resist the temptation to beat the shit out of you." He paused, scowling at me. "Goddamn it, why does Jack Benton stick up for you anyway?"

I knew he didn't want an answer to that, so I remained silent. I also knew he was too professional to work me over even though he was certainly angry enough to do it.

Lytle shook his head and pulled a cigar out of his coat pocket. Soon smoke drifted toward the fluorescent lights, one of which was blinking like a bug zapper on a hot summer night.

I gave him time to cool down. Then I said, "Look, Lieutenant, I know you're mad about what happened tonight, but remember I've alerted you to two or three bad guys you might not have caught otherwise."

"You've given us a couple of leads, but that doesn't buy you a pass on whatever trouble you're mixed up in. I'm talking about how you keep getting shot at by folks you don't even know . . . or claim not to."

He knocked ash from his cigar. "Now you're shooting back, with permanent effect on somebody."

That made me remember how the dead man had looked as he lay sprawled on the pavement. "I don't know who's after me. If I did, I'd tell you, and then you could lock them up so they couldn't shoot at me again. I'd like that."

"I bet you would—next time they might hit what they're aiming at. That's assuming this guy wasn't the only one gunning for you. Think he was flying solo?"

"I doubt it although I don't have anything to base that on. Any ID yet?"

"They'll call me as soon as they have a positive." Lytle took the cigar out of his mouth and looked at me. "You look a little pale, Robert. Reckon you could use a drink, and even if you couldn't, I could. I'm getting too old to be dragged out of bed this late—or this early." He dug in a desk drawer and pulled out the whiskey.

He uncapped the bottle and poured each of us what my father would have deemed "a healthy slug." He pushed a cup across to me. "Here. This will help—I know."

For a moment I wasn't sure what he meant, but then I did, and I realized he must know exactly how I felt. "Uh, how many for you? If you don't mind my asking."

He gave me a sharp look before answering. "What if I do mind?"

"Then I withdraw the question."

"That's not the kind of thing you can withdraw, Robert."

"Sorry. I didn't mean to . . . pry. I just wondered."

Lytle had some whiskey. Then he put the cup down and stared at it. "Three. The first was just a kid—seventeen. I practically begged him to drop the gun, but he wouldn't. So I did what I had to do . . .

and I've thought about that kid every day since."

"It sounds as though you had no choice."

"No, we all have choices. I didn't have to become a police officer, and maybe I didn't have to shoot that kid. If I'd given him a little more time, he might've put the gun down. I'll never know."

He paused, then looked at me. "And you didn't have to get mixed up in this blackmail shit. Now you've killed a man because of it."

"A man who was trying to kill me."

"That will keep you out of prison—probably. But I don't know if it will help you sleep nights."

He raised his cup, and I drank too, watching his face, which told me nothing more than it ever had at Jack's poker games.

"Okay, Robert, you know I'm on your side in this. I want to help you if I can. Understood?"

I nodded.

"But you got to come clean with me. It's a whole different game now. As my father would say, 'These boys are playin' hardball and you ain't wearin' no glove.' No cup neither." He smiled faintly. "So exactly what are you working on?"

"Sorry. I know there's a dead guy, but I'm the one who shot him, not my client, so I still can't tell you." *Former client*, I thought, *but the information is still privileged.* "I wish I could, but I don't know enough yet to do more than get the client in trouble if I say anything."

"I understand your desire to protect your client, and I don't blame you for what you did out there on the street. I even respect you for it—maybe you saved some cop's life down the line. But it's not just about you and your client anymore. They're putting other people in danger, like that little Oriental secretary you and Jack have."

"Vietnamese American."

"Okay, Vietnamese American. Don't forget I was over there when they were called . . . well, 'Oriental' was considered an enlightened term."

I wondered if he was going to ask what I'd been doing at Georgia's apartment at four in the morning, but I decided he probably knew and didn't care.

"And once they start endangering folks in the community, that's what's most important." Lytle paused, looking down at his cup as though trying to divine something from the dregs. "I think you're investigating the death of that stripper, the one shot in her apartment downtown." Then he looked into my eyes. "Are you?"

"What makes you think something like that?"

"Cops talk to other cops. Maybe a D.C. homicide detective talked to one of the stripper's coworkers and got a pretty good description of some guy who was asking a lot of questions about the girl not long after she was killed. Maybe that detective passed the description along to me, and it reminded me of someone I know."

When I didn't reply, he added, "Don't tell me you're surprised, Robert—you know how word gets around. The detective called me because the coworker said the guy was a polite, well-educated Southerner. That made the detective wonder if someone from my town was doing a little legwork across the river."

"Saying the man had a Southern accent doesn't pin it on me."

"No, but combined with a close physical description, it sure makes me wonder what you were doing Monday night. Somehow I don't think you were watching the football game. What about it? Are you investigating the murder of Cate Gaulois?"

So he knew her name. *Hell, he's probably read the whole case file, including the part about how her death was reported.*

I tried to keep my voice casual. "As the CIA says, I can neither confirm nor deny. I wish I could be more help."

"You can be if you want to." He leaned forward, making the chair creak. "So what about it? I need to know *now.*"

I finished the whiskey. Then I looked straight at Lytle. "As I said, I can't tell you, not yet anyway. If that means I have to stay in jail tonight, well, I've slept in worse places." I tried to think of any, but even a rack right under a carrier flight deck was better.

I could see from the working of Lytle's jaw muscles how close the big man was to losing his notorious temper. After several seconds he spoke in a hoarse voice I had never heard. "All right, I think we can accommodate you."

I knew he wasn't given to puns, so I didn't laugh. Instead I waited, hoping the tension in the room would subside a notch or two.

"Fine, what's the charge?"

"Oh, so now it's the fucking charge you're worried about? Well, how about second-degree homicide, assault, battery, and probably illegal possession of a firearm? How about those, just for starters?"

I set my cup on the desk and stood. "Let's go."

"*You* don't decide when we go, Mr. Lawyer." He rose, towering over me.

The telephone rang and he snatched up the receiver. "Yeah? What's that? From where? No, no, wait a minute, goddamn it!" He scrambled for paper and pen and bent to scribble, snapping into the phone from time to time. Eventually he said, "All right, call me when you have more." Then he slammed down the handset.

"Well," he said with a grin like the devil's on Saturday night, "I've got some news about the dude you planted. He's a contractor from New York. A political bagman, someone willing to do dirty jobs for a price. Even disposal jobs although he didn't handle this one very well."

"If he'd been just a little better, I'd be in the morgue and he'd on his next assignment."

"Yeah, so you better sit down and tell me why someone sent a hitter after you. Was it a guy named Thomas Osborn?"

I didn't answer, but he must have seen my eyes widen.

"So you've heard of him, huh? We found his phone number on a slip of paper taped inside one of the dead man's shoes and ran a search to put a name to the number."

Was Osborn the blackmailer—or just working for someone who was? In either case, could someone else have killed Cate Gaulois? Why? Her death had to be linked to the blackmail scheme—didn't it?

"Yes, I know the name. I talked to him—he said he didn't know anything about what I'm investigating."

"Well, maybe this Osborn knows more than he told you. And maybe he has a reason to come after you. If he does, it's to keep you from digging any deeper."

I thought some more. *That phone number might mean Osborn was mixed up in this mess—or it might not. Osborn could have hired the guy to do some other dirty job, something unconnected with Lisa and Cate.* I'd have to talk to Osborn again and see if I could find out.

Lytle sensed the wheels turning in my head. "That shooter may not be the only one out there, Robert. Lots of folks are willing to pull a trigger for a price, and you're not lovable enough to discourage them."

I knew he was right—given this week's events, I was probably still in danger.

Lytle waited until it was clear I had nothing to say. "Okay, have it your way, smart guy. *Now* it's time to go."

He took me to the desk sergeant, a stocky man with a pitted face. The sergeant looked jaded, as though the many strange things he'd seen on the job had left him incapable of surprise.

"Sergeant Pratt, I've got a joker here who'd rather bullshit me than sleep in his own bed tonight." Lytle pushed me toward the desk. "Book him and find him an empty rack."

"Book him for what, Lieutenant?"

"Anything you can think of, damn it! Start with homicide. Assault and battery. Illegal possession of a handgun. Hell, disturbing the peace and indecent exposure! Feel free to add to that. Use your imagination, Sergeant." Lytle gave me a cold look and left.

Then I felt the walls close in around me.

CHAPTER TWENTY-NINE

"Okay, buddy, welcome to the Alexandria Hilton." The desk sergeant shoved a dirty plastic tray across the scarred counter. "Empty your pockets."

I patted my trousers and came up with the wallet, watch, and keys I'd left there the night before. I dumped them on the tray.

The sergeant extracted my driver's license. He peered at the photograph, then at my face, grunted, and logged my information on a form, tongue snaking between thin lips. He shoved the license back in the wallet and slid everything into a manila envelope. He sealed it and had me sign my name across the flap.

The sergeant pressed a button on the phone. "Get your butt out here, we're open for business."

Less than a minute later a young police officer sauntered up. "Here he is," the sergeant said. "Shoot him, print him, and find him a rack. But watch yourself—he and Little John are friends. Or maybe not, since we're locking him up. Anyway, the lieutenant knows him."

The officer, who had a cocky air to go with his crew cut, looked skeptically at me. "Right. Come on, we've got a nice soft bed all picked out for you."

Half an hour later, after the tedious business of being photographed and fingerprinted, the officer took me to a cell with two sets of bunk beds, each bed occupied by a sleeping man. The men were snoring as loudly as I had ever heard, even in the Navy.

"Oops." The cop gave me an ugly grin. "Looks like someone got here ahead of you and took the last rack. Well, I'm sure you won't mind sitting on the floor. Can't show you any special favors, even if you do know Lieutenant Lytle."

He looked me up and down. "You ain't wearing a belt, but give me those shoelaces." After I did so, he unlocked the door and motioned me inside. "Have a nice rest."

The cell was fairly clean, as jail cells go, but smelled like a ripe locker room. The smell was worse near the toilet. Graffiti covered a good portion of the walls, most of it misspelled and all of it sexual or scatological.

The sad, lonely feeling of the place was almost physical. I could understand why the jailers were concerned about suicide attempts.

I glanced at my wrist before remembering the sergeant had taken my watch. I found the least-dirty spot on the concrete floor, stretched out, and made myself as comfortable as possible in the stuffy semi-darkness. I closed my eyes and waited a long time for sleep.

It came, finally, but brought dreams of a dead man.

□ □ □

Too soon to be rested, I woke with a start to the clang of metal on metal as the morning-shift officers began distributing breakfast trays. I'd gotten little sleep and every muscle ached.

I blinked in the strong artificial light. I watched as a young cop who looked and acted much like his counterpart from the night before brought powdered scrambled eggs, tough bacon, cold toast, watery orange juice, and coffee that wouldn't keep a baby awake. Still, all of the prisoners, myself included, wolfed down the food and polished the trays with scraps of toast.

Breakfast seemed to be the big event of the morning. As soon as the meal was over, two of my cellmates retreated into mental worlds of fantasy, fear, or regret—maybe all three. The other two began bragging to each other about how many jobs they'd pulled, how much they'd stolen, and what master criminals they were. Most of their claims sounded like complete lies.

Sitting on a bottom bunk, one of the dime-store Dillingers looked menacingly in my direction as though evaluating whether he could mess with the newbie. I pretended to ignore the stare and turned my back on the man by going to the sink and splashing my face. Straightening, I stretched and rolled my shoulders as though to get the kinks out.

Then I turned around and stepped into the middle of the room. Keeping my face blank, I glanced around casually, ending my survey by looking the man in the eye. He stared back for a few seconds, shrugged almost imperceptibly, and resumed his conversation.

Then I sat on the floor, made myself as comfortable as possible, and waited. Nothing happened for the next couple of hours except that an officer came to collect our empty trays and another came to take away one of my cellmates, freeing one of the top bunks. I climbed gratefully into the empty bunk and closed my eyes. I was just drifting off when the young cop returned and yelled, "Hey, Shipley, wake up! Lieutenant Lytle wants to see you."

A few minutes later I was escorted into Lytle's office and left standing like some jailbird beneath his notice. Reading through a file, occasionally making notes, Lytle looked as fresh as though he'd gotten a full night's sleep. I rubbed a hand across my stubbled cheek and glanced down at my dirty, rumpled clothes.

Lytle had a cup of steaming coffee on his desk—the best coffee I'd ever smelled. As I watched, he took a long sip and, without turning his head, replaced the cup on the freshest brown ring staining a pile of papers.

I waited but he didn't offer me any. He didn't ask me to sit either.

After a minute he looked up at me. "Appears you had a rough night. Good."

I didn't say anything.

"Now you ready to tell me what's going on?"

I still didn't say anything.

"Why that fellow came after you? What all this has to do with that dead girl downtown?"

I was exhausted, dehydrated, and angry. I had the worst headache of my life and wanted to crawl into my own bed and sleep for days. But I forced myself to wait a moment before answering.

"I'm sorry, Lieutenant, I can't tell you, not yet. I hope I can soon, maybe when I know more myself."

"Damn it to hell!" Lytle threw down his pen. "You know I can toss you back in that fucking cell, don't you? Keep you there all goddamn day if I want to?"

"Yes."

"That's 'yes, sir,' to you, counselor, even if you are Jack Benton's partner."

"Yes, *sir*, and I don't expect any favors just because you and Jack are old friends."

"Good, 'cause you won't get any." He paused, started to speak—loudly, it appeared—but then closed his mouth.

He picked up the ballpoint and clicked it a few times. He made another note in the file and closed it. Then he reached for the coffee and drank slowly.

Finally he spoke. "Last chance, Robert. You gonna talk to me or not?"

"Yes, but not now. I know you can hold me, at least for a while, on account of the shooting last night. But I can do a lot more good out on the street and not just for my client. Maybe I can help you and the guys downtown figure out who killed Cate Gaulois."

"Yeah, and maybe you can get yourself killed. At the moment that seems a lot more likely."

"I'm willing to take the chance."

"I know, but you could be putting other people in danger, maybe even your client, whoever he is. Or is it 'she'? Maybe someone you're . . . close to?"

It was a good guess, but I didn't think it was more than that, so I didn't react.

Lytle looked at me for several seconds, then made an angry gesture. "All right, smart guy. I'm going to let you go. I shouldn't, but if I keep you locked up Jack will be down here in an hour talking lawyer shit and waving a bunch of papers around. Besides, there's always the chance that you'll get lucky and stumble across the truth."

"I think I'm getting close—or closer, at least."

"Maybe—but will you know the truth if you find it?" He didn't wait for me to answer. "Understand one thing, counselor. I don't have to like your refusing to cooperate with us, and I don't like it. Remember that. It'll make a difference if we pick you up again."

"I understand. Of course, you may not arrest me again, at least not before this thing's over."

"I'll bet my next paycheck we do. You can't stop getting into trouble any more than you can stop breathing. Unless somebody stops you—us or someone like that fellow last night."

"Well, better you than another shooter. But I hope that if I am here again, you'll be as generous with your coffee as you were with your whiskey."

"We'll see. Depending on the situation, either of them can be the lifeblood of tired men."

It took me a few seconds to catch the reference. "I didn't know you'd read Chandler."

"Like you, I don't always tell everything I know. You might want to remember that too."

"I will."

"One more thing. I've got to keep your gun for a while even

though I think you may need it. I can't let you have it until after the inquest."

"Okay."

"Didn't you tell me at one of Jack's poker games you've got the handgun your daddy carried during Vietnam?"

"Not his service pistol, the Colt .45. I've got his backup gun, a Smith and Wesson .32, the two-inch."

"A .32? The Regulation Police model no cop ever carries? Shit, can't stop nothin' with that. But if it's all you've got, might be a good idea to take it out and clean it, make sure it's in working order." He paused, frowning. "Bet you don't have a permit for it."

"No."

"Well, then don't let us catch you carrying it, and get a permit as soon as you can. You hear?"

"Yes, sir. Thanks."

He jabbed a button on his phone. "Get in here. We're letting him go."

An awkward minute passed while he and I looked at each other across the big desk. Then a cop came and took me to the desk sergeant, a different one this time, a scrawny, balding man with squinty eyes.

The sergeant thumbed through some manila envelopes stacked on the counter and pulled one out. He broke the seal, making sure I saw him do it, and dumped out the contents, including an inventory sheet. "Check over your personal property and sign for it. You're free to go."

I gathered my things. The lawyer in me made me ask, "What was the charge you used to hold me?"

"Charge? Charge?" The sergeant pretended to root around for a scrap of paper. "I don't see anything on that. Guess you might say you was here as a guest of the City of Alexandria."

He gave me a mocking grin. "The way I heard it, Lieutenant Lytle didn't want you to get hurt out there, wandering around all alone."

"Well, I appreciate that . . . even if it did mean spending a night in jail without being charged with anything."

"The lieutenant's only trying to keep you from gettin' shot full of holes. God knows why."

I managed to hold back my own anger long enough to see the logic in his words. "Maybe you're right, Sergeant. Thanks for reminding me."

□ □ □

Although there were public telephones in the police station, I headed for one down the street. The daylight hurt my eyes, but the fresh air made my head feel better. A little.

Georgia answered after one ring. "Benton Law Group."

"Georgie, do you think it will be ironic if our firm's initials ever are 'BS'?"

"Robert! How are you? *Where* are you?"

"Just left the police station. I'm at a pay phone."

"Are you all right?"

"Sure, nothing injured but my pride. How're you?"

"Okay. The police spent two hours at my apartment, taking photos inside and outside and checking for fingerprints on the window. They asked me a lot of questions—well, actually, the same questions over and over. They didn't seem to believe me when I told them I didn't know anything about it. Then they asked me about . . . us."

"Bet that made you mad."

"You know it did! It's none of their business!"

"You're right, Georgie, it's not. You don't have to answer questions like that."

"I didn't. They didn't like it much, but eventually they left. Then I phoned the police station, and they wouldn't tell me anything. Finally I called Jack—waking him up—and he said a Lieutenant Lytle is a good friend of his and would look out for you."

"He looked out for me, all right. He's the one who kept me in a holding cell until this morning."

"I was really worried about you, and I think Jack was too even though he tried not to show it. He was just about ready to call out the Marines to go get you."

I laughed, which made my head throb. "He'd do it too. In fact, Jack would welcome a chance to call up his old buddies and give them some honest work. He could probably find most of them at the racetrack."

"You're hopeless, you know that?"

"I just need the love of a good woman . . . one with a lot of money." At last I got a laugh out of her. "That's better. Now what are the chances of your picking me up?"

"Oh, pretty good, I guess. I like picking up men," she said, and I knew that line was for my benefit. "Just stay there, try not to get into any more trouble with the police, and I'll be there as quickly as I can."

"Okay, I'll be the guy on the corner who looks like he's trying not to get arrested."

She said something very unladylike and hung up. The sun, now riding high, still hurt my eyes but felt good on my skin. I sat on the curb to wait for Georgia.

CHAPTER THIRTY

Georgia drove up in less than half an hour and looked at me over the rolled-down passenger's window. "Hi, sailor. New in town?"

"Yep, and looking for some action."

She pushed back her hair and smiled. "Think you're man enough to handle me?"

"I hope so, and if I'm not, I can always die trying."

As soon as the words left my mouth, I knew I'd said the wrong thing. Georgia sank back in the seat, her smile gone. "You almost did last night, remember?"

"Unfortunately, yes."

"I'm still scared . . . and you should be too. Well, come on, I'll take you home. You don't want Jack to see you looking like that."

I slid into the car. "Why not? I look as good now as he does most Monday mornings."

"A close call, I'll admit." She pulled away from the curb and drove silently for a minute before glancing at me. "What's going on, Robert? Why did the police keep you all night? Don't they know it was self-defense?"

"Maybe they just wanted to teach me a lesson. A few months ago I did something they didn't like—blew the whistle on a cop who'd planted evidence. Also . . . ."

"What?"

"Well, in addition to squeezing me for information, Lieutenant Lytle might've been trying to keep me from getting killed."

"Then that explains it. But who was that man last night? Do you know anything about him?"

"The police say he was from New York, hired to come after me."

"Who hired him? Who wants you . . . ?"

"Dead?"

She glanced at me again, then looked back at the road. "Yes."

"I don't know, Georgie. I finally paid my bookie, so that can't be it."

"Uh huh. I suppose you're trying to keep me from worrying, but you know this is really serious."

I thought of the man I'd killed, the one who'd tried so hard to kill me. For once the cliché "deadly serious" was actually true. "You're right—it is."

"That man must've had some connection with Lisa Lindstrom and her political enemies—hers or her husband's. I suppose they're the same."

"That's a reasonable theory, but I don't have any proof yet. Either people won't talk to me or they lie. Even worse, they mix truth with lies so I can't tell which is which."

"You're surprised at that?"

"No, I've learned to expect it, but it never stops being frustrating."

"Any chance it's someone in their own party?"

"Less likely but possible. Maybe it's someone who's jealous of Lisa or the senator or just resentful of their power. They have a lot of pull in Washington, which means they have a lot of friends—and people posing as friends."

"I guess this isn't helping much."

"No, it does help, Georgie. Sometimes you just have to brainstorm."

"Well, I'd better get you to the office as soon as possible so you can brainstorm while billing clients."

"Jack'll appreciate that." I watched Old Town slip past in the mid-morning sunshine, the Colonial-era buildings standing in stately contrast to the more modern and generally less appealing structures.

"I didn't know whether you'd want to pick up your car from my place this morning or after work, so I brought your briefcase."

"Thanks. Lisa's case file is in it, and I want to review my notes."

I fell silent, unable to think anymore or to do anything but stare out the window. Perhaps sensing my mood, Georgia didn't speak again while we drove the rest of the way to my house. I picked up the newspaper from the steps, unlocked the door, and followed her inside.

While she read the paper, I made coffee. "We're in luck—the milk's still okay." I put a small pitcher of milk next to her cup and then brought over sugar and sweetener.

As Georgia fixed her coffee the Vietnamese way, I remembered scenes from my favorite restaurant in Arlington's Little Saigon. I wanted to take her there even though their food might not be as good as what she remembered from her childhood.

I gave myself a moment to enjoy that thought, but then I looked at my watch and swore softly. "We need to get going. I'll get dressed and we'll head straight for the office. I'll pick up my car after work."

"Okay. Mind if I look at the case file while you get ready?"

"No, maybe you'll see something I didn't." After I dug the file out of my briefcase, I refilled the cups and took mine upstairs.

Twenty minutes later, putting on a tie, I frowned at myself in the mirror.

Man, you've really screwed up this case. Letting Lisa crawl into your bed, seduce you, try to tell you how to do your job. Treat you the way she did in law school. Then bringing Georgie into it, leading a hired killer to her place, putting her in danger.

I didn't like those thoughts, but I couldn't stop them from coming.

And making love to her, risking her happiness, when you don't even know what your feelings are. . . .

For a moment I stood there, listening to the silence.

Or maybe you do. Maybe you really do, but you're just scared, especially after Lisa.

Those were things to think about, but I didn't have time for them at the moment. I opened a dresser drawer and took out my father's gun, a dark, slightly oily .32 wrapped in a white towel. I unfolded the towel on top of the dresser, releasing the tangy odor of polished steel mixed with the sweeter smell of gun oil.

I wiped away the excess oil, checked the revolver to make sure it wasn't loaded, and looked it over carefully. I'd cleaned the gun after the last time I'd taken it to the range, a couple of years earlier, and there was very little dust on it. I tested the trigger action—it was firm but smooth and ended in a tight snap when the hammer hit home.

I took a small box of ammunition from the drawer and loaded the revolver, the shiny brass cartridges cool in my hand. My belt-clip holster was at Georgia's place, so I stuck the gun in a pocket of my suit coat and went downstairs.

I found Georgia in the study, reading the last couple of pages from Lisa Lindstrom's slim file. She picked up the framed photograph I'd taken from Cate Gaulois's apartment.

From where I stood I couldn't see the picture clearly, but I remembered what it showed: a man helping a young girl build a sand castle at the beach—the two of them admiring their handiwork before the tide washed it away.

"Who's this?" Georgia asked, turning the picture toward me.

"I'm not sure, but I think the little girl is Cate Gaulois."

"You found it in her apartment?"

"Yes, and I'll bet the police would love me even more if they knew about that. Not to mention the state bar."

"Who's the man with her?" Georgia leaned the frame on its cardboard stand and sat back, looking at it thoughtfully as she sipped her coffee.

"I don't know. It's hard to tell much with his face in profile. But this was the only framed photo in her apartment, so it must've been important to her."

"Hmm, he looks familiar. I think I've seen him somewhere or at least a picture of him." She studied the photograph some more. "Hey, wait a minute!"

She clattered her cup onto its saucer and started flicking through the papers in the file, almost ripping some in her excitement. She quickly found what she wanted. She plucked up a printout from *The Washington Post* and stabbed at it.

"See? See? I told you about this one." She thrust the piece of paper in my face.

I looked at the grainy news photo: a group of middle-aged white guys in business suits clustered around a lectern at which another middle-aged white guy in a suit was making a speech. All had the "former class president" look of most politicians.

I didn't recognize the speaker. I read the caption out loud: "Virginia Representative Alexander Wheaton echoes Senator Talbot Lindstrom's call for Congressional task force on Appalachian economic development."

I turned back to Georgia. "You think the guy in the framed photograph is Congressman Wheaton? I don't see much resemblance."

"No, Robert, *this* one!" She tapped the paper. "Look at him."

Bill Murphy was standing off to one side, hands clasped over his belt buckle, looking at the congressman rather than into the camera the way the other men were. His pose reminded me of the picture in which a presidential staffer appears to be taking a leak against the wall of the Pentagon rather than intrude on his boss's photo op.

I studied the pictures, glancing from one to the other. Then I looked at Georgia. "I don't know. It could be the same guy. What makes you think it is?"

"Something I learned in my photography course—we had to study faces from different angles." She put the two pictures next to each other. "See how the nose and chin are alike, the shape of the head?"

"Yes, I see now. There's a certain resemblance. You might be on to something, Georgie."

"Who is he?"

"Bill Murphy, Congressman Wheaton's chief of staff. I talked to him about Lisa's case. He admitted he'd known Cate Gaulois, but that's about all he would say. I couldn't tell if they'd been lovers, close friends, or simply acquaintances."

"Well, he must've been holding something back."

"Could be. I'll show him this picture and see if he's a little more forthcoming." I gathered up the papers and put them back in the file. "Let's go. I think I want to get my car first after all."

CHAPTER THIRTY-ONE

When we walked into the office, Jack was standing at the coffeepot, a cup in his hand and a sour look on his face. "My God, this coffee is awful. I only wish *I* hadn't made it so I'd have somebody else to blame!"

Georgia arched her eyebrows at me and set about making a fresh pot.

"Good morning to you too, Jack."

"Good afternoon—almost. Glad you could make it in today. Guess I should thank Georgia for getting you here at all. I hope you slept well."

"Not particularly—the city jail isn't all that comfortable. Georgia told me you know where I spent the night."

"Yes, she called me early this morning, and then Little John called about an hour ago, gave me the whole story. He said if you're too stupid to keep yourself out of trouble, I should try to keep you out, for the sake of the firm if nothing else."

"What did you tell him?"

"I told him nobody has ever had much luck keeping you out of trouble, and I know better than to try."

"Thanks, Jack. I know I can always count on you."

"Stow the sarcasm, Commander. Little John is serious about this and I am too. You're letting your personal feelings for your client interfere with your professional judgment."

I could almost feel the hurt and anger in the look Georgia shot at Jack. "Come on, partner, let's discuss this in my office. Georgia's got work to do, and we're keeping her from it."

She watched us start up the stairs. "I'll give you two a few minutes to settle the problems of the world, and then I'll bring you some decent coffee. Maybe."

Hearing the edge in her voice, I turned toward her. "Thanks, Georgie, that'd be great." After a moment I added, "It's going to be all right."

She held my gaze, her dark eyes too far away to read. Then she nodded and went to her desk.

I walked into my office, where Jack was already sprawled in a chair and unwrapping a cigar. As I closed the door he bit off the end of the cigar and spat it into the wastebasket.

"Excuse me for being crude, Robert, but I'm feeling that way since I got my ass chewed by Little John. As you're well aware, nobody chews ass like a Marine."

"Yep." I dropped into the desk chair. "My drill instructor taught me that lesson during a long, hot summer in Pensacola. You've reinforced it a few times, and I got a refresher course in Little John's office last night."

I dumped paper clips out of a decorative glass dish and put it in front of Jack. He grunted his thanks and lit the cigar.

When he had it going, he dropped the match into the dish and said, "Look, I know you're only trying to help your client—ours, actually—but you killed a man last night. Granted, in self-defense—still it changes everything. It's time you talked to the police."

"I thought I'd been talking to them, before and after they locked me up."

"Come on, Robert! I mean it's time to tell them something besides your name, rank, and serial number." He waved the cigar for emphasis. "You can't solve this case by yourself, at least not before someone else gets hurt, maybe even killed. Most likely you."

"I'm willing to take that chance—in fact, I'm already taking it."

"I know you're not afraid. But if something happens to you, who'd do the scut work around here? Talk to the difficult clients? Free me up to go to lunch once in a while?"

"Oh, you wouldn't have much trouble replacing me."

"That might be harder than you think." He puffed on the cigar. "Okay, what's the next step?"

"Based on something Georgia pointed out to me this morning, I want to talk to Bill Murphy again. And a guy named Tommy Osborn, if he'll talk to me. If that doesn't get me anywhere, I promise I'll turn it over to the police."

"Later today, you mean?"

"Yes. I've been working under a one-week deadline anyway. Today's the last day, and I haven't found the blackmailer yet."

"All right. I told Little John I'd try to talk some sense into you. I hope some of what I said sticks."

"I appreciate your concern, Jack, really."

"I'm here if you need me." He shoved himself out of the chair and stuck the cigar in his mouth. "Fortunately, you're too ornery to get killed, so I guess I won't worry . . . much." He smiled—a bit grimly, I thought—and walked out, his tread making the floor vibrate.

For a long moment I just sat there, not moving, thinking about what Jack had said. Then I found Osborn's number and called him. The receptionist said he'd gone out of town on business and wouldn't be back until Monday. She wouldn't give me his cell phone number but took a message for him to return my call. *Fat chance that'll happen*, I thought.

Then I dialed Murphy's number. I went through the drill with the receptionist and eventually got him on the line.

"It's Shipley. I need to talk to you."

"Ah, my persistent young friend. Well, Mr. Shipley, for the last time let me tell you that I'm a very busy man, and I don't have time to talk to you. Moreover, I don't *want* to talk to you, so if you'll excuse—"

"I've got a photograph you should see."

"A photograph?" Caution came into his voice. "Of what?"

"You'll know when you see the picture."

"I don't know what you're getting at, Shipley. Remember blackmail's a crime."

"Yes and also a dirty business—like politics, as you've told me—and I should've known that when I got into this mess. But it's too late for me to stop now."

"No, you're wrong—you can stop right where you are, right now."

"I'm not a blackmailer, Mr. Murphy, but I am trying to solve a murder. The murder of Cate Gaulois."

I waited while he thought about it. Finally he said, "All right, I'll talk to you. My office, two o'clock. But this is the last time, the very last time."

I hung up the phone and went to the little bathroom on the second floor, where I splashed my face with hot and then cold water.

After I dried my face, I looked in the mirror. My reflection didn't say anything this time—it just looked at me blankly, the way you look at someone about to do something he shouldn't.

When I went back to the office, I saw that Georgia had left a sandwich and a glass of iced tea on my desk. I ate lunch quickly and then it was time to go.

I put on my coat, feeling the weight of the Smith and Wesson. For a moment I considered taking the gun with me even though I knew

I couldn't carry it into the House office building.

Then I decided the revolver wouldn't do me much good if I had to leave it in the car. Anyway, a daylight attack on me seemed unlikely—at least judging from the past few days. And I didn't want the police to catch me with an unlicensed gun. I locked it in the desk.

I grabbed my briefcase and headed downstairs. Georgia was bent over the desk, long hair veiling her face. The photographs from Vietnam were spread in front of her.

"Thanks for lunch, Georgie. How it's going?"

She looked up, pushed her hair back, and gave me a weak smile. "Fine, Robert. I'm just—well, I'm concerned about you, about this thing you're working on."

"Don't worry—I'll be careful."

"I hope so. And then, I don't know why, but I keep staring at these pictures my aunt sent me. Maybe I'm hoping they'll tell me something."

"Maybe they will."

She looked back at the photos. "My ancestors. People I never knew, probably never will know. Like my father, whoever he was."

I saw the liquid light in her eyes—tears about to fall. I leaned down to hug her.

"It's okay, Georgie, it's okay. We're your family now, Jack and I. We're here for you."

She hugged me back, hard. Then she wiped her eyes with the back of her hand and nodded.

I stood and looked at the photos scattered across the desk. "Do you have any more pictures of your mother?"

She glanced over the photos and handed me one of a Vietnamese woman in her late teens or early 20s standing next to a disheveled white man about the same age. A pair of dog tags hung outside the man's sweat-stained shirt. He had one arm around the woman and a cigarette in his free hand. He looked drunk.

"Who's this with her?"

"I don't know. My father maybe—any of them might be." She tried to smile again but didn't quite make it. "I guess that happens in wartime."

"Yes, it does." I picked up a picture of the same young woman standing next to a large, solidly-built man in fatigue trousers and a T-shirt with "DOGS" on it. The man's hat shadowed his face. "I remember seeing this one before. But you don't know who this guy is either?"

"Tôi không biết." She spoke slowly as though reluctant to use her mother tongue. "I don't know. Another friend of my mother's, another GI. Who knows? What do you think that means: 'DOGS'?"

I thought for a moment. "Well, it could be that he was in D, or Dog, Company. You know, like Alpha, Bravo, Charlie. D was usually Delta, but sometimes they used Dog. Maybe it's short for 'dogfaces'—slang for infantrymen. Or it could be a reference to *Teufelshunde*, German for 'devil dogs'."

"What?"

"That's what the Germans called American Marines after they fought them in World War I—a compliment to the way the Marines fought like hounds from hell. Maybe this guy was a Marine."

I looked at the photo more closely. "Could be anything really. In Vietnam during the war? Could be anything at all." There was something else about the snapshot. I studied the picture for a moment but couldn't figure out what was bothering me. "Let me keep this one for a while, Georgie, if you don't mind."

"Sure, but why?"

"Oh, I don't know—maybe if I put it into my pocket and carry it around for a while, I'll get a sense of what your mother must have been like. All I know about her now is that she was a lovely woman who would've been very proud of her daughter."

Georgia blushed. "Well, I don't know whether she would've been proud of me, but she *was* beautiful, as anyone can see."

"Almost as pretty as you." I leaned to kiss her forehead. Then I cupped her chin in my palm and looked into her eyes. "Now I've got to go see my friend Mr. Murphy one more time."

"You be careful, Robert, just like you said."

"I will, Georgie. I promise."

At the door I turned and glanced back at her. She was sitting quietly at her desk, hands folded in her lap, staring at the fading shadows of her unknown past.

CHAPTER THIRTY-TWO

This time when I walked into his office, Bill Murphy neither rose nor invited me to sit. He just leaned back and looked at me—hard. "What the hell do you want now?"

"The truth."

He gave a harsh laugh. "The truth? Shit, what's that? Who knows? Who would tell it even if they knew?"

"I want the truth about Cate Gaulois."

"I've told you what I know."

"Not all of it."

"You calling me a liar, young man?"

From my coat pocket I pulled the framed photograph of the little girl and the man at the beach. I laid the picture on Murphy's desk.

Murphy glanced at the photo, then glared at me, his face reddening. He looked at the photo again, longer this time. His shoulders sagged, and suddenly he seemed old. He said nothing for several seconds, slumped in the deep leather chair, his head bowed so low that I could see the bald spot beginning to spread under the carefully combed hair.

I thought about the bull fight I'd gone to during a port call in Spain—how a bull looks in the ring when he's too spent to run anymore and the matador's closing in.

Finally Murphy spoke, emotion thickening his voice. "Where . . . where did you get this?"

"In Cate Gaulois's apartment. I'm the one who discovered her body and called the police."

"Then I suppose you've told them what you know about her and that you've talked to me?"

"No, to protect my client I've told the cops as little as possible, including about you and Cate. In fact, when I called them, I didn't give my name."

"That could be dangerous for a lawyer—an officer of the court."

"Lots of things are dangerous. I did what I thought best at the time."

Murphy turned to the window. The afternoon sky was a dull,

leaden color that seemed to chill the office even though the room wasn't cold. He looked out on the street below and the buildings beyond as though seeing years and worlds past.

He was silent so long that I was about to press him again, but then he spoke, his voice still thick. "I loved Cate, you know. Very much. I loved her mother too."

He turned back from the window. "More than her mother knew, perhaps. Certainly more than I knew at the time. But sometimes you can't do what you want to. Or can't bring yourself to do what you know you should.

"Anyway, that's how it seemed to me then." He picked up the photograph and held it gently. "Looking back . . . well, I'd do it differently."

"Cate Gaulois was your daughter."

After a long moment Murphy nodded, and now his eyes were just sad. "I never wanted her to be a dancer—a stripper—in some seedy club. She was too smart for that."

I waited for him to continue.

"She *was* smart, you know. She read philosophy and wrote poetry and loved to paint. I think she had real talent. But she didn't seem to want to do anything with her life—she was content just to *be*. You know?"

"This town could use a few more people like that. I'd like to try it myself sometime. That's why she became a dancer?"

"Yeah, I guess so. Cate was always very athletic, kept herself in good shape. She loved to dance, loved music, liked to sing along with the radio. I guess she figured she could make more money dancing—at least more per hour—than doing anything else. It left her time to read and paint. I kept hoping she'd go back to school, finish her degree,"

"How do you think she got mixed up with political blackmail?"

"I have no idea. She never cared much for politics—or for politicians. In fact, I don't think she had much respect for my line of work."

"You told me before that you'd seen Frank Nelson at the 1776 Club. Do you think Cate knew him?"

Murphy's mouth twisted. "Yes, very well, much better than I would have liked. Frank's a strong-willed man who knows what he wants, and Cate may have responded to that despite her general dislike of politicians. Of course, I've heard that a lot of women find

Frank Nelson attractive, so perhaps he has some hidden charm."

"Did Cate knew Lisa Lindstrom?"

"Yes, in fact I think Cate was . . . well, attracted to Lisa. Based on a couple of comments she made." He paused. "I didn't think I'd ever be able to say that. But, yes, Cate was attracted to her. Lisa's very pretty. And she can be engaging although you might not see that side of her unless she wants something from you."

"I know. Firsthand."

"Oh?" Murphy studied my face a moment before continuing. "Then you understand what I'm talking about. Well, I think she played that game with Cate, who was very pretty and charming herself, only she didn't know it was a game and actually fell for Lisa."

"That's probably how she got mixed up in this," I said, more to myself than to Murphy.

"What's the blackmail scheme? Attorney-client privilege shouldn't protect an ongoing crime unless your client is behind it."

"My client didn't tell me who killed Cate, and somebody's shot at me, a couple of times, to keep me from finding out. So I'm sufficiently pissed off not to give a damn what my client—now my ex-client—thinks about what I've found or might find."

"And that is . . . ?"

"Sure you want to hear? It isn't pretty although I don't know that Cate was actively involved in the blackmail scheme."

"Yes, I want to know."

"Someone videotaped Cate being intimate with another woman and tried to use the tape for political purposes."

He was silent for several seconds, taking it in. Then he said, "Obviously, you're leaving out some key details—to protect your client, I suppose. But you've told me what I most want to know, and I can guess who the other woman was."

"Yes, that wouldn't be hard. Any idea who might have done it? Or even which side?"

"It's hard to know where the sides are anymore. With all the polls they conduct nowadays, one side steals the other's positions before breakfast. I do know that Cate and Lisa had very different views about a lot of things."

"So they didn't have much in common?"

"Maybe just a need to test the limits, to see how far they could take something."

"How much did Cate tell you about her relationship with Lisa?"

"Not much. She never told me a lot about her personal life. She resented the fact that I hadn't married her mother, and for the last couple of years the only place she'd see me—or even talk to me at any length—was that club where she worked. I think she wanted to rub my nose in how she'd chosen to make a living."

He paused a moment before continuing. "But she did mention Lisa. She probably didn't want me to be surprised if I heard that the two of them were . . . involved."

"Did she say how they met?"

"No, but I assumed it was probably through Frank Nelson. Or maybe through somebody he knows. Frank doesn't have a lot of scruples, but he's clever. Maybe once he heard about the two of them, he was hoping for some kind of kinky setup."

"A *menage-a-trois*."

"Yes, but if that's what he wanted, he was playing a dangerous game. I mean, his boss's daughter, a senator's daughter. . . ."

"Maybe Nelson wasn't thinking clearly."

"Thinking with his dick, you mean."

I nodded. "Could be. It happens to most guys at one time or another."

A smile ghosted across Murphy's face. "Sure. You're in the bar at two a.m., half gassed, some sweet young thing breathing in your ear, your fly braced tight as a pup tent. I remember."

"There's another possibility though."

"What?"

"Maybe Nelson was willing to play a dangerous game because he figured the stakes were worth it."

"Sleeping with two women?" His lip curled. "Sure, a lot of guys have that fantasy, but—"

"That's not what I mean. Maybe Nelson wanted them to meet so he'd have something on Lisa, something that didn't involve him."

"You think Frank's working with the blackmailers? That's pretty hard to believe. Frank's a son of a bitch, but he's a loyal one—at least, I've always thought so."

"Maybe he is and maybe he isn't. That's what I've got to figure out. As well as who killed Cate."

"Yes, that's the important thing. Who killed Cate. My daughter . . . who was never really mine." He swallowed hard.

Then, not looking at me, maybe not looking at anything visible, he spoke in the voice of a man with little left to lose. "Was that what you wanted, counselor?"

"Some of it. I'm convinced now that you didn't kill Cate. I still don't know who did, but I was hired to do a job, and I'm going to finish it."

"A real crusader, aren't you, Mr. Shipley? All you need now is a cape." His tone softened the sarcasm.

"Maybe. Given my track record, you might say crusading is a fault of mine. But do you have any idea who might've mailed that videotape to Lisa?"

"I don't know anything about the tape or how it got to her."

His words made me pause, but I wasn't sure why. As I was groping for the reason, he added, "But I appreciate what you've been trying to do. I know Cate would also."

"Trying isn't the same as succeeding."

"Oh, I'm sure you're not done yet. Ask enough questions and you'll find the truth—at least what passes for it in this town."

The irony wasn't lost on me. I stood. "I'm sorry to have bothered you again, Mr. Murphy. I'll be going now."

"That's all right. I hope I was some help."

"Yes, sir, you were. Well, goodbye."

He walked around the desk. "Please let me know what you find."

"I will, however it comes out."

Suddenly, impulsively, I held out my hand. Murphy took it and pumped hard.

I thought I recognized something of Cate Gaulois in his face, mostly around the eyes—a look that was knowing, even jaded, but hadn't always been that way. Once it had been young and open and eager.

As I walked out, I thought of Cate's self-portrait and the pain in her eyes, a look that I knew I would never—could never—forget.

CHAPTER THIRTY-THREE

Back in the parking garage I sat in the car, hands on the wheel, replaying the conversation with Bill Murphy. I took the new pieces of information and tried to connect them to what I'd already known.

The picture was beginning to form, but it was far from finished. And the blackmailer's deadline had arrived—either Lisa announced today that she wasn't running for the Senate or the sex tape would become public tomorrow.

I glanced at my watch: 3:15 p.m. *Out of time . . . out of time.*

It was like being on a river dammed within sight of the sea. I wrenched the key in the ignition, paid the attendant, and turned onto the crowded streets of Capitol Hill.

I had slow going until I crossed back into Virginia and got on the G.W. Parkway. As I drove south, I caught glimpses of the Potomac on my left, the broad river rolling slowly toward the Chesapeake Bay. A few boats, sails cloud-white, cut through the water, which was several shades bluer than the sky it reflected.

Should be out there. Even a bad day on a boat is better than a good day anywhere else, and this isn't one of my better days—or weeks. But what was it my father said? "Never give up. You're not beaten until you think you are."

When I got to Old Town, I passed an angular Postal Service truck, dirty white with the big blue eagle. The carrier emerged with a heavy-looking bag slung over his shoulder and letters, magazines, and a package in his hands.

I glanced over, and something made me focus on the package. I stared at the book-sized brown box. Then I knew.

Goddamn it! That lying son of a bitch!

I mashed the accelerator and savagely shifted gears. I grabbed the phone and dialed Lisa, almost sideswiping a parked car when I glanced down at the keypad. Then I drove very fast through Old Town, listening to the phone ring. I was cursing out loud when she finally answered.

"Hello?"

"It's me. Thank God you're home."

"Robert? Is that you?"

"Yes—wait a minute." I juked right and went down a side street. I pulled to the curb and sat there with the engine running. Then I took a deep breath, held it a moment, and exhaled slowly.

"Have you made any announcement yet?"

"No. I haven't even told anybody that I'm going to make one. But I plan to call a local news station at 5:00 p.m. At this point I don't think I have any other choice."

"Yes, you do! I've figured out what's going on."

"Really?" She sucked in her breath.

"Yes, I'm pretty sure. You told me you hadn't discussed the videotape with anyone, right?"

"I haven't told anyone but you. There's no one else I can trust." She paused. "That's assuming I can still trust you. You certainly haven't been willing to handle things my way."

"Let's not go through that again. You asked me to find out who's blackmailing you. I think I've done that."

"Robert, I fired you. Didn't I make myself clear?"

"Yes, very clear, but I still want the truth."

"All right, who's the blackmailer?"

"You're sure you didn't tell anyone? Not even Frank Nelson?"

"You must be kidding. Frank would just use the information against me, keep me in 'my place,' wherever that is."

"Okay, that means I'm almost certainly right. I've got to make sure, though, and I need you to help me."

"How?"

"You'll see. Is your husband home?"

"No, he's playing golf with some other rich techies. They're going to have dinner at the country club afterward."

"Where's Nelson?"

"Frank? Probably at his office. Why?"

"Is the maid or anyone else around?"

"No, she's off today. I'm here by myself."

"Good. I'm in Old Town. I have to stop by the office for a minute, and then I'll head for your house in McLean."

"What for?" She spoke sharply. "Why do you need to see me?"

"I need to see Nelson, and I want the meeting to be at your place."

"Frank? What does Frank have to do with this? I told you he

doesn't even know about it. And why here?"

"I believe he knows more than you think—a lot more. To find out, I need to question him in front of you, see how he reacts."

I knew she wouldn't like the idea, and she didn't. "You don't need me for this, Robert. That's what you're for—to keep me out of everything."

"Yeah, but you fired me, remember?"

"It sounds like I need to do that again! Maybe you'll stayed fired this time."

"Come on, Lisa! I know who the blackmailer is, but I need you to help me prove it."

She paused, and I listened to the hum of the telephone, barely audible above the muted sound of the engine. "Well . . . if you really need me, I'll be here." She paused again. "I suppose the blackmailer killed Cate."

I'd expected that. "It's a reasonable assumption."

"Certainly." She paused. "Okay, just give me time to shower, get dressed, and put on some makeup."

"You don't need to. It's not a fashion show."

"I've been moping around the house all day, knowing I have to phone reporters later and tell them I'm not going to run. I'm a complete wreck. How soon will you be here?"

"Forty-five minutes, maybe a little less."

"Then I'll hurry. Do you need the address?"

"I have it. See you soon."

I cleared the phone and dug for Nelson's number. When the receptionist answered, I identified myself and asked for Nelson.

"Just a moment, please." I waited impatiently until she came back on the line. "I'm sorry, Mr. Nelson's unavailable right now. May I take a message?"

"Try him again. Tell him I want to talk about blackmail and murder."

She was well trained, but her surprise still came through. "Blackmail and—"

"Murder. That's right."

"Wait, please."

The wait was a lot shorter this time. "Goddamn it, Shipley, what the hell do you mean telling the girl that—'blackmail and murder'! Don't you know how people gossip in an office?"

"I had to get you on the phone."

"Okay, you've got me. What the fuck do you want?"

"I want to talk to you at Lisa Lindstrom's house."

"At Lisa's . . . why there? What about?"

"About blackmail and murder, just like I said. She's waiting for us—I want her to hear what you have to say."

"Well, I'm not going to do it. I've let you jerk me around long enough. I'm going to report you to the Virginia State Bar."

"Report away. While you're doing that I'll have a little talk with the police. I'll tell them everything I know about this case, which I haven't up to now."

There was silence for several seconds. Then Nelson said, "All right. Maybe I can finally convince you that I had nothing to do with the black—uh, with whatever you're investigating."

"Fair enough. Meet me at Lisa's in an hour."

"But the traffic at this time of—"

"Just be there."

I clicked the phone off and dropped it on the passenger's seat. As I began to pull away, a sudden gust of wind blew dust and scraps of paper toward the car.

The dust made me sneeze and blink. The sun dimmed and the trees tossed in the breeze. Then, as quickly as it had come, the wind was gone, leaving the sky bright and clear again.

The dust left a film on my hands and face, and I tasted grit all the way to the office.

CHAPTER THIRTY-FOUR

I pulled into the parking lot behind the office and turned off the engine. I felt very tired. Despite the need to hurry, I sat listening to Old Town in the late afternoon. I heard the low rumble of traffic, the staccato pounding of a jackhammer, the sharp clang of a garbage can lid.

I closed my eyes and imagined myself in a sailboat heeled over in Vieques Sound off the eastern end of Puerto Rico, the smaller islands to the east rising from the sea like great green whales. I pictured Georgia there with me, dark eyes flashing in the sunlight, long hair blowing in the sea breeze.

Then I snapped back to reality, remembering that I had a date with a lady. A date with my former lover to talk to a gentleman who was also her lover. A date to discuss a dead woman who'd been the lover of the lady and perhaps of the gentleman.

I shook my head. *How had it gotten so complicated . . . why were there so many lies?* I got out of the car and walked into the office.

Georgia looked up from her desk, her expression anxious. "Hi, Robert. How'd it go?"

I gave her what he hoped was a reassuring smile. "Pretty well, I think. Things seem to be falling into place—finally."

"Good! Then you're done with the investigation?"

"Almost. There's just one more thing to do."

"What's that?"

"Meet Frank Nelson and Lisa at her house, confront them with what I know, and see if I can't shake the rest out of them. That's assuming they know more than they've told me, and I'm positive they do."

"Oh, please be careful, Robert. I have a bad feeling about this. You know?"

"I know." I tried to give her another smile but couldn't find one. "I think you're right. But I've got to keep going—'marching forward,' as Jack would say. Hey, can you get directions to this address?" I pulled Lisa's card out of my wallet and handed it to her.

Georgia looked at the card, pulled out a map book, and headed to the photocopier. As I took the copied page, I squeezed her hand. "You'll be here when I get back, won't you?"

"You just get back."

I looked into her eyes and nodded. Then I went upstairs for my father's Smith and Wesson.

□ □ □

Just over half an hour later I exited the G.W. Parkway onto Route 123 and drove south into McLean. Imposing homes surrounded by big trees were set well back from the four-lane highway and largely concealed by manicured shrubbery.

A mix of company presidents, doctors, lawyers, bankers, and a few famous journalists and successful artists lived in McLean. Several cabinet secretaries and members of Congress also had their Washington homes there. New money rubbed against old—the latest residents were dot-com millionaires like Daniel Strawbridge who wanted a short commute to the sprawling, traffic-choked mess that was Tysons Corner.

After about a mile I turned left between twin blue spruce trees into a neighborhood of big houses, mostly Colonials with a couple of Tudors for variety, situated on lawns as green as golf courses and almost as big. I slowed and looked for the number of Lisa's house.

Hers turned out to be a red brick Colonial with white columns and shutters looming over a semi-circular drive and flanked by tall trees. The property looked as though it should be on the cover of *Southern Living*. My little townhouse, which actually dated from the period this house had been built to recall, would probably fit into the garage and the rooms above it.

I parked three-quarters of the way around the drive. I slid the Smith and Wesson in the left side of my waistband and put on the suit coat. Unbuttoned and hanging loosely, the coat hid the gun.

I walked to the front door—white-painted wood with a gleaming brass kick plate—and rang the bell. I heard chimes reverberating inside. Outside the late-afternoon sun played hide-and-seek behind the clouds scudding across the sky, which was pale blue where the light gray clouds didn't obscure it.

The weather finally felt like fall. It was time for the harvest—time to reap what had been sown.

I waited a while for Lisa to come to the door and then impatiently rang the bell again, longer this time. Several seconds later she opened the door.

"Hello." Her voice had the husky quality I'd always liked but lacked some of its usual self-assurance. Her hand, the one holding a cigarette, trembled slightly.

"Hi. You took a while."

Lisa didn't explain her delay. She merely stepped back and motioned me inside with a tilt of her head.

I squeezed past her, smelling her familiar perfume, and stood on the oriental rug in the octagonal foyer while she closed the door. She wore a short red skirt and a clinging white blouse so sheer I could've counted the swirls of lace on her low-cut bra. Her hair appeared slightly damp from a shower.

Lisa didn't stretch up to kiss me. I noticed that her eyes seemed unusually bright and large and that she was blinking very rapidly, her long eyelashes fluttering like butterfly wings.

"Are you okay?"

"Sure, why not? I mean, don't I seem fine?"

"Just a little . . . wired. Maybe you took something, huh?"

She tried to laugh but didn't sound very mirthful. "Oh, Robert, stay out of my personal business, won't you? That includes my medicine cabinet."

"To stay out of your personal life is a pretty strange request coming from a woman who hired me to find her blackmailer."

"And you found him—or them—didn't you? So everything's going to be all right."

"I hope so. We'll see." I saw in her face that she'd hoped for more reassurance. "Nelson should be here soon. Where's the best place to talk to him?"

"I would've said his office."

"No, I mean in your house. I told you before why I wanted to meet here."

She sucked hard on the cigarette, leaned her head back, and shot out smoke. "You've said a lot of things over the years, Robert. I haven't found all of them convincing."

The remark stung but hurt me less than she wanted. "Really?"

"Yes, like how you said you'd look out for me on this case."

"I said I'd try to find the blackmailer. I never said I could do that and keep your skirts out of the mud. You know blackmail's a crime."

"Of course I do."

"Well, so is murder."

She held my gaze a few seconds, then turned toward a table on which a large vase of fresh flowers stood in front of a long mirror. She carefully shifted the vase half an inch to the right. She looked at herself in the mirror, brushed her hair back with one hand, and glanced at my reflected image. "Let's go into the library."

I followed her into a spacious room off the foyer. Another oriental rug, thicker and larger than that in the foyer, covered most of the hardwood floor. Built-in bookshelves ran from the floor to the ceiling, broken only by a marble fireplace and the tall windows that looked out on the emerald lawn.

Two comfortable-looking wing chairs were near the fireplace, and a long, low sofa, prefaced by a mahogany coffee table, anchored one edge of a considerable expanse of rug. An antique rosewood table with a matching straight-back chair behind it stood on one side of the room. Over by the windows was a small wooden cart with an ice bucket and cocktail glasses on top and several liquor bottles underneath, handy for any drinking that needed to be done.

I glanced at the books filling but not overcrowding the shelves. Most of the volumes, some of them leather-bound, seemed to be works of biography, history, or political theory. A few looked as though they'd actually been read.

The only artwork in the room was a large painting of the Capitol seen from the Mall. The artist had depicted the building in the late afternoon on a day apparently much like this one: the marble shone brilliantly white in the sun but dulled to lunar gray in the shadows of the clouds.

I turned to Lisa. "This'll do. Bring Nelson in here as soon as he arrives."

"Okay—boss." She took another drag on the cigarette, this time blowing the smoke toward me. "Thanks for complimenting my decorating."

I grunted at the sarcasm. "Nice room. Reminds me of my study at home except that it's four times as large, has hardbacks instead of paperbacks, and all the books are in order. Plus I don't have a drinks cart."

"Serves me right for fishing. Speaking of drinks, would you like one?"

"Yes, but not now. Maybe later."

"Well, I'm going to have one—perhaps several."

"Okay. I can carry you to your room if necessary."

"Just like old times, huh, Robert?"

"In some ways, maybe. Not in others."

I noticed framed photographs on the table and stepped over to look at them. "Nice wedding picture. They say all brides are beautiful, but you must've set a record."

"Thanks. That was my mother's dress."

"And this is you and your father? On a sailboat, looks like. With you at the helm."

"Yes, that's my favorite of us together. We'd gone to the beach for a long weekend." She paused. "I was thirteen then. It seems like a long time ago."

"I know that feeling. Looks like you two had a good time."

"We did. That was before . . . . well, when we were still happy."

I tried to think of something comforting to say but couldn't come up with anything. What can you say to someone who'd been through what she had? The best I could do was, "Well, regardless of anything else, I'm sure he's proud of you."

She stabbed her cigarette out in a silver ashtray. "I wish that were true, Robert. It's nice you think so."

I didn't reply, leaving her with her thoughts of her father, whatever they were.

Chimes interrupted the silence. "That's Frank," she said, keeping her voice low although there was no way Nelson could've heard her normal tone.

"Yes." Without meaning to, I'd lowered my voice to match hers.

"I still don't think he knows anything about this."

"We'll see."

"After I let him in, you're on your own."

"Fine. I'm used to that."

She gave me a look and then swept by, muttering, "This'd better be good, Robert, or so help me. . . ." She left the room, closing the door behind her.

Good? It may be a lot of things, but it won't be good.

CHAPTER THIRTY-FIVE

I heard the front door open and, a few seconds later, close. I heard voices but couldn't make out the words.

Still standing by the table, I noticed that the shallow drawer in its center wasn't fully closed. Light glinted off something metallic inside. I reached out to open the drawer but withdrew my hand when I heard steps.

Lisa returned, followed closely by Nelson. Both looked displeased, whether with each other or with me I didn't know or care.

Not at this point . . . too many lies and too much death.

"Good afternoon, Mr. Nelson, thanks for coming out." I didn't offer to shake hands, and neither did Nelson.

"Skip the pleasantries, Shipley." He unfastened the one closed button on his suit coat but didn't remove the coat. I saw something bulging in the right pocket, causing the coat to hang lower on that side and making his tall, lean frame look slightly crooked. "What the hell's this about?"

"Blackmail and murder. Dirty politics too although that by itself isn't against the law. If it were, hardly anybody would be left in Congress."

The remark didn't faze him at all. "It's very easy to criticize the system from the outside—especially when you don't understand it."

"I understand a young woman didn't need to die to further someone's political agenda."

"Goddamn it! I've already told you that I know nothing about that."

"Yes, I remember what you said." I paused. "Look, let's sit down. We can be comfortable even if we can't be pleasant. This shouldn't take long."

"Sit here, Frank." Lisa gestured toward one of the chairs by the fireplace.

Nelson glared at me and lowered himself into the chair, careful not to sit on his coat. I watched him as I began to pull the straight-back chair away from the table, but Lisa stopped me by saying, "No, Robert, that one might be too rickety for you—it's an antique.

Take the other wing chair."

The antique looked sturdy enough, but I didn't argue. Still watching Nelson, I went over by the fireplace and sat, leaning toward him so that the gun didn't press into my side.

Lisa sat on the sofa and crossed her long legs negligently, exposing a lot of tanned, waxed skin. She put her arm on the back of the sofa and said in a cool tone, "Well, Robert, it's your party."

I gave her the best grin I could muster and turned to Nelson. "As you and I discussed last evening, someone's blackmailing Lisa, trying to get her not to run to replace her dad in the Senate. The blackmail involves a videotape of Lisa and another woman—Cate Gaulois, who was murdered last weekend."

"Yes, yes, I know all that, but why keep asking me about it?"

"Because I know who's blackmailing her."

Nelson's eyes widened. "Well, that's great. Good news for the senator as well as Lisa." He shifted, moving his right hand toward his coat pocket. "Obviously, I want you to share that information with me."

"Sure, that's why we're here."

"Then please get on with it." Nelson glanced at his watch. "I've got a very important appointment downtown in fifty-three minutes."

"I'll try to keep that in mind," I said, "but you may be a little late." I paused to let him wonder about that, then continued. "Lisa's being blackmailed by a political opponent—an opponent of her and possibly of Senator Lindstrom as well."

"Well, you don't have to be a rocket scientist to see that. It's self-evident."

With his left hand he took a snowy handkerchief out of his breast pocket and patted his forehead. *It's not that hot. Not even especially humid now.*

"But go on," he said. "What other brilliant deductions have you made?"

"Whoever's behind this—and for now assume it's just one person—knows Lisa personally and also knew Cate Gaulois."

Lisa shifted but said nothing.

"Well, I think I understand the part about knowing the Gaulois woman. That connection was necessary to make the videotape." Nelson put the handkerchief back in his pocket. "But why do you think the blackmailer knows Lisa?"

"Once he found out about the relationship between Lisa and

Cate, the blackmailer must've had a high level of confidence that the relationship would continue long enough for him to hide a camera in Cate's apartment and capture the two women on tape. Otherwise, he would've thought of some other way of catching Lisa in a compromising position." I turned toward her. "Sorry to have to say it, Lisa, but that wouldn't be terribly difficult."

She frowned. "Fuck you, Robert."

"Nice language, especially from someone who sees herself as a U.S. senator. Okay, assuming the blackmailer was working without Cate's cooperation or even knowledge—and I believe that to be the case—he would have to be able to retrieve the camera secretly. All of which strongly implies he had personal knowledge about both women and perhaps even had a relationship with each of them."

"You're just jumping to conclusions," Nelson said. "Maybe the blackmailer only knew Cate and heard from her that she and Lisa were lovers. And maybe the blackmailer didn't retrieve the camera secretly at all. Maybe the blackmailer killed Cate when she got the camera."

"'She'? Why 'she'?"

"Your chauvinism's showing, counselor. The killer could be a woman—we don't know."

I sensed Lisa stiffen. "I suppose that's possible, but we know the blackmailer's a man. In fact, we even know who he is, don't we?"

Nelson moved his right hand half an inch toward his coat pocket. "You may know or think you know, but I'm sure I don't."

"Yes, you do, Mr. Nelson. In fact, you told me who it is."

"*I* did? How could I when I don't know that myself?"

Without turning toward her, I said, "Lisa, you said you haven't discussed this matter with him."

"That's right, Robert—no one but you. I knew if I said anything to Frank, he'd tell my father. You would've, too, wouldn't you, Frank?"

Nelson seemed to be thinking fast. Still, he was a beat late in saying, "Well, yes, I suppose so."

I looked at Lisa. She'd always been smart and beautiful, but since the long-ago days of our affair she'd also become ruthless, even dangerous. Maybe whatever her father had done to her had slowly changed her. Maybe it was a love of money and power. Maybe it was just ambition.

Whatever the cause, she'd stayed beautiful but had become hard, like a diamond.

A flawed diamond.

Remembering how she'd lied and tried to manipulate me over the last few days and knowing what I'd have to say to her in another minute, I didn't feel much sympathy for her. Yet, given our intertwined pasts, I couldn't help feeling some.

"I wish I didn't have to do this to you, Lisa, but it can't be helped." I turned back to Nelson. "You're the blackmailer."

His hand twitched but his face turned to stone. "You're crazy."

"Maybe, but you're still the blackmailer. Remember when we talked in the bar? You said you didn't know who'd mailed the tape to Lisa."

"I don't!"

"But you know she received it in the mail."

He looked confused for a moment. "Oh, hell, I just assumed she did. I mean, that would be a logical way to get the tape to her. What I said certainly doesn't prove I'm blackmailing Lisa."

"That alone might not be enough to convict you in court, but it's certainly enough to make the police want to talk to you. It shouldn't be hard to prove you knew Cate. Someone may have seen you entering or leaving her apartment."

Suddenly I remembered the tall, slim figure I'd passed on the stairs in Cate's building. "In fact, I think it's very possible somebody saw you. You were probably there on several occasions—planting the camera, retrieving it, maybe putting it back a time or two if the tape didn't show what you needed. You wouldn't have trusted anyone else to do that."

The man's gaze was murderous.

"You had keys to her apartment, didn't you? Either a set Cate gave you or one you copied from Lisa's. And I think that after you had the tape, you went back one last time just to make sure you hadn't left any clue that you were ever there. What you found in the bedroom must've scared you—I know it scared me."

"Complete fantasy, of course, but at least it's amusing. Don't you think so, Lisa?" He turned to look at her, and I glanced the same way.

She was staring at him, her skin flushed, her features ugly with hatred.

From the corner of my eye I saw his hand dive into his coat pocket. I started to reach for my gun, but Nelson, moving with surprising speed, won the race as he brought up a semiautomatic and pointed it at me.

"Hold it!"

I froze, hand just inside my coat. I calculated the chance of getting the .32 out before Nelson shot me. Virtually zero. I slowly brought my hand back into view.

"That's right." He smiled, but his expression wasn't pleasant. "Don't even breathe wrong. I can't miss at this distance. Show me both your hands, empty."

I complied.

"Okay. Put your hands together behind your back and keep them there."

I bent slightly at the waist and moved my hands behind me, not quite touching. I heard Lisa's breathing but didn't look away from Nelson.

"Now sit against the back of the chair. We don't want you tempted to try anything heroic." He kept the pistol on target as I leaned backward.

"Good, very good." He seemed to relax slightly, shifting in his chair but keeping the gun pointed at me. "Yes, an amusing little fantasy. Too bad I'm not in the mood for amusement."

He was still smiling, and I wanted to punch his face—hard.

"Really, though, couldn't you come up with something more believable? As you said, the blackmailer is undoubtedly a political opponent of the Lindstroms. I'm the senator's chief of staff, for God's sake! You should be talking to people in the other party. Bill Murphy, for example. He knew Cate Gaulois."

"Interesting you know that." I saw him stiffen as he realized his slip. "I have talked to Mr. Murphy, and I know about his relationship with Cate. I'm talking to you now. You'd be Lisa's opponent if you wanted to get her out of the way so you could run for office yourself."

"Yes, *if*, a very big if."

"But plausible." Lisa's voice was tight but controlled.

She stood and stepped to the table, where she opened the drawer and took out a pack of cigarettes and an elegant gold lighter. She didn't close the drawer.

"You can't be serious." Nelson was looking at her, but his gun hand hadn't moved.

She lit a cigarette. "I know how ambitious you are even if you've been careful to conceal it from Dad. I also know how ruthless you can be when you want something bad enough." She touched her cheek and frowned as though it hurt. "My God, do I know. I think all your talk of how much you care for me is just . . . talk."

"That's crazy. I meant every word of it."

While he kept looking at Lisa, I leaned forward slightly and moved my hands a few inches apart.

"You're a politician, Frank. You haven't really meant anything you've said in your whole life." She exhaled a plume of smoke as an exclamation point. "You're smart, though, smart enough to figure out how you could benefit from me being in a compromising position. I may not be a very good wife—"

He laughed.

"—but I'd never intentionally do anything to hurt Daniel. If that tape gets out, it would hurt him deeply and probably ruin his career. You knew just what kind of pressure would keep me from running whether or not I had any chance of being elected." Her eyes widened as she inhaled sharply. "That's it, isn't it? You found out I was having a fling with Cate, and you saw your chance."

"By the way," I said, "how did you learn about their relationship? I'm guessing Tommy Osborn told you."

Nelson didn't deny it, which confirmed my suspicion. "Osborn was there the night they met," I said, "and he asked Lisa about Cate later. I'll bet that once he figured out they might be having an affair, he came straight to you with that information. Naturally, he'd want you, as a possible successor to Senator Lindstrom, to owe him something. He may not have known Cate's name, but with your connections it wouldn't have been hard for you to find out who she was."

Lisa ground her cigarette into the ashtray. "Frank, you bastard, you used that against me—and after you encouraged me to try something like that." She mimicked his voice. "'Go on—you're curious and the experience will be good for you.' You son of a bitch."

She thrust her hand into the open drawer and pulled out a small, snub-nosed revolver. By the time she had her gun pointed at Nelson, he'd swung his toward her.

"Not so fast. You can call me all the names you like, but at least I haven't killed anyone. Not yet."

I leaned forward a little more and got my hands out from behind my back. I began inching my right hand forward, keeping it down on the seat of the chair.

Nelson looked at Lisa as though he expected to her to say something, perhaps ask him what he meant. She remained silent, her face twisted.

After a moment he said, "I may be a blackmailer, but you've done something a lot worse. So now we're in this together."

"No! You're wrong! I didn't murder Cate. I couldn't have—I loved her."

He shook his head slowly. "Sorry, darling. You killed her."

CHAPTER THIRTY-SIX

Lisa raised her gun toward Nelson, and he steadied his aim on her. I held my breath.

After several tense seconds her expression softened and her lip trembled. "I—I didn't want her dead." Tears started down her cheeks. "I didn't want that. I just wanted to talk to her, find out what she knew about the tape."

"She didn't know anything about it." Nelson rested his gun hand on his knee. "Cate wasn't a manipulative person. If she'd known about my scheme, she wouldn't have had anything to do with it."

"That's what she said, but I didn't believe her." Lisa was sobbing now. "I tried to force her to tell me what was going on. We—we struggled, and the gun went off. That's all. I didn't mean to do it."

For a minute the only sound in the room was Lisa's crying. She wiped her eyes with her free hand, keeping the gun pointed toward Nelson. He kept his pointed at her, but he looked as though he didn't know what to do next.

I moved my hands forward a few more inches before saying, "Nice try, Lisa. I've always thought you should've been an actress. But I know you too well to buy that story."

Nelson's eyes widened, and Lisa looked angry, her tears stopping almost as quickly as they'd started. She turned her revolver on me and came around the table toward my chair.

I nodded. "I've seen you turn on the waterworks when you thought it'd get you what you wanted. And I taught you to shoot, so I know you can handle a gun. You shot Cate because you were furious about that tape, furious enough to kill her. Partly for revenge, I guess, but also to keep her from talking about it."

"You're full of shit, Robert, as usual. I don't know why I thought you'd help me with this mess. You've just fucked up everything the way you fucked up your career and the rest of your life!"

The words stung, but I said nothing.

"And how can you accuse me of anything? I hired you as my lawyer, for God's sake!"

"Yeah, but you fired me, remember? And then I figured out you killed Cate—you didn't tell me. Even if I can't report you to the police, I don't want you to think you can fool me with that fairy tale about 'accidentally' shooting her."

"But it's true! Frank, you believe me, don't you?"

"Okay, Lisa, just calm down," he said. "It doesn't matter how Cate died. The important thing is that the story of why she died will ruin us politically—both of us—if it ever gets out."

She paused a moment, biting her lip. Then she seemed to decide. "Yes—*if*."

"Fortunately, there's only one other person who knows the story, and we're about to take care of that. I tried to take care of it earlier, but apparently the man I hired wasn't up to the job."

So Nelson hired the gunman, I thought. *Or maybe had Osborn hire him—not that it made any difference now.*

Both of them looked at me, and I felt a chill. I wondered whether I could draw the gun before either—or both—of them shot me. I noticed that although Lisa had her revolver aimed in my direction, Nelson had his pistol pointed about halfway between Lisa and me as if keeping his options open.

"Killing me won't solve your problem. I've already told my partner all about this case, including who's blackmailing Lisa and who shot Cate. Jack knows that Lisa and I met here to confront you, Nelson. The trail won't end with me."

"You're lying," Nelson said. "If you'd been sure of all that, you'd have brought the police. This thing will end with you if we shoot in self-defense."

I did my best to look skeptical. "Defense against what? What's my motive for attacking you?"

"Jealousy. It's obvious you and Lisa were lovers in law school. I'll bet she's let you do it again so she can keep you on a leash." Lisa said nothing but gave Nelson a venomous look.

"So if she and I just keep quiet, there's no blackmail case against me and no murder case against her. Right, darling?"

She nodded. "Self-defense sounds like a great idea." She took two steps toward Nelson. "Especially if you shot Robert for identifying you as the blackmailer and then I had to shoot you to keep from being killed as a witness."

Nelson's eyes widened. He was moving his gun toward her and opening his mouth when she turned and shot him in the center of the chest.

The shot wasn't loud, no louder than dropping a heavy book on a tile floor. A small black hole fringed with red appeared on Nelson's white shirt, and he made a strangling noise. Then he slumped to one side, his gun falling softly onto the oriental rug.

Lisa scooped up Nelson's gun in her left hand and spun to aim it at me as I stood and reached for the .32. I drew the revolver and steadied it on Lisa an instant before she got the semiautomatic pointed at me, but it was close.

She gave me a sardonic smile. "You were a good shooting instructor. Thanks. Now drop your gun."

I looked into her eyes, twin pools of blue ice. "No."

Her smile vanished. "I'm not kidding, Robert. Drop the fucking gun."

"Lisa, you don't have to do this. They'll go easy on a blackmailed woman, especially a senator's daughter."

"But Daddy would be so ashamed. He's always thought I'm perfect. So I can't let him end all his years in the Senate this way— with some tawdry scandal."

"Shooting Nelson has probably already done that."

"We'll see. At any rate, there'll be no one left to contradict my story."

We looked at each other. I could hear the ticking of the wall clock. *Something must be wrong with it—time can't be going by that slowly.*

"Even if you're faster and straighter—and that'll be hard, left-handed—it's going to be a tough story to sell."

She seemed to think about that for a moment. Then she cocked her hip in the short skirt and, using the snub-nose in her right hand, toyed with the top button of her blouse.

"I guess it doesn't have to be that way, Robert. You and I were really good friends once, and we could be again, if only—"

"If only you'd stop lying to me, yourself, everybody. But it's too late for that—it has been for a while."

She smiled again, dazzling this time, the smile I remembered so well. "You think so? Well, I'll come through all right. I always do, don't I?"

Then I said, speaking to myself as much as to Lisa, "Who'd have thought it would end this way. . . ."

I sensed rather than saw Lisa's finger tightening on the trigger. I made a quick movement to throw off her aim, and our guns fired almost simultaneously.

The bullet slammed into my left shoulder. I lurched backward and grabbed the top of the chair to keep from falling.

I looked across the room and saw Lisa on the floor. She was lying on her side, left arm outstretched, Nelson's gun still in her hand. As I watched, she took a shallow breath, then another.

A red stain was spreading on Lisa's blouse like the blossoming of a rose. *A rose with thorns. Beautiful but deadly.*

I felt dizzy. I squeezed my eyes shut, held them closed, opened them again. The room was revolving slowly. I shook my head, but that only made the room turn faster.

There was a phone on the far end of the table, and I started for it. I managed to take three steps before I fell into deep darkness that had no bottom.

CHAPTER THIRTY-SEVEN

I awoke in a hospital bed, shoulder heavily bandaged, head swimming from medication. A nurse stood by the bed, writing on a clipboard.

She smiled when she saw me looking at her. "Good afternoon, Mr. Shipley. How're you feeling?"

My mouth was dry, but I managed a sort of a croak. "Lousy."

"Good. Lousy's normal for someone who's been shot."

"Is she . . ." A wave of nausea swept over me and my vision blurred. I fought to keep from vomiting.

"Better take it easy—you need to rest."

After the nausea receded, I looked up again, and the nurse, now bending over me, gradually came into focus. "Lisa Lindstrom, the woman who was with me." I swallowed hard. "Did she make it?"

"No, I'm sorry." The nurse paused. "She died in the ambulance. The emergency technicians did all they could."

My eyes felt hot and wet, and I turned my face to the wall. "And the man, Frank Nelson?"

"I understand he was dead when they got there."

I lay still, thinking of a book I'd read years before—*Red Harvest*. After the last few days the title made more sense.

The nurse was sensitive enough to let me be. She finished writing on the chart and quietly replaced the clipboard on a hook at the foot of the bed.

"Can I get you anything?" Her voice was soothing.

"Just some water."

She held a plastic cup close to my mouth, and I drank through a straw.

"Thanks." I leaned back on the pillow. "I guess I need to let my business partner know where I am."

"Is that Mr. Benton?"

"Yes, how do you know?"

"He's here now, in the visitors' lounge with a young woman, the one who found you and called the ambulance."

"Georgia? Georgia Nguyen?"

"That's her. I think she rode in with the ambulance and then called your partner. They stayed last night until you were out of surgery and came back this afternoon, not long after I started my shift."

"May I see them?"

"Yes, I'll let them know you're awake." She smiled. "Mr. Benton seems to hold you in high regard. He told me to take good care of you. I would've done that anyway, but I'm glad he explained how you ended up with a bullet in your shoulder."

"Great. Now if he can just explain it to me. . . ."

She looked puzzled. "Don't you remember?"

Yes, and I'll never forget it, no matter how hard I try. My stomach surged again, and I couldn't answer.

"Here, let me give you something. It'll make you feel more comfortable."

"No, thanks, I'll be fine," I said through gritted teeth. "I do remember what happened. I'm just not sure why it happened."

"I'm afraid I don't understand."

"Never mind. I'll see Jack and Georgia now."

The nurse's bedside manner gave way to a look of embarrassment. "Well, actually, I'm afraid there's someone else you have to see first."

"Let me guess: a big cop named Lytle."

"Yes, he's sitting right outside. He said he wanted to talk to you as soon as you were awake. Feel up to it?"

"No, but I'll see him anyway. Might as well get it over with. Please show him in."

The nurse looked as though she might dispute my decision on medical grounds but then seemed to realize objecting would be futile. "Yes, sir." She turned smartly on her heel and left.

A few seconds later the dark bulk of Lieutenant John Lytle filled the doorway. He looked at me with an expression hard enough to break glass and came over to the side of the bed.

"Well, well, got those eyes open now, Mr. Shipley? Good! No point in reaming your ass if you're still asleep!"

I didn't say anything.

"I'm pissed and got a right to be! I told you to let the police handle this. But you had to act stubborn, as usual. Now two more people are dead, and you didn't miss being dead by much."

I didn't say anything to that either.

"You had no right to take this into your own hands, become some self-appointed avenging angel."

When I still didn't say anything, he lowered himself into the chair beside my bed. The chair sagged but held.

"Maybe you think self-defense will get you off, but don't be so sure. I got a lot of charges I could throw at you, and some of them would probably stick. The way I feel, I'd enjoy makin' them stick."

"I'm sorry." My mouth was still dry, so the words came out softly.

"What?"

I swallowed and tried again. "I said, 'I'm sorry'."

"Sorry for what?"

"Sorry for your having to deal with this. Sorry for dragging Jack and Georgia into it. And sorry that four people had to die because two of them wanted to be elected to the Senate."

"Maybe they didn't have to die, Robert—not all of them anyway."

"I know. That's just the way things worked out."

He sighed and shifted in the chair. "I talked the Fairfax County detectives into letting me see you first even though McLean's in their jurisdiction. Maybe I can help you, but it won't be easy to explain this one away."

"Probably not. But what happened is that a murderer shot a blackmailer and then shot me."

"That may work—if it's the truth. So who was who in this setup?"

There was less anger in his voice, but he was still giving me one of those cop looks, the kind that said he knew when I'd been tardy in first grade. "Maybe I should have a lawyer here if I'm going to answer any questions. Jack's in the building."

Lytle snorted. "Lucky for you—no other shyster in town would represent such a goddamn cowboy. Hell, it's easy to lose count of the bodies on this one." He paused. "I'll get Jack if you want, but I figured you were man enough to give it to me straight."

I took a deep breath. "Okay. Lisa Lindstrom, daughter of Senator Talbot Lindstrom and wife of the dot-com CEO Daniel Strawbridge, was a law school classmate of mine. She shot Frank Nelson and then shot me. She shot Nelson because he was trying to blackmail her over a sexual indiscretion."

"And why did she shoot you?"

"I told her I knew she murdered Cate Gaulois."

"Cate Gaulois? The stripper? You're telling me this Lisa Lindstrom killed her?"

"Yes."

"For what reason?"

"Because Lisa thought—incorrectly, as it turned out—that Cate was in on the blackmail attempt. The two women were lovers, and someone had secretly made a videotape of them in bed together."

"You've seen the tape?"

"Yes, Lisa received it last weekend and brought it to me on Monday. I didn't know she'd already confronted Cate about it. Cate claimed to be innocent, but Lisa didn't believe her, so she shot her."

"Where's the tape now? You'll need it if you expect anyone to buy this crazy story."

"Locked in my office desk. I'm sure Nelson had at least one more copy, perhaps several. Maybe at his home or, if he was careful, in a safe-deposit box. You'll find them."

"You know, some folks might call that evidence. Might even say you should've told the police about it."

"I'm telling you now."

"Yeah, now that three more people are dead and another's been wounded. Who deserves the blame for that?"

"I guess I do, at least for some of it, but I don't see how I could have done things any differently."

Lytle looked away as though thinking about what I had said. I followed his gaze to the wall where the afternoon sun, streaming through the blinds, painted a pattern of black-and-white stripes.

Finally he spoke. "Well, maybe not for the shootings—especially that contractor you planted. Not if you didn't start any of the gunplay, just finished it. But you are to blame for not coming to me with evidence of a crime."

"My client wouldn't let me, and I didn't know for sure who'd killed Cate until I confronted Frank Nelson about his blackmail scheme. I figured that either he or Lisa was the killer and the one who wasn't might accuse the other if I put some pressure on."

"Well, it worked, but now both of them are dead and you're damn lucky you're not dead too."

"I know, but remember that Lisa was my client. I was bound by attorney-client privilege."

"Not for a murder she committed before she hired you and didn't tell you about. And anyway, counselor, that privilege is supposed to be a shield, not a sword."

"I don't think you can chop logic that fine, Lieutenant. I couldn't reveal what she'd told me, so I tried to solve the puzzle myself."

"You surely did, Robert." Lytle shook his head. "You surely did that."

"Well, with help from Georgia. I couldn't have done it without her."

"Jack and I could have helped you too. Remember that the next time you're in over your head."

"I will. And now comes the part where you tell me I'm under arrest, right?"

Lytle rubbed a hand over his face. "Should be—and you know I'd do it. But technically you've solved two murders for us, and you shot the Lindstrom woman in self-defense. So I don't see much point in arresting you—*this* time. You hear me, don't you?"

"Loud and clear. Thanks, Lieutenant. I appreciate it."

He stood. "Well, gotta go. Come see me when you get out of here—and bring Jack. We'll have dinner, drink some whiskey, and swap sea stories."

"That sounds good."

Lytle nodded and walked toward the door. As he put his hand on the knob, he looked back at me. "I think Jack's waiting to see you. And there's a pretty young woman with him. Should I send them in?"

"Please do. Their medicine's got to taste better than yours."

He grinned, a little evilly I thought. Then he left, and in a moment Georgia burst in, followed closely by Jack.

CHAPTER THIRTY-EIGHT

"Oh, Robert!" Georgia rushed to the bed and bent to kiss me on the cheek. "I've been so worried! Jack was too. I don't think either of us slept at all last night."

Although she was careful not to touch the bandages, even the light pressure of her body sent pain knifing into my shoulder. I brought up my good arm to stroke her hair. After a few seconds the pain receded to a throbbing ache.

She wiped her eyes and smiled. "The doctor says you're going to be all right. No permanent damage although you may need some physical therapy."

"Sure, he's going to be all right," Jack said. "It'd take more than this to keep Robert down."

He came closer to the bed but not so close as to interrupt Georgia's intimacy with me. "He's tough—and stubborn too. Isn't that right, Robert?"

"I'm not feeling too tough right now." I paused, remembering what Lytle had said. "But I guess I'm stubborn—to a fault."

"What's that, Robert?" Georgia carefully slid off the bed and stood by it.

"Oh, nothing, just thinking about what someone, a friend, told me recently."

"Good. You should listen to your friends more."

"I think you're right."

Jack laughed. Georgia tried to hide a smile and then shook her head in mock exasperation.

Jack pulled a pint of whiskey from his coat pocket, slipped it into the drawer of the bedside table, and winked at me. "Anything else we can do for you?"

"Don't suppose you brought any cigars?"

"No, I thought that might be pushing it. There's no smoking in here, you know."

"Not supposed to be any drinking either, but some rules were made to be broken."

"And some weren't. That's a good thing to keep in mind."

"I'll remember—and I'm sure if I forget, you'll remind me."

Jack laughed again. "Probably. Well, I'll leave you two in peace."

"Thanks for coming by, Jack. I'm all right, really. I'll be up and around in a day or two—probably faster than the doctor wants."

Georgia thumped the bed rail. "Robert Edward Shipley, you won't move from that bed until the doctor says you can. For once in your life you won't be stupid about yourself."

"Now, that would be a first," Jack said. "If you can make Robert do that, Georgia, I'll know you're having a positive effect on him."

I smiled and tried to sit up, but the pain surged back. I closed my eyes and waited for it to subside. Then I blinked and looked Georgia.

"Okay, I'll follow the doctor's orders. Now, Georgie, could you please wait in the hall a few minutes? I need to talk to Jack privately."

She started to protest, but I said, "I know, I know. Normally there's nothing I'd say to Jack that I wouldn't say in front of you, but this is different. Trust me."

She looked at Jack and then, arching her eyebrows, at me. "All right, *Mister* Shipley. I'll wait outside until you men have finished your important business."

After she left, Jack eased himself into the bedside chair. "Women. Can't live with 'em . . ."

"Yeah. I hope Georgie will understand about Lisa."

"You mean—"

"I mean about my shooting her. Granted, that was after she'd killed two people and was trying to kill me."

"From what the police told me, you had no choice. Did you?"

I thought for a moment. "No, I guess I didn't, at least not after Lisa decided killing me was her only way out."

"I agree. So don't blame yourself."

"Okay, I'll try not to. Even though I was shot at several times—and didn't even get paid for it."

Jack sat up straight. "What? She didn't pay you? Not even a retainer?"

"Nope. Sorry, partner."

"Well, maybe this will give me some leverage to keep you in the office instead of out on that boat."

"Think it'll be enough?"

"No, probably not, but I can always dream, can't I?"

"Sure." I paused. "Jack, I want you to do something."

"Anything for you, Robert, you know that."

"It's not for me, Jack, something for Georgie. Well, partly for you too."

He gave me a wary look. "What's that?"

"You've got to tell her."

In the ensuing quiet I heard the soft push of the ventilation system and the low muttering of a television in the next room. I heard someone walking down the hall and cars going by on the street outside.

When Jack finally spoke, his voice was hoarse. "Tell her what?"

I glanced at him, then looked out the window. The sun was sliding down the deep-blue sky, beginning to paint the west with shades of green and gold and red.

"You know."

Jack didn't pretend he didn't understand. "How long have you known?"

I looked back at him. Jack had his hands on his knees and appeared to be counting the floor tiles. "Not long. Georgie's been showing me the pictures her aunt sent her from Vietnam, and I just figured it out."

"From what? I mean, what gave it away?"

"Oh, lots of things, nothing in particular. A big, muscular man wearing a DOGS T-shirt in one of those pictures. You graduated from the University of Georgia before you went to Vietnam and still follow Bulldogs football and basketball."

"Yeah, but for those dogs it's usually spelled D-A-W-G-S."

"Okay, maybe it meant devil dogs. Whatever. The point is it made me think. And then there's her middle name—Georgia, the name she began using here. Her mother must've picked it to please you."

Jack smiled, and I could tell he was remembering the lovely young woman in the fading photographs. "Well, it *is* a pretty name."

"Yes, it is. There's that, plus the way you look out for her, like she's much more than just a law student working with us. Maybe it's Georgia's eyes most of all. She looks more like her mother otherwise, but she has your eyes—especially when she's mad at me."

He chuckled but said nothing as he continued to study the floor. I gave it a few seconds, then asked, "Why haven't you told her?"

"I don't know. I've meant to several times. I just . . . well, it's harder than you'd think." He looked up at me. "I mean, to tell a kid that you're her father and that you left her and her mother behind. Of course, I didn't know when my tour was up that Linh—her mother—was pregnant and was certain I was the father."

"How'd you find out she's your daughter?"

"Years later at a Marine Corps reunion. I ran into one of my buddies, a guy who'd also been . . . close to her mother. He didn't leave Vietnam until several months after I did."

He paused, and I could tell he was thinking about when he was a young man in what was then an old war. "My friend and I did some drinking that night and got to telling stories. You know how it is."

I nodded and waited.

"Well, finally he asked me if I knew I'd left a baby girl in 'Nam. I figured he was just drunk, kidding me, but he insisted he wasn't. He knew enough details to make the story sound like it could be true, so after the reunion I started checking, working with the Red Cross and groups like that. Took me a couple of years to find out he was right."

"What'd you do then?"

"I learned that Linh had died when Georgia was an infant and that they put the baby in an orphanage. Probably not a pleasant place, especially for an Amerasian child."

Jack had squeezed his clamped fingers white. I started to speak, to say something to comfort him, but then he continued, voice rough with emotion.

"When she was a teenager she was sent to the United States along with a number of other *Việt kiều*. That means—"

"Children of the war. Georgie told me."

"Right. Well, eventually I learned she'd been sent to live with a Vietnamese American family in upstate New York. I felt awful that she'd never known her mother or . . . me, so I offered to pay for her to go to college here in the D.C. area. To cover my tracks, I pitched it as though my Marine Corps buddies and I had come up with an idea for a scholarship fund."

"And when she started going to law school you hired her to work at the firm so you could be close to her."

His expression mixed shame and defiance. "Yes, damn it, I did. Of course, it wasn't until after you came that Georgia said she wanted to stay until she graduated. She said it was good training for practicing law, but even I could see through that."

Silence filled the room again while I thought about what he'd told me. Finally I said, "Well, Jack, it looks like you and I have one more thing in common: we both like to kid ourselves. She's wonderful, isn't she?"

"Yes, she is. I've known that for a while, Robert, but I'm glad you know it too. Now, what're you going to do about it?"

"Spend a lot of time making up for not realizing it sooner. How's that?"

"Pretty good although I don't think it'll be hardship duty for you. Sounds like you know what you want."

"Yes—finally. But do you?"

"What?"

"Do you want your daughter? I mean, as a daughter, not just as a good employee? If you do, you'll have to tell her the truth and take the consequences, whatever they are."

"Easy for you to say, Robert. You don't have to do it."

"Bullshit, Jack. You've known for years that you're her father, but you've never had the guts to tell her. She has a right to know."

He flushed and for an instant looked as though he might take a swing at me. But then he looked at the floor again, jaw muscles working.

Neither of us spoke for a while. Eventually Jack said, "Well, counselor, I guess you're right. First time for everything, huh?"

"Yeah, I guess so. Of course, I've had some experience—more than I would've liked—taking consequences. I'd like to cut down on that in the future."

"Good idea. Maybe you can avoid getting shot by another client."

"That's the goal—one of them anyway. Now go talk to your daughter."

Jack stood. "All right, I will. But tell me this: afterward, when my daughter needs a shoulder to cry on, someone other than her father, will you be there for her?"

My gaze met his. "What do you think?"

□ □ □

Sometime later—I didn't know the time—I woke to find Georgia sleeping in the chair by my bed. Night had fallen and the room was dark except for a glow from the hallway.

I sat up, wincing. I used my good arm to pull the blanket up from the foot of the bed and spread it awkwardly over Georgia. She stirred and opened her eyes.

At first she seemed disoriented, but then she saw me and smiled. Despite the dimness, she stretched like a cat in the sun. "Hi, Robert, how're you feeling?"

"Better. How are you doing?"

Her smile faded. "Okay—I think. It's been a big day. First, you here in the hospital. Then Jack told me . . . well, he said you know."

"Yes, I do."

"He said you figured it out somehow."

"Let's say I made a good guess. Those photos of your mother got me thinking."

"I guess a girl could do worse for a father." Georgia looked at me as though seeking agreement.

"You couldn't do better. You know how much I think of Jack."

"Yes, I always have. He's almost like your father too. I just wonder how he could've gone so long without telling me."

"I'm sure he wanted to tell you. He was probably worried about how it might affect you, how it could change your relationship. Maybe he feels guilty about having left you in Vietnam."

"But he didn't even know about me then!"

Hearing Georgia defend her father, I thought that things would probably work out. "That's right—he didn't."

She was silent for a while. Then she said, "It's going to be different, having a father."

"Yes, it will."

"And I'll be a daughter again, something I haven't been in a long time."

"That's true too."

She fell silent again and closed her eyes.

Then I thought about two other daughters, both dead now, one killed by the other. I was sure that both of their fathers were grieving but for different reasons.

Reasons they could never undo.

But there is little we can undo in life. I couldn't undo what had happened to me at the big firm downtown, what had caused me to lose my dream of being a partner there. A dream that didn't seem as sweet now as it once had, but still it had been mine.

And I couldn't undo what had happened at Lisa's house, especially that last part I'd always want to forget but never could—the part where she and I pointed guns at each other. The part where I killed a woman I'd once loved. . . .

No, we can't undo much. The past catches up with us one way or another. And now it had caught up with Georgia. And with me.

I looked at her again and saw she'd gone back to sleep. Well, that was the best thing for her—for both of us. Sleep and heal.

Soon both of us would be better, and then we'd see what the future held. I liked that thought, and I held onto it as I let myself drift into a comforting darkness.

The future. Maybe it was more important than the past. Neither Georgia nor I could change the past, but we could make the future whatever we wanted. Yes, whatever we wanted.

Anyway, I hoped so.

THE END

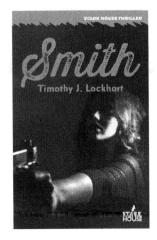